ROSE BLISS COOKS UP MAGIC

U-710-010

B000 000 015 3817

ABERDEEN LIBRARIES

Also available:

The Bliss Bakery Trilogy — BLISS BAKERY
The Bliss Bakery Trilogy — SWEET

ROSE BLISS COOKS UP MAGIC

Kathryn Littlewood

HarperCollins *Children's Books*

First published in Great Britain
by HarperCollins *Children's Books* 2015
HarperCollins *Children's Books* is a division of HarperCollins*Publishers* Ltd,
HarperCollins Publishers
1 London Bridge Street
London SE1 9GF
The HarperCollins *Children's Books* website address is
www.harpercollins.co.uk

1

Text copyright © 2015 by The Inkhouse

The author asserts the moral right to be identified as the author of
this work.

ISBN 978-0-00-745178-4

Set in Albertina MT by Palimpsest Book Production Limited,
Falkirk, Stirlingshire

Printed and bound in England by Clays Ltd, St Ives plc

Conditions of Sale
This book is sold subject to the condition that it shall not, by way of
trade or otherwise, be lent, re-sold, hired out or otherwise circulated
without the publisher's prior written consent in any form of binding or
cover other than that in which it is published and without a similar
condition including this condition being imposed on the subsequent
purchaser.

MIX
Paper from
responsible sources
FSC
www.fsc.org   FSC™ C007454

FSC™ is a non-profit international organisation established to
promote the responsible management of the world's forests.
Products carrying the FSC label are independently certified to assure
consumers that they come from forests that are managed to meet
the social, economic and ecological needs of present and future
generations, and other controlled sources.

Find out more about HarperCollins and the environment at
www.harpercollins.co.uk/green

For Katherine Tegen,
who makes magic with books

Contents

WHATEVER WILL BE, WILL BEE

ROSEMARY BLISS'S DREAMS had come true.

She was the most famous baker in all the world. She was the youngest chef ever to have won France's famed Gala des Gâteaux Grands. She was the twelve-year-old girl who'd out-baked celebrity TV chef Lily Le Fay and stopped her aunt's nefarious schemes. She was the local kid who'd saved her hometown and rescued the Bliss family's magical *Cookery Booke*.

So why wasn't she happy?

On the thirteenth morning after returning from Paris, she got up and pulled open the curtains of her bedroom.

Snap. Flash. Click. Click.

That was why.

"Look, up there, it's Rose!" *Click. Flash. Snap.* "Rose, how

do you feel about your victory?" *Click. Flash. Flash. Snap.*
"Rose! How does it feel to be the best baker in the
world?" *Snap. Flash. Click.* "And at only twelve years old?"
Click. Flash. Snap.

Ugh, Rose thought. *They're still here.* Gone were the
soothing sounds of morning, the wind chimes, the rope
of the tire swing creaking against the branch of the old
oak outside her window. Instead, the new sounds came
courtesy of the group of paparazzi that had taken up
permanent residence outside the Follow Your Bliss
Bakery. Each morning they waited for Rose to open her
curtains and then snapped hundreds of pictures, while
calling out for a quote about her prodigious victory.

Rose had always harboured a secret curiosity about
what fame would feel like, and now she knew. It felt
like being a goldfish: hundreds of big googly eyes staring
in at you, leaving you nowhere to run and nowhere
to hide, except maybe a little plastic castle.

Rose snapped the curtains shut, and wondered if
she'd had enough of baking. It wasn't worth it, not if
it meant *this.*

"I wish I never had to bake again," Rose said to no
one in particular.

A furry grey head, its ears flattened, appeared from a

mound of dirty clothes at the foot of her bed. "Be careful what you wish for," Gus said. "Wishes before birthdays have a strange way of coming true." The Scottish Fold cat raised a paw and began licking carefully between each sheathed claw.

"That's just silly," Rose said. "My birthday isn't until the end of summer. Anyway, I didn't really mean it." She scratched his head and he purred. "I'd just like to *not* have to bake for a little bit, you know?" She'd become a baker because she loved her family and her town, and baking was in her blood – but thanks to her victory at the Gala des Gâteaux Grands, everything had been turned upside down.

She knew it had only been a measly two weeks, but the past fourteen days had been the longest of her life. No peace and quiet. No time to enjoy the summer. Baking wasn't fun anymore; it was something she was *expected* to do – like homework.

And that was no fun at all. As far as Rose was concerned, unless something changed this summer, she was done with baking for good.

Downstairs, inside the kitchen of the Bliss Family Bakery, the situation was no better. Camera flashes burst through the drawn curtains like stuttering flickers of lightning, and the barking of reporters outside the door made it sound like there were a thousand people outside instead of just a few hundred. Why wouldn't they leave her alone?

The mail was almost worse.

Rose's brothers, Sage and Ty, were already sitting in the bakery kitchen, tearing through yesterday's mail, throwing the unimportant letters into a giant black trash bag and placing the ones that needed answers in a pile. Rose knew the letters were for her ("Your fans *love* us – I mean, you," Ty liked to say) but she was tired of having to read them. She didn't want to look at another letter now – or ever. She just wanted to get back to a normal life.

"Junk," announced Sage, throwing a stack of balled-up paper into the trash. Rose's pudgy-cheeked younger brother had just turned ten, but he didn't look a day older than eight. He had curly, strawberry-blond hair, and the only thing that had grown on him over the past year was the number of freckles on his nose.

"What was in it?" asked Ty. Rose's handsome older brother *had* grown, but not enough – lately he had confided in Rose that he was worried that his dreams of NBA superstardom were out of reach.

"The prime minister of Spain wants a cake," Sage said, flipping through the letters, "Warren Buffett wants an enormous pie-chart pie, with a different flavour for every section."

"What's a pie chart?" Ty asked.

"Who's Warren Buffett?" Rose asked.

"Some nobody who likes pie, I guess," Sage said, and read another letter. "The United Nations General Assembly wants us to make a cupcake for every ambassador for their next meeting – frosted with the country's flag, and – listen to this – 'the flavour of each ambassador's homeland in every single nibble.'"

"Ugh," Ty replied. "When is someone *important* gonna write to us?"

Sage opened the next letter, a heavy pink envelope that wafted out a gentle breath of sweet perfume. He fell to the floor and clutched his chest like a man dying of heartache.

"Now!" he cried, handing the letter to Ty and Rose.

Rose scanned the delicate sheet of stationery:

Dear Wonderful Rose and the Rest of the Follow Your Bliss Bakery!

Please send me a cake. Please. I don't care what kind. I

have to have one of your cakes. I will die without it. I will
pay you anything. You can even play in the band on my
next tour.
Send the cake soon.
Katy Perry

"No!" Ty gasped. "She must have been watching the competition, seen me, and fallen in love. The *cake* is just a way to get to *me*."

Rose sighed. She knew she should be excited, but all these letters from famous people just made her tired. Baking wasn't about getting notes from celebrities. It was about mixing and stirring and folding, about flour and butter and sugar and heart, and love, and—

"We're rich!" cried Ty, holding up a letter embossed with the cartoon image of Kathy Keegan, the name of a big baked goods conglomerate.

"Rose," Ty said, "they're offering seven hundred and seventy-seven thousand dollars just for doing a single thirty-second commercial endorsing their products."

"Why all the sevens?" Sage asked.

"All you have to do is eat a Keegan Kake and say, 'I'm Rosemary Bliss, youngest winner in history of the Gala des Gâteaux Grands,' and, um, 'Kathy Keegan is my inspiration!'" Ty handed her the letter and stared moonily at the ceiling. "If I were married to Katy Perry, and you signed this endorsement deal... none of us would ever have to work again!"

"Kathy Keegan isn't even real," Rose answered. "The Keegan Corporation was founded by a group of businessmen. How can I say someone is my inspiration when she isn't even an actual person? Besides, I would never eat a Keegan Kake. You know what Mum says about cakes that come wrapped in plastic." She stuffed the letter into her pocket and turned away. She'd had enough of letters.

That's when she noticed that every available surface in the kitchen was covered in cookie sheets lined with parchment.

Her mother, Purdy Bliss, burst through the saloon doors from the front room of the bakery, her arms laden with grocery bags. She was a sturdy woman with a sweet face and curly black hair and bangs that flopped wildly over her forehead.

"Boys, the buttons!" she cried. "I told you to pipe the buttons and not stop until all these cookie sheets are filled!"

The boys grumbled as they each picked up a pastry

bag. Purdy tousled their red hair as they set about piping little blobs of chocolate dough onto the sheets in tidy rows.

"What's going on?" Rose asked.

"Those reporters," Purdy said, kissing Rose on the forehead. "We'll never get on with our lives until they vamoose."

"I'll help," Rose said, feeling enthusiastic for the first time in days. Maybe she could actually be useful.

"Rose, honey," said Purdy, unpacking the groceries, "you should probably go back upstairs. You're the one who really sets them off."

"Am I just supposed to stay in my tower, like Rapunzel?" Rose asked, throwing up her arms. "I don't think so." She seized a pastry bag filled with chocolate dough and squeezed out a few orderly blobs as her brothers finished the rest.

"Three hundred buttons," Purdy said, counting. "Just enough. Children, come here." She drew Rose and her brothers close to her, gently settling her arms on their shoulders.

The door to the walk-in fridge swung open, and Rose's great-great-great-grandfather Balthazar emerged carrying a massive blue mason jar lined with chicken wire. From inside it came a sound like ten thousand electric toothbrushes all buzzing at the same time. "You ready?" he asked.

Purdy nodded and cried, "Release the bees!"

Balthazar set the jar down in the center of the kitchen floor, then cracked open the lid. A swarm of bees tumbled forth, filling the kitchen like a horrible fuzzy cloud of buzzing black-and-yellow smoke.

"Behold, the Dread Swarm of the Tubertine!" Balthazar cried, tugging at his beard.

"The cookies are Mind Your Own Beeswax Buttons," explained Purdy over the sound of the buzzing. "If you eat a cookie imbued with one sting from the Dread Swarm of the Tubertine, you'll mind your own business. They were first used on the Trappist monks; as a matter of fact, before the fateful day when the monks in the order feasted on these, you couldn't shut them up. Gab gab gab! After devouring these buttons, the monks took the first vows of silence in the history of monkdom." Purdy pulled a kazoo from the pocket of her apron. "Behold!"

She pursed her lips and puffed out a rhythmic tango. The swarm of bees immediately stood perfectly still in the air, then scrambled around until each bee hovered over a tiny mound of chocolate dough. The bees looked to Purdy, wide-eyed and ready. Rose could feel a steady flutter of wind from their buzzing wings.

At Purdy's next blast on the kazoo, each of the three hundred bees plunged their stingers into their mound of dough. They seemed to sigh, and their buzzing grew quieter, and then they looked away from Purdy and one another and flew single file back into the jar.

Balthazar snapped the lid closed.

Ty and Sage crawled out from beneath the table in the breakfast nook, sighing with relief.

"Ew," said Sage. Rose noticed that the walls and floor were smeared with yellow goop. Sage swiped his finger through a patch. "They slimed the place."

Balthazar scratched his bald head, and his finger came away dripping with the sticky yellow stuff. He held it to the tip of his tongue. "It's honey," he grumbled.

Purdy and Rose shoved tray after tray of the newly stung chocolate buttons into the oven. A few minutes later, they transferred the hot cookies onto a serving tray, and soon after that, Ty and Sage were outside distributing the buttons to the teeming mass of reporters and photographers.

As each reporter bit into a cookie, his eyes flashed

as gold as the scruffy neck of a bee, and he quickly hurried off the lawn. Within ten minutes, the flock had vanished from the backyard – cameras, boom microphones, flashbulbs, and all.

Ty and Sage re-entered the kitchen with their empty serving trays. Ty's hair, which he'd started to gel into three-inch spikes since the Gala, was wilting like a patch of broken weeds, and Sage had a bright pink welt across his forehead.

"Someone hit me with a microphone," Sage said, fuming. "Those people are animals. *Animals*, I say!"

Ty held up a sheet of orange paper and said, "Once they'd cleared out, I found this on the front door – they're taped all over the building." The edges of the orange sheet trailed bits of tape.

Purdy took the paper from him and read it out loud. "By Order of the American Bureau of Business and Congressional Act HC 213, this Place of Business is CLOSED FOR BUSINESS immediately."

"Can they do that?" Sage asked. "Don't they have to talk with us first?"

"We only just hit the big-time!" Ty said, exasperated. "Katy Perry wants cake!"

Purdy furrowed her brow and read further. "The

American Big Bakery Discrimination Act states that bakeries employing fewer than a thousand people must cease and desist operation. Big bakeries are suffering due to the unfair advantages of mom-and-pop bakeries throughout the United States. You are to cease and desist selling baked goods for profit henceforward. Violations will be punishable to the full extent of the law."

Rose gulped and felt something soft butt against her ankle. She looked down and found Gus the cat, who looked up at her. "A wayward wish is a bitter dish," he said, then threaded himself around her legs. "Told you so!"

Chapter 1

THE CAT'S IN THE BAG

EXACTLY TWENTY-SEVEN DAYS later, Rose woke to find her bedroom toasty warm like the inside of a sock fresh from the dryer.

She had suffered through twenty-seven days of waking to morning cold throughout the house, the ovens turned off, the front windows shuttered, the bakery closed for business. Twenty-seven days of living with the guilt that she, Rosemary Bliss, had brought a chill onto her town just by making a simple little wish.

She stretched in her bed and listened to her bones creak and was thankful that it was a warm Saturday in June. There was no need to drag herself through the sad-sack halls of Calamity Falls Middle School. Like everyone else in town, her fellow students had taken a turn for the worse since the Follow Your Bliss Bakery had closed. The teachers lost their pep, the sports teams lost their matches – even the cheerleaders had lost their enthusiasm. "Rah," they'd mumble at games, halfheartedly shaking their pompoms.

Worst of all, Devin Stetson was affected too, his blond bangs sitting lank and greasy on his forehead. Rose wondered what she'd ever seen in him at all.

And Rose was droopier than anyone: she alone, among all the people in Calamity Falls, knew that she was the reason the bakery had closed.

"Just another week," she muttered to herself as she lay there.

"Shhhhhh!" a little voice cried from beside her. "Sleeping!"

Rose whipped back the covers, exposing the snoring bundle of pyjamas that was her younger sister, Leigh, curled up like a comma in the space where the bed met the wall.

"Leigh," Rose said, "you've got to stop sneaking into my bed!"

"But I get scared," Leigh said, batting her dark eyelashes, and Rose felt guilty all over again. Her four-year-old sister's sudden night frights were probably Rose's fault, too.

"Another week of what?" someone else purred. Curled up in a tight comma against her sister's chest was Gus. He opened one green eye and glared at her. The cat had been able to talk as long as Rose had known him – ever since he'd eaten some Chattering Cheddar Biscuits her great-great-great-grandfather had made, in fact. But she was shocked anew every time he opened his tiny whiskered mouth and spoke. "Cat got your tongue?" he asked.

"Until school is out for the summer," Rose said. "I can't take it anymore. Everyone's so mopey!" She sucked in a deep lungful of air and felt comforted by the soft scent of cinnamon and nutmeg. "Someone's baking!" she exclaimed.

Gus stretched out his front paws and leaned forward, his tail rising straight like an exclamation point. "This *is* a bakery, you know."

"But, but, but – we've been closed! By order of the government!"

Leigh blinked and scratched Gus's rumpled grey ears. Since being freed from Lily's awful spell that caused her to praise her aunt incessantly, Leigh had taken on a Buddha-like serenity, and rarely opened her mouth except to speak the simple truth.

"Closed," the little girl said calmly, touching the wrinkle in Rose's forehead, "is just an opportunity to be open in a different way."

Rose scrunched up her face. "Well, open or closed, if we're baking, we're breaking the law," she said. "We'd better get downstairs."

Dressed in a red T-shirt and tan shorts, Rose arrived in the kitchen with Leigh and Gus just as Chip entered from the bakery – Chip was an ex-marine who usually helped customers in the store. Rose didn't know *what* they'd do without him.

"I don't understand why I'm here," he said. "The sign on the front still says CLOSED. The blinds are still drawn. The lights are still off."

"Good, Chip," Purdy said. "Now take a seat so I can explain to everyone what's going on."

He sat on a stool at the head of the table in the breakfast nook, where Rose's parents, brothers, and Balthazar were huddled around the table, with its overflowing pile of fan mail. Rose's father, Albert, held the official letter that had come from the United States government, reading it over and over, as if he expected to find some tiny footnote that negated the whole thing. "This law makes no sense – no sense at all!" he muttered under his breath. Leigh crawled under the breakfast table and re-emerged in her mother's lap. Rose slid in beside her brothers.

"I agree: It makes no sense," Rose's mother announced. "That's why, beginning today, the Follow Your *Bliss Bakery* is back in business."

"But, Purdy!" Albert protested. "That would be breaking the law!"

"Honey, the government says we *can't* operate," said Balthazar, wiping the top of his bald head with a handkerchief. "This document is perfectly clear: unless we employ more than a thousand people, we are shut down. That fancy lawyer, Bob Solomon, hasn't been able to find a single loophole. And our congresswoman, Big Nell Katey – well, she hasn't made a bit of headway with those other politicians down in Washington. They've got good hearts, the both of them, but we're up against something sneaky here."

Gus arched his back and hissed. He began to scratch at the wooden base of the breakfast table like it was a cage full of mice.

"Gus," Purdy said gently. "No scratching, please."

Gus sank to the ground and twisted miserably until

he was lying on his back. "I'm sorry. It's how Scottish Folds cope with sneakiness."

"The law says that we can't operate for *profit*," Purdy explained with a strange glint in her eye. "It says nothing about operating as a charitable organization. We have to stop *selling* baked goods, but we don't have to stop *baking!*"

Ty's jaw dropped. "You can't be suggesting that we—"

"—give our baked goods away for *free!*" Sage finished.

Ty put his head in his hands, careful not to mess up his hair. "I can't believe what I'm hearing. We'll *never* get rich this way!"

"Giving our goods away is exactly what I'm suggesting," Purdy said. "Our work is bigger than simple profits. Calamity Falls needs us."

Sage groaned theatrically.

Beside her, Albert smiled and folded up the letter. "We won't be able to give away our Bliss baked goods forever – we can't afford to do that. But we can at least do so until we find some way around this backward law."

"I just know this is Lily's fault." Balthazar rose from the breakfast table and began to pace around the room, scratching his beard. "May none of you forget: Lily never returned *Albatross's Apocrypha*. I'll bet you a loaf of Betray-Yourself Banana Bread that Lily is using the sinister recipes in that little booklet to wreak havoc on the government. I should have destroyed it when I had the chance back in 1972."

Rose's great-great-great-grandfather was fond of warning the family about the dangers of *Albatross's Apocrypha*, a pamphlet of particularly meddlesome and nasty recipes written long-ago by a black sheep in the Bliss family. Usually, the *Apocrypha* was tucked into a pocket at the back of the *Bliss Cookery Booke*, but when Lily had returned the *Booke* after she lost the Gala des Gâteaux Grands in Paris, the *Apocrypha* was missing.

"We don't actually know that, Balthazar," Albert protested, though Rose thought he looked more like he was trying to convince himself than Balthazar. Rose's great-great-great-grandfather just harrumphed.

"Never mind any of that!" Ty shouted. "The solution to our problems is so obvious! All Rose has to do is one commercial for Kathy Keegan Snack Kakes, and we can all retire to Tahiti. None of us will have to approach an oven again. *They'll* be baking for *us*!" He and Sage gave each other a high five.

"It's not about the money, Thyme," Purdy said, flicking her oldest son on the side of his head. "It's about the people of this town. They need us. And we need them. Baking is our grand purpose."

"Besides," said her father, "we can afford it – for now. We've always scrimped and saved in case of an emergency. And this? This is as much an emergency as Calamity Falls has ever faced."

Somewhere deep within her, Rose felt a tiny flame kindle, a fire of hope and a desire to do some good the only way she knew how. "What are we going to do?" she asked her mum.

Purdy smiled, and Rose felt the dreariness of the past twenty-seven days burn away like a cloud at sunrise. "We are now the Bliss Bakery Underground," Purdy announced. "We will bake all day and all night, and beginning tomorrow morning, we will personally deliver the cakes and pies and muffins to everyone in town. The people of Calamity Falls stuck with us through our hard times, when we didn't have the *Booke*. Now we're going to stick by them."

Albert tore the official government letter dramatically down the center. "I think that's the best idea I've ever heard."

Purdy moved Leigh to her father's lap. She stood up and began pacing the cramped bakery kitchen. "Chip will make a major grocery store run," Purdy said, looking at her burly assistant. "Albert – will you inventory our magical ingredients?" Standing tall, she added, "We shall not cease."

"I'll help," Rose said, happy for the opportunity to reverse her careless wish and, for the first time in nearly a month, to cut loose and bake – no cameras, no reporters, just three generations of Blisses, doing what they had always done best.

Making kitchen magic.

It was three in the morning.

The heat in the kitchen was as thick as grape jelly. Rose cracked the red egg of a masked lovebird into a bowl of zucchini muffin batter to make a batch of Love Muffins for Mr and Mrs Bastable-Thistle, who, without the magical intervention of the Bliss Bakery, became shy strangers to each other.

"Mum, look," Rose said as she mixed in the egg, watching the batter thicken and hiss as tiny hearts of flour exploded into the air.

But Purdy couldn't hear Rose – not over the Malaysian

Toucan of Fortune, whose confident squawk she released into a bowlful of pastry cream, then stuffed the cream into a batch of Choral Cream Puffs for the Calamity Falls Community Chorus, whose voices were meek and thin without them. "What was that, honey?" Purdy asked.

"Never mind," Rose said, continuing with the muffin batter as Balthazar unleashed the gaze of a medieval Third Eye onto a batch of Father-Daughter Fudge for Mr Borzini and his daughter, Lindsey – after eating the fudge, each could more easily glimpse where the other was coming from. "You never want to look a Third Eye directly in its, erm, eye," Balthazar told Rose. "It could blind you."

Mental note, Rose thought. *Don't go blind.*

The family had been at it for sixteen hours, and Purdy's master list of baked goods was still only half complete.

The kitchen itself was strewn with blue mason jars filled with various sniffs and snorts and fairies and gnomes and ancient lizards and talking mushrooms and googly eyes and woogly flies and jittering, glowing bobbles of every sort. Hints of cinnamon and nutmeg and vanilla swirled in the air, and all the various sounds coming from the kitchen made Rose hope the neighbours wouldn't think the Blisses were running a zoo.

Albert had ferried jar after jar of magical ingredients from the secret cellar beneath the walk-in fridge – "Watch your heads, Blisses!" – until the dingy wooden shelves were practically empty.

Ty and Sage had long since gone to bed. At one point, they'd come downstairs for a snack, but they took one look at the magical mayhem, at the chomping teeth and flying rabbits and the explosions of colour coming from dozens of metal mixing bowls, then scurried back upstairs.

There were Cookies of Truth for the infamous fibber Mrs Havegood, Calm-Down-Crepes for the angry, overwrought Scottish babysitter Mrs Carlson, and Adventurous-Apple-Turnovers for the reserved League of Lady Librarians.

There was Seeing-Eye Shortbread for Florence the Florist, who was nearly blind, Frugal Framboise Cake for the French restaurateur Pierre Guillaume, who had a notorious shopping problem, and even something for Devin Stetson, the blond boy whom Rose had thought about at least twice a day for approximately one year, five months, and eleven days. She had made him Breathe-Easy Sticky Buns to help with his frequent sinus infections, which, as far as Rose was concerned, were the only things wrong with Devin Stetson.

By four a.m., Rose felt that the heat from the ovens was slapping her on the head. She told Purdy she needed to lie down just for a minute, and she nuzzled onto the bench at the breakfast table and promptly fell asleep.

Rose woke to bright buttery sunshine and the swatting and drooling of Gus the Scottish Fold cat. "Deliveries, Rose!" he said, batting her on the shoulder with his thick paw. "The list is complete!"

Rose bolted upright and found her mother, father, and Balthazar snoring on the floor. Every surface of the kitchen was covered in white bakery boxes tied with red-and-white-striped twine.

Ty and Sage had already started loading boxes into the back of the Bliss family van. Leigh helped by sitting beside the boxes and patting them with her frosting-covered hands. "Pat-a-cake," she said over and over again.

Sage strapped her into her car seat and climbed in beside her.

"I'm driving," Ty said proudly. He was fond of reminding everyone that at sixteen he was old enough to drive, and now he reached into the back pocket of his dark jeans and pulled out his licence. The picture on the front captured the full height of his red spiky hair, though it cut off everything below his top lip. "Phew," he said. "Just making sure I had my licence. My *driver's* licence."

Rose rolled her eyes.

"Let's go, *hermana*," he said. "I'll drive."

"Actually, I think I'm going to make a few personal deliveries on my bike, if that's OK," Rose said.

Ty looked at her sideways, then shrugged. "Whatever *hermana* wants, *hermana* gets." Ever since Ty had taken Spanish in school, he added foreign words to what he said in an effort to sound foreign and sophisticated.

Sage called out through the van's window. "You do know there's no air-conditioning on a bike, right?"

"I know," said Rose. While her brothers waited, she rifled through the back of the van and grabbed a few choice boxes. She loaded them in the front basket of her bike and carefully put one special box into her backpack. Just as she was about to set off, Gus hopped inside the basket, too.

"Onward!" he cried.

"Do stop at the Reginald Calamity Fountain, sweet Rose, so that I can catch myself some breakfast."

The fuzzy grey blob of Gus's head peeked out from Rose's basket as she pedalled through the streets.

"Gus, there are no fish in the fountain," Rose answered, "only nickels and dimes that people throw in there for good luck. It's a tradition."

"Well, then, I shall collect those nickels and dimes and buy myself some delectable smoked fish."

Without stopping at the fountain, Rose parked her bike in front of the ivy-covered bungalow owned by Mr and Mrs Bastable-Thistle.

"No talking, Gus," she said, opening her backpack.

Gus leaped inside, wiggled around until he was comfortable, then poked his head out. "Oh, I know." He sighed. "If only the sight of a talking cat didn't cause such violent fainting among humans."

Rose pulled aside a tapestry of ivy and pressed her finger into the doorbell, which was shaped like a frog.

After a moment, Mr Bastable, wearing a frog-printed T-shirt that read KISS ME, answered the door. "Hello, Rose," he said. He seemed a bit droopy, though his stringy white hair was as wild as ever. "What brings you here?"

Rose stared at the welcome mat, which said FROGS AND CERTAIN HUMANS WELCOME. "As you know, the Bliss

Bakery has been closed," she said. "But we wanted to say thank you for supporting us while we were away at the Gala, so we brought you some of your favourite Love – I mean, *zucchini* muffins."

"My my," he said quietly. Rose could tell by the soft twinkle in his eye that he was touched, but Mr Bastable had always been shy, hence the need for Love Muffins.

Mr Bastable noticed Gus's folded ears peeking out from Rose's backpack. "Hey, is that a cat? What's wrong with its ears?"

Rose felt Gus's body tense inside her backpack.

"Oh, nothing! He's a breed called a Scottish Fold. They just have folded ears."

"Huh," Mr Bastable mused, biting absentmindedly into one of the Love Muffins. "Somewhat like the ear of a frog, all folded up on its face."

Gus dug his claws into Rose's back. "Ow!" She jumped.

"What?" Mr Bastable said.

"Nothing," said Rose.

Ignoring her, Mr Bastable took another crumbly bite and swallowed loudly. Suddenly, his eyes flashed a bright green, his back straightened, and he cleared his throat. "Felidia!" he shouted. "I must woo my beloved Felidia once more, for she is a supreme woman, and supreme women must be wooed daily! I'm coming, Felidia!"

Then Mr Bastable turned away, the box of muffins tucked under his arm. He slammed the door in Rose's face.

"I guess it worked," Rose said, though she didn't want to think about what was about to transpire inside the Bastable-Thistle bungalow.

"Ears like a *frog*," said Gus. "Of all the ridiculous nonsense."

Florence the Florist thought that Rose was a burglar until she took a bite out of a piece of Seeing-Eye Shortbread. "Ah! Rose Bliss!" she cried out, and sighed with relief that the Blisses hadn't forgotten about her.

Rose caught Pierre Guillaume on his day off. "*Sacré bleu!*" he cried as he took a bite of Frugal Framboise Cake, which promptly dissuaded him from buying a yacht on eBay. "That mother of yours, Purdy, she eez always looking out for me," he said.

Box by box, Rose went around town, narrowly averting small disasters, until just one box remained: the one in her backpack, the one she'd really wanted to deliver, for which all the others had been only an excuse.

She pedalled up the impossible incline of Sparrow Hill and parked her bike in front of Stetson's Doughnuts and Automotive Repair.

Rose wondered whether Devin had seen her new haircut. She had got what the hairdresser called "side bangs," which meant that her black bangs now sloped down from one end of her forehead to the other, instead of the usual straight line that she gave herself in the bathroom mirror. Rose hadn't said a word to Devin in school, but she thought that maybe he'd seen her bangs in the paper, or in a TV news report. She hated to admit how much the side bangs made her feel like a sophisticated woman, but she couldn't help it. They just did.

Walking in a sophisticated manner, Rose wandered into the store carrying the box of Breathe-Easy Sticky Buns. They were gooey pillows of sweet dough covered in sticky cinnamon frosting. In the very centre of each was a dollop of crème infused with Arctic Wind – the buns instantaneously cleared the lungs and sinuses of any unwanted goop. Purdy used to make them for Rose when she was home sick from school with a stuffy nose, and they were far more fun to eat than chicken soup.

Rose spotted Devin behind the checkout counter. He sported side bangs of his own, only his were a rich, sandy blond. To her they looked like spun gold. His nostrils were bright red and his eyes were clouded and dull. He blew his nose into a tissue.

"He looks like a sickly version of that Justin Boo Boo character," Gus whispered from his perch in the backpack.

"Shush!" she hissed, gliding over to the checkout counter.

She gathered herself and took a deep breath. "Hi, Devin."

Devin quickly wiped his nose, then smoothed his bangs. "Hi, Rose," he replied gloomily.

"Are you OK?" Rose asked. "Sick again?"

"Yeah, you doh me," he said, sniffling. He nervously drummed his fingers on the glass countertop. "You're, like, this celebrity dow. It's weird."

Rose's heart sank. "Bad weird, or good weird?"

Devin stumbled over his words. "Good weird. Oh, defidently good weird. I... uh..." He trailed off. His eyes darted between her face and an empty corner of the ceiling.

Is he nervous? Rose thought. *I'm usually the nervous one.*

Aloud, she said, "I came because even though the bakery is closed, I wanted to bring you your favourite – Sticky Buns! So you're not forlorn without them."

Rose nearly kicked herself as the words left her mouth. *Forlorn?* Why did she say that? She sounded like a ninety-year-old granny. Devin probably thought she was a word-obsessed moron.

Devin opened the box and sank his teeth into one of the thick, pillowy buns. "Mmmmmmmmm!" he exclaimed. "My oh my, that is one gnarly bun." The *m*'s and *n*'s came out crystal clear. "Weird! I can breathe again!" He smiled, and his eyes lost their sleepy look.

"Good weird or bad weird?" Rose teased.

"Good weird," he replied, smiling.

Back outside, Gus whispered, "He's not even that cute," as Rose skipped toward her bike, her feet so light that she felt like she might be receiving assistance from unseen fairies.

"Says you." Rose squealed, already replaying the moment in her mind like a beloved DVD.

"The basket of your bike is decidedly uncomfortable for travel," Gus observed, squinting up at the empty wire basket. "And cold. The wind, you know."

"Would you like to ride in my backpack?" Rose said.

"I thought you'd never ask."

She knelt down and opened the flap, and Gus leaped inside. From the dark, she could hear him moving around and saying, "Much warmer! This is more like it!"

She reshouldered the pack and had very nearly reached her bike when a voice called out to her from the lookout fence at the top of the hill.

"Are you Rose Bliss?"

Rose turned and saw a hulking figure silhouetted against the afternoon sky. The only person she'd ever seen with such enormous shoulders was Chip – but this man sure didn't sound like Chip. She moved closer.

"You're Rose Bliss, aren't you?" he repeated in a deep, gravelly voice.

. The man had a nice-looking face – at least for someone almost as old as her dad – rugged, with a huge head, a square jaw, and narrow, beady eyes. He had thick black hair and wore a track suit made of fuzzy maroon velour. His fingers and the front of his track suit seemed to be covered with a light dusting of flour.

"I don't like this," Gus whispered. "What's that on his

fingers? What sort of grown man wears a maroon velour track suit?"

Rose's parents had always told her not to talk to strangers, but ever since she'd won the Gala des Gâteaux Grands, everyone knew who she was. There was no real point in denying it. "Yes, I'm Rose Bliss."

"I thought so." The man gestured over the tranquil pastures of Calamity Falls. "You know what's a travesty, Rose? The new bakery law."

Rose softened a bit. "Yeah, it makes no sense."

"Those people out there," the man went on, sounding passionate, "they need cake and pie and cookies and doughnuts. Just a little sweet thing once in a while reminds a person of how sweet life is." He rested his hand on his chest, like someone about to sing "The Star-Spangled Banner."

Rose nodded. She thought of the lives she had brightened this morning. The people she and her family had helped. But how long would they be able to keep it up? The Blisses had provided enough magic that morning to last the town a couple of days, but they couldn't really go on baking and delivering everything to people's homes without being paid. They weren't broke, not yet, but they couldn't support the whole town.

"A life without the occasional slice of cake is... it's an empty life," he continued, inching closer. "Look out there," he said, gesturing again at Calamity Falls. "Emptiness. That's what's going to become of all those lives."

Gus reached a paw out of the backpack and swatted Rose's ear. "I don't like this!" he whispered.

The strange behemoth of a man bent over so they were eye to eye. "Would you... I mean, do you want to help those people?"

"Of course!" Rose said. She thought of the wish she'd made. She didn't really believe what the cat had told her (did she?). A wish couldn't change the world (could it?). But even so, she would take it back if she could. "It's what I want most in the world."

"Oh good!" said the man. "In that case..."

He snapped his fingers.

Before Rose could take a deep breath to scream, darkness closed over her and Gus as they were enveloped in a giant empty flour sack.

Chapter 2

MAKING THE MOSTESS OF
A BAD SITUATION

THE TWO HOURS that Rose spent trapped in the burlap sack with Gus were by far the worst of her life.

First of all, no one likes to be kidnapped by strangers and tossed into a bag. Questions such as *Where are they taking me?* and *Will I ever return?* naturally arise. Second, being trapped in a burlap sack inside a moving vehicle in summer feels essentially like being kept in an itchy oven. A bouncing, jouncing, *moving* oven. Third, the residual flour that dusted the walls of the bag mingled with her sweat to form a disgusting paste. She scrabbled at the neck of the sack with her nails, but it was firmly tied shut.

Then there was the matter of Gus. "I have claws," he kept whispering to her. "Just remember that, Rose. They are weapons of mass destruction, these claws."

Luckily, the man who had stuffed her in the sack seemed not to be able to hear the whispers of the Scottish Fold cat over the hum of the van and the honking of traffic. All Rose could do was keep her wits about her and, every so often, yell, "Where are we going? Let me out of here!"

But there was never any answer.

When the van finally came to a stop, a pair of sturdy arms lifted the sack containing Rose and Gus out of the van. She heard the opening of doors and felt a sudden rush of air-conditioning.

Then the arms set her down in a chair, and the burlap sack was pulled away.

Rose was instantly blinded by fluorescent lights.

She found herself sitting on a rusted metal chair in the centre of a room made of grey concrete. Feeble light peeked through tiny windows near the ceiling. At one end of the room was a grey metal desk covered in manila file folders. The wall behind the desk was lined with filing cabinets of rusted grey metal. The rows of rectangular fluorescent lights that hung from the ceiling sputtered and hummed in the awful way that fluorescent lights do, as if they were actually prisons for thousands of radioactive fireflies.

The room smelled like metal and disinfectant, and Rose suddenly felt a wave of longing for the scents of home: butter and chocolate and cakes just pulled from the oven.

"I don't like this place," Gus whispered, digging flour out of the spaces beneath his crumpled ears with his paws. "It looks like an office from a movie about... how terrible offices are."

She petted the cat on the head. "It's OK. You've got those claws, remember?"

"Indeed," the cat purred.

Rose shook out her hair. She dusted flour off her red T-shirt and her eyelids and from behind her ears and even flicked some out of her armpits.

"Where am I?" she yelled.

When no one answered, Rose spun around and saw two men standing by a grimy, empty water cooler in the opposite corner of the room. One of them was the hulking, squinty gentleman in the maroon velour track suit who had approached her on top of Sparrow Hill, and the other was a tall bespectacled man. He had a tiny face and a bulbous white head that was entirely hairless. He looked like an illustration of an alien wearing a suit.

"Hello?" she hollered again. "Where am I?"

Neither of the men so much as turned to acknowledge her – they kept chatting at the water cooler, sipping from little paper cones.

"What is this?" said the bald man, gesturing at Rose, so that water splashed from his little paper cone onto the floor. "You were supposed to get the BOOK."

"It was a no-go on the book, boss," the man wearing the track suit answered. "The bakery is closed. I couldn't get in there. So I brought the *cook* instead."

Rose gasped. These two had been after the *Bliss Family Cookery Booke* – but what could they possibly want with it? It was bad enough when Aunt Lily had gotten her hands on the *Booke*, but when she'd given it back, Rose had thought that she – and her family – were safe.

The wiry bald man refilled his cone of water. "No, not the *cook*, the *book*. What we need is the book."

The bulky man let out a long huff. "But, sir, the *cook* is the next best thing to the *book*. She won that French baking contest. She can do it."

The bald man goggled his eyes at Rose. "But she's so young!" he said in a sharp, quiet voice. "So scrawny! And she has a cat in her backpack, with broken ears!"

"I can hear you, you know," Rose fumed. "I'm right here. And if you don't tell me where I am, I will set my cat on you."

Gus jumped out of the backpack and sat back on his hind legs, hissing and swiping, with his front legs extended and his claws bared. He looked like a praying mantis.

"And his ears are *not* malformed," Rose added. "They are a distinctive feature of the breed."

"Don't worry, little lady," said the thin man. "We'll explain everything, just calm that old cat down."

Rose gave Gus a stern look. He shrugged and retracted his claws. "Good kitty," she said, pulling Gus into her lap and petting him until he was purring. "There," Rose said. "Now, I repeat: where am I?"

The two men inched along the perimeter of the room toward the desk, keeping as far away from Gus as they could.

The bald man sat in the chair behind the desk, while the man in the velour track suit settled in behind him, leaning against the row of rusted metal filing cabinets.

"Where you aaaaaare," said the thin man, "is the finest bakery in the universe: the Mostess Snack Cake Corporation." He tapped his long index fingers together and stared at Rose through his spectacles. He had no lips to speak of – it was as if the skin beneath his nose and above his chin just decided, at a certain point, to stop. "I am Mr Butter, and my muscular associate, whom you've already had the pleasure of meeting, is Mr Kerr."

"Mostess, huh," Rose said. She had heard of Mostess Snack Cakes, of course. Everyone had. They were the ones with the little white cow in the corner of the package.

At school, Rose's friends sometimes pulled out packages of Mostess Snack Cakes at the lunch table – little chocolate cakes stuffed with marshmallow, black cupcakes covered in white dots, vanilla cakes stuffed with chocolate cream – each with different names that bore no resemblance to the cake itself, like Dinky Cakes, Moony Pyes, and King Things. Rose never thought to try a bite of her friends' Dinky Cakes or King Things, because her mother always packed her a delicious homemade treat, and anyway, the snack cakes were gobbled and gone in two bites.

"Misters Butter and Kerr, of the Mostess Snack Cake Company," Rose repeated. "Got it. Now I can tell the police who kidnapped me."

Mr Butter opened his non-lips and let out a crisp

ha-ha. "Kidnapped! Do you hear that, Mr Kerr? The poor thing thinks that *we kidnapped* her!"

Mr Kerr stared nervously at Rose. "Ha," he replied.

"You carried me here in a flour sack," Rose said. "Against my will."

"Oh, you've misinterpreted the day's events, Miss Bliss," Mr Butter went on smoothly. "We haven't *kidnapped* you, we've brought you here to offer you a *job!*"

Rose furrowed her brow. "A job? What kind of job?"

"We need help with our recipes," Mr Kerr said bluntly, rubbing his hands over the smooth velour of his track suit.

Mr Butter glared at Mr Kerr a moment, then turned back to Rose, all smiles. "Yes, that's the gist of it," he said, tapping his fingers on the desk. "You see, Rose, we here at the Mostess Snack Cake Corporation were just as horrified as you were by the passage of the Big Bakery Discrimination Act. Of course, the law does happen to benefit our bakery, as we employ well over a thousand people. So we wanted to help a newly unemployed small-town baker like yourself by putting *you* to work for *us.*"

Gus fidgeted on her lap. It suddenly dawned on Rose that neither of them had seen a bathroom for hours.

"Think of it as an exchange programme," Mr Kerr added matter-of-factly. His voice was so deep that it sounded like his throat was trying to swallow the words before they escaped. "Like you kids do in school."

"*Exactly*," said Mr Butter. "You see, Rose, we have something wonderful to offer each other."

"We do?" Rose said.

"Mostess has the finest baking facilities in the world, thousands of square feet of floor space, the most cutting-edge machinery, and a staff of thousands of qualified baking professionals." Mr Butter paused a moment to savour the thought of it. "That is what you lack. *You*, Rosemary Bliss, are a baker without a bakery."

Rose hung her head. Mr Butter was wrong. The Bliss family had a bakery; they just weren't legally allowed to *operate* it. She thought of last night, how cramped and hot the tiny kitchen had been, and how little they could really afford to support the town's baked-goods needs. How exhausted she and her parents were. They couldn't go on like that.

"What *we* lack is the kind of attention that you small-town bakers can afford to lavish on each loaf of bread, each crumpet, each swirl of cupcake frosting, each—"

"I understand," Rose interrupted.

Mr Butter bristled. "You know as well as I do that a perfect dessert sweetens life like nothing else. People in every town, students at every school, from every walk of life, they all depend upon that little bit of goodness that they can find within, say, a Bliss tart. Or slice of cake."

"Or a muffin," Mr Kerr continued. "Or a croissant. Or clafouti. Or—"

"I get it," Rose snapped.

Mr Butter cleared his throat and ran his fingers along the bald arches where his eyebrows should have been. "At the Mostess Snack Cake Corporation, we believe our snack cakes are nearly perfect, but our recent sales record has not reflected this. Our snack cakes can't compete with the love and the... how do I describe it... the *magic* that you small bakeries provide."

Rose eyed Mr Butter suspiciously and felt something flutter nervously in her stomach. *Magic?* she thought. *He couldn't possibly know about the magic.*

"And shouldn't every town have what Calamity Falls has? Readily available, forever fresh, fabulous, delicious gourmet treats?" Mr Butter went on. "Before your fortuitous arrival, we had—"

"You *kidnapped* me," Rose said again. On her lap, Gus growled.

"—we had the assistance of a master baker who had very nearly perfected our recipes. Sadly, she competed in a baking contest in Paris, and after events there never returned." Rose immediately knew there was only one person he could be talking about – her devious aunt Lily. "And that's why we need *you*," Mr Butter said. "To perfect the recipes. To make our snack cakes the best in the world. To finish what the previous director started but failed to finish."

Rose looked down at Gus, who stared back at her with wide eyes, as if to say, *Don't you dare*. The point of his tail flicked.

"Why me?" Rose asked. "Why not any of the other bakers at any of the millions of bakeries around the country that were just put out of business by that crazy new law?"

Mr Butter tapped his finger on the tip of his broad nose. "You come highly recommended."

"By whom?"

"Well… Jean-Pierre Jeanpierre, of the Gala des Gâteaux Grands, of course. He selected you as the winner of the most prestigious baking competition in the world, didn't he? Wouldn't it make sense that we would seek your help above everyone else's?"

Rose blushed. It was flattering, if highly suspicious. Apparently she was never going to live down that competition. "But you said before that you wanted the book instead of the cook. What book were you talking about?"

"We heard that at the Bliss Bakery you use a... special book that makes your treats magically delicious," Mr Butter said. "That the secret of your success is thanks to—"

"Nope!" Rose lied. *How could they know about the* Booke? "No special book! We do all our baking from memory. Whoever told you about a special book was pulling your leg. Yanking your chain. Lying through their teeth—"

"And that is precisely why we brought you here," said Mr Butter. "You are our only hope, Rosemary Bliss. We desperately need your help. Not just for us, but for the good of anyone who has ever turned for hope and happiness to a sweet baked good." He removed his glasses and dabbed at his eyes with the corner of his handkerchief. "Will you help us in this, our time of greatest need?"

Mr Butter obviously cared about baking, Rose thought. True, he *had* kidnapped her, but her mother would never have let her go anyway, so in a sense, Mr Butter had no choice if he wanted Rose's expertise.

And her family was going to need the money.

Maybe she could do a little bit of good and earn some money for her family. True, she'd made that wish that she could be done with baking, but maybe baking wasn't done with her.

"I can help you," said Rose. Gus dug his claws into her leg, which made Rose yelp. *"I wasn't done!"* she muttered to the cat through her teeth. She turned to Mr Butter. "I can only help if you *if* you let me call my parents and tell them where I am. They are probably insanely worried by now."

"Of course you can call your parents," Mr Butter said. "After you bake."

The hair on Rose's neck stood on end. "So you're holding me hostage!"

"Hostage!" Mr Butter laughed. "I don't even know the meaning of the word. You're free to go at any time." He examined the fingernails of his right hand. "After you've completed your duties, of course."

"You can't keep me here against my will!" Rose cried.

"Against your will?" Mr Butter fanned the idea away with his hand. "We are not holding you here. You may come and go as you wish… once our five main recipes are perfected."

Rose was getting nowhere with this man. She thought of her parents, how Ty and Sage would have returned from their deliveries by now. Albert and Purdy would ask where Rose was, and they would say that she'd wanted to make a few deliveries on her bike. It would be conceivable that Rose was still out and about. Maybe her family wouldn't start worrying until sundown. She could finish the baking here by then, or at least find a phone.

"Fine," she said at last, gripping Gus so tightly that he knew not to scratch. "I'll bake first."

"Come," said Mr Butter with a smile. "Let me show you where we work."

Mr Butter led Rose down a bright corridor, with Mr Kerr taking up the rear. From within her backpack, Gus leaned forward, both his paws on her left shoulder, the sound of his constant low growl a comfort in her ear.

Mr Butter opened a steel door and Rose was hit with

the smell of sugar and chocolate and bleach, the heat of roaring ovens, and the sounds of industrial hissing and churning and buzzing and pounding.

Mr Butter led them out onto a steel catwalk – with railings, of course – overlooking a vast factory of gleaming stainless steel. Giant metal paddles churned enormous vats of chocolate. Dozens of hairnetted workers piped white dots onto hundreds of chocolate cupcakes that rode on a conveyor belt, like luggage at an airport. A monstrous mechanical press sealed snack cake after snack cake into plastic wrappers, then another conveyor belt dropped the packages into cartons.

Rose stared down at the scene in distaste. She was used to individually packing each precious cake in a white box and tying it off with baker's twine.

"Gorgeous, isn't it?" said Mr Butter, inhaling deeply and spreading his arms majestically. "We produce eight thousand snacks of one sort or another every minute. Our facilities here are larger than the Pentagon, and we have more delivery trucks working for us than the U.S. Postal Service."

When they reached the end of the catwalk, Mr Butter led Rose and Gus into a tiny glass-walled room that was suspended precariously over the factory floor. She looked down at the tangled mess of conveyor belts and was reminded of the stomach-churning feeling she'd had when she looked over the railing at the top of the Eiffel Tower.

The suspended room was empty except for an illuminated glass pedestal, on top of which sat a glass dome. Inside the glass dome was a small hemisphere of chocolate cake, stuffed with white pastry cream. She recognized it instantly as a Dinky Cake.

"Why do you have an entire room devoted to a Dinky Cake?" she asked.

"It's not *just* a Dinky Cake," said Mr Kerr, squinting his dark eyes.

"Beneath this hallowed dome," Mr Butter began, like he was delivering a sermon, "lies the very genesis of the Mostess Snack Cake Corporation. Our empire was built on the Dinky Cake. Each year, the average person in the United States devours upward of seven pounds of Dinkies."

"Ugh," said Rose, remembering the way some of the kids at school used to gobble up the cakes in two bites. "So, why is this one in a jar?"

"This," Mr Butter said, once again lifting his glasses

and wiping his eyes, "is the first Dinky Cake we ever made. And it's every bit as fresh as it was the day it was manufactured by my grandfather back in 1927."

Rose was horrified. The Dinky Cake was almost a century old – it should already have rotted away. "That's vile."

"It's *sensational*," Mr Butter spat, pressing his spindly arms close to his sides. "It's the power of preservatives – something your homespun cookies lack. Two days after you bake a cake, it dries out and winds up in the garbage. But with preservatives, each Dinky is guaranteed to be as delicious as the day you bought it, no matter when you eat it. The cakes are, in a way, immortal."

Gus, who was staring at the Dinky, began to heave.

"Oops! My cat has a hairball!" Rose cried as she whisked Gus out of the room and placed him gently on the catwalk, where he continued to dry heave. "I would like to leave now," he said quietly so that only Rose could hear him.

"I want to go home, too," said Rose, equally quiet. "But we have to find a way out of here."

"We want you to go home as well!" said Mr Butter, who had stepped out of the glass Dinky shrine just in time to hear Rose. "But there is work to do first, so now we are going to bring you to our main test kitchen. It's the happiest place on Earth."

"I thought that was Disneyland," Gus whispered.

Mr Butter put his thin arm around Rose's shoulder. "Your mission, which you've already accepted, will be to perfect the recipes for our five key products. After that, you will be absolutely free to go. With our thanks, of course."

"Of course," Rose said with a gulp. "Perfecting a few recipes should be easy." She looked at Gus.

But the cat only shook his head and sighed.

Chapter 3

FLCP

Outside the main factory building, Mr Butter and Mr Kerr ushered Rose and Gus into the back seat of a golf cart.

"Now we are off!" Mr Butter shouted. "To the place where the magic happens!"

"Magic?" Rose repeated. *Were there kitchen magicians here? No, that couldn't be... could it?*

"A figure of speech," Mr Butter said. "I'm speaking, of course, of the magic of industry!"

"Oh," Rose said, breathing a sigh of relief.

From her backpack, the cat whispered, "Spare me, please."

Mr Kerr drove the cart past dozens of box-shaped warehouses, all painted a lifeless grey. Rose looked up the alleyways between the warehouses and all she could see were other warehouses, as if she'd entered a labyrinth of grey blocks from which there was no escape. The buildings were so tall and so close together that even the late-afternoon sun failed to penetrate to the ground below, and the streets of the Mostess Snack Cake Corporation were dark as night.

The sun would be setting in an hour or so, and she knew that her parents would have officially started worrying that she hadn't returned. She considered hopping off the cart and making a run for it, but in which direction? The buildings seemed to go on forever.

"How many buildings are there?" Rose asked, trying to seem casual.

"More than one hundred and seventy-five units in this compound alone," Mr Butter answered proudly. "Then there's our other production facility in Canada. That one has only one hundred and twenty-five buildings."

After what seemed like a long drive, Mr Kerr stopped the cart in front of a grey warehouse with a giant 67 painted on the side. He pulled a walkie-talkie from his suit jacket pocket and spoke softly into it. "Marge, FLCPC landing, over."

Suddenly, a part of the warehouse wall lifted into the roof, like an automated garage door, and Mr Kerr drove the cart through the opening. The door closed behind them, locking the golf cart into a pitch-black, air-conditioned box.

When the floor underneath started rumbling, Rose realized they were in an elevator. After a minute, the car emerged on the floor of a giant kitchen with rust-colored linoleum tiles on the floor, stainless steel prep tables, and a row of top-of-the-line ovens.

The perimeter of the room was lined with every conceivable kitchen appliance: restaurant-sized stand mixers, deep fryers, toasters and blenders, salamanders and broilers, stainless steel pots and pans, and a rack containing twenty spatulas of various sizes and colours.

Rose gasped. She didn't like being brought here against her will, but she certainly didn't mind the kitchen itself. It was almost perfect – the only thing missing was a secret pantry of magical blue mason jars like they had back home.

"Quite something, isn't it?" Mr Butter asked. "This is our test kitchen."

He snapped his fingers, and a row of men and women in white lab coats, aprons, and chef's toques marched in from a small door at the far corner of the room labelled BAKERS' QUARTERS. In perfect unison, the six bakers filed in behind the row of metal prep tables and stood at attention.

The six bakers were all nearly the same height – that is, on the shorter side, just about as tall as Rose herself. And they were all round. You might not notice it if you were just looking at one of the bakers, but seeing them all together in a row, it was clear they all were alike in one way: they were all overweight.

Also, they were smiling. Not like genuinely happy men and women, but more like people whose mouths were being stretched up at the sides by invisible fish hooks.

"Why are they so round?" Gus whispered, cradled in Rose's arms. "They look as though they might roll away with just one push."

"Shh," she replied. "I don't know."

Mr Butter sauntered over to the prep tables and leaned in close. "A spot." He smiled, pointing at the perfectly clean stainless steel surface. "Someone missed a spot."

Then he snapped his fingers.

One of the bakers gasped, ran to the back wall, and grabbed a fresh towel and some spray. He hurried back to the table and scrubbed vigorously at the spot.

Mr Butter pulled a magnifying glass out of his pocket and peered at the tabletop. "Better," he said. Then he stood straight again, cleared his throat theatrically, and addressed Rose. "These are our very best bakers, specialists in every facet of the creation of our great line of products. They now all answer to you, Rosemary Bliss."

"Um, OK," Rose said. The bakers' eyes swivelled from Mr Butter to Rose. One on the end farthest away from her audibly gulped.

"And this is our Head Baker, Marge."

The woman standing closest to Rose had round pink cheeks and short brown hair that peeked out from beneath her chef's toque. Her lips were as plump as maraschino cherries, and her nose was as round as a tiny cupcake. The pockets of her apron bulged with paper and recipe cards.

"I'm Marge, and I'm in charge," she said. "Let me introduce you to our specialists. This is Ning, he's our Icing Tech."

Ning, a gentleman with a black crew cut, pointy eyebrows, and a large mole above his lip, gave Rose a salute.

"This is Jasmine, our CTM – Cake Texture Modifier,"

Marge said, moving down the line. Jasmine, a woman with two long black braids, nodded, and the wide grin plastered across her face grew even wider. "The texture of a cake is, as I'm certain you know, the most important thing."

"Next we have Gene, our VP of Fillings, both marshmallowy and fruity." Gene had a brown mustache and long, curly hair that he wore tied back in a hairnet.

"And down at the end there," said Marge, "we've got the twins, Melanie and Felanie. Nut Chunk and Sprinkle Maestros, respectively."

At the end of the line stood two young women with short blonde hair and freckles. They waved to Rose and smiled so widely that Rose could see their gums.

These people are smiling, thought Rose, *out of fear.* They were all terrified of Mr Butter, she realized.

"That's it," said Marge. "That's the gang."

"And this," announced Mr Butter with a flourish of his bony, fishy-white hand, "is Miss Rosemary Bliss, your new FLCP Director."

"She's a lot younger than the last one," said Marge, then rushed to add, "but worthy of our respect all the same!"

Rose furrowed her brow. "FLCP? What's that? It sounds like the noise Gus makes when he gets a hairball."

The bakers began to titter good-naturedly.

"FLCPs," said Mr Butter, "are the things we bake. The products. Dinkies, King Things, all of them – they are all different types of FLCPs: Food-Like Consumer Products."

"Food-*like?*" Rose repeated.

"Because of the mix of preservatives and chemicals we use in our delicious treats, the government has classified them as Not Food, but Food-Like." Mr Butter shrugged as though he were talking about a minor embarrassment. He winked at Rose. "But you and I both know that the government makes mistakes all the time, don't we?"

Rose thought about the wrongheaded law that had closed down the Follow Your Bliss Bakery and nodded. "We sure do."

Marge came around behind her and spotted the grey furball nestled in Rose's arms. "Wow! A cat!" she cooed, lifting Gus out and cradling him like an infant. "There is nothing I love more on this sweet, sad dumpling of a planet than a funny-looking, alien-eyed, fat cat with crinkled ears."

Gus wore a look of sheer contempt as he gazed into the eyes of the round-headed baker.

"No cats in the kitchen," said Mr Kerr, pulling Gus from Marge's arms and dropping him back inside Rose's backpack. She heard the Scottish Fold sigh deeply over the ratchet of the zipper.

"Do I start baking now?" Rose asked, eager to get this whole charade over with so she could return to her family. They'd be worrying, she knew.

"That's the spirit!" said Mr Butter. "But no. It's too late today. You'll start in the morning."

"You expect me to *sleep* here?" Rose asked, outraged. "That wasn't part of the deal."

Mr Butter gritted his teeth, but said cheerfully, "If you are to perfect the five recipes in the five days we've allotted you—"

"Five days?!" Rose repeated, shocked. She had expected to spend a few hours here at the most – not *days*.

"It's not enough time for an average baker, I know," Mr Butter said, stroking his lip, "but are you not the great" – he coughed into his hand – "Rosemary Bliss? The youngest baker to win the Gala blah blah blah?"

"It was the Gala des Gâteaux—"

"Yes, I know what it was called. I said 'blah blah blah' to show you that I am not impressed. As I was saying, to make the most of the five days until… well, the five days we have allotted you, you will live here. Your bedroom is up those stairs there, in the office that overlooks the FLCP Development Kitchens. Tomorrow you'll get started, and Marge and the team will execute your marvelous ideas. The team is always here. If you have an inspirational dream and come up with something brilliant at three in the morning, just wake Marge, and the team will rally behind you."

"The bakers *all* live here?" Rose asked, looking around uneasily.

"Of course," said Mr Butter. "They sleep right back there, in the Bakers' Quarters. Where else would they live?"

"In town, maybe? With their families?" Rose offered.

"Oh," said Mr Butter, laughing as though Rose had told a funny joke. "Goodness, no. We are in recipe crisis here, Rose, and recipe crisis requires round-the-clock attention. What are families and homes when there are snack cakes to perfect? Nothing! The only thing that matters – to me, the Mostess Corporation, and to you – is that these recipes be perfected." He dropped one of his bony hands on her shoulder; it was like having a bag of hangers draped across her back. "The bakers won't be going anywhere until our little problem is solved. And neither, for that matter, will you. Good night, Rose. We'll see you in the morning."

Rose climbed the spiral stainless steel staircase in the corner of the test kitchen, which led to a room suspended from the corner of the ceiling. She could hear Gus snoring from inside of her backpack, so she knew he was OK.

The room had glass walls and looked out over the test kitchen like a fishbowl on a shelf, with Rose the fish. Marge had turned off the lights and the bakers had returned to their quarters at the back of the kitchens. Rose's room had a single, tiny window to the outside world, just one foot square, above the bed. Through it, June twilight filtered in and glinted on the prep tables in the darkened kitchen below.

The room was filled by a twin bed with a white duvet, a metal desk and desk lamp, and a little wooden dresser. Past a door on the back wall was a white-tiled bathroom, complete with little monogrammed towels. MOSTESS spelled the red thread. Sitting on top of the desk was a glass of milk and a few dry-looking biscuits. *Dinner?* Rose thought.

Rose breathed deeply – the room had an oddly familiar smell, though she couldn't place her finger on it. Was it the faintest whiff of old perfume? A faintly flowery hint of... she couldn't recall where she knew the scent from. Maybe it was just the trusty old smell of a bakery?

White curtains were tied in bunches in the corners of the room; Rose untied them, covering the glass walls for privacy. Then she unzipped her backpack and Gus tumbled out onto the bed.

"Ah!" he said, waking up from his nap. "Are we home yet?" He glanced from side to side, then sat back and curled his tail round his feet. "I was hoping this place was all a bad dream."

"I'm afraid not," Rose said. She took a biscuit and broke it in half, popping one of the pieces into her mouth and giving the other to Gus. Then she took a swig of milk.

"It's OK, Rosie," the cat said between bites. "We will triumph! Are we not cats? Are we not the slyest, smartest, most surprising foes in all of creation? Are we not—"

"You're a cat," Rose said, frowning. "I'm a girl."

"A technicality," Gus said. "My point, though, was simple. We shall get through this. We have each other." He yawned.

Rose cracked open the window above the bed and stuck her head out. The room was pretty high up. All she could see were the tops of other warehouses. They seemed to go on forever. On the very edge of the horizon was a barbed-wire fence. There'd be no escaping through this window.

The sky was a dark purple, the color of a summer plum, with little rivulets of bright orange winding their way through the deep clouds. Her parents would definitely be panicking by now. They would notify the police, they would search Calamity Falls, they would find her bike outside Stetson's on Sparrow Hill, and Devin Stetson would tell them she had made her final delivery at around three that afternoon. They would know she'd been missing ever since.

Rose gave a trembling sigh. She just wanted to go home. She missed her sister and her parents, Balthazar and Chip – she even missed her brothers! "I wish I'd never made that wish," she muttered. "To stop baking. Then none of this would have happened."

"This isn't happening to you because of a little wish," the cat said, "so don't go beating yourself up over it. Just get a good night's sleep. That's a cat's solution to everything, you know: sleep. The right thing to do is always obvious in the morning. Oh, and by the way – had you considered sharing your milk?"

Rose stared at the half-empty glass. "I'm sorry, Gus. How rude of me." She tipped the glass over on the floor and let Gus lap up the rest of it with his tongue.

"Oh no," Rose moaned, staring at her clothes. "I don't have any pyjamas."

"Neither do I," Gus said, looking up at her. "But you don't see me complaining about it!"

Rose rolled her eyes and went to the dresser and tugged open the drawers. They were stuffed with white linen trousers in all sizes, white chef's coats, white chef's hats, and boy's underwear.

"Seriously?" she said, holding up an unopened package of briefs. "I have to wear *these?*"

Gus did his best to twist his head around so that he could clean his back. "Ugh! Out, out, spot! I've been cleaning since we got here, and there is *still* flour stuck in my fur."

Rose sat down again on the bed, right next to Gus.

The two of them huddled against each other, and Rose thought about what her family would be doing right about now if she'd been at home.

Leigh would have been pulled out of her filthy trousers and T-shirt and been loudly unhappy until she was zipped up into her pyjamas. Sage would be using the head of Rose's desk lamp to create a spotlight, and then performing in its beam, telling the jokes he'd written and then raising his hands to quiet the nonexistent audience. Ty would be making plans for what he called "the Grand Finale" – the stunts he hoped to pull off during the last week of school. And her parents...

It was too much. Rose blinked back tears. She knew her family wouldn't be doing any of these things. They'd all be awake, so worried about Rose they'd be unable to eat dinner, let alone sleep. She had to find a way to contact them.

Through the curtains, Rose gazed down at the shadowy appliances looming in the test kitchen and looked in vain for something she could use to get help.

"Something is seriously wrong with this place," she said.

"I'll say," Gus replied. "Linoleum flooring with stainless steel prep tables? Dreadful."

"Besides that," Rose said, scratching beneath Gus's chin so that he purred and closed his eyes. "Those bakers are terrified of that Mr Butter. And the things they make here: Food-*Like* Consumer Products? A baked good is natural, wholesome. It's food. Not a consumer product that's *like* food."

"To say nothing of the fact that they kidnapped us," Gus reminded her.

"I don't want to fix their stupid FLCPs," Rose said. "We need to escape. Maybe if we find the button for that elevator, we could get down to the ground floor."

"And then what?" said Gus. "I suppose you intend to climb that barbed-wire fence in the distance?" Rose fell silent as the cat opened his eyes and resumed cleaning his back. "Would you mind turning on that lamp, Rose? I can't see what I'm doing over here."

"I thought cats could see in the dark!" Rose exclaimed.

"That's just something we say to impress people. My night vision is actually just as poor as yours," Gus admitted.

Rose switched on the lamp, then peered out of the window. It was now pitch-dark outside.

"My parents must be flipping out right now," Rose said. "They probably think I'm dead." She rolled over and buried her head in the pillow. Gus stopped his cleaning and sat on her head, which was his way of saying that he didn't know what to say.

Then, after a moment, he leaped across the room and landed on the dresser.

"The Caterwaul!" he exclaimed.

"What?" Rose asked, rolling over.

Gus sat back on his hind legs and clapped his front paws together. "I can't believe I forgot about the Caterwaul! It won't get you out of here, but it will get word to your family that you are safe. Trapped, but safe. So they won't worry."

"Good!" Rose said, feeling relief wash over her. "But what *is* the cay-ter-wall?"

"The Caterwaul is a network," Gus explained. "At some point in our feline history, all the breeds came together and decided that while we each may privately feel that our own breed is the best – which is silly, given that the Scottish Fold is objectively the superior breed – in times of crisis we ought to unite for the common good. Long before Facebook, we formed the world's first social network. And we named it the Caterwaul.

"If I tell any cat a message," Gus continued, "he will carry it to another cat, and the message will be passed from cat to cat until eventually it falls on the correct ears. It takes a little while to get information back and forth, but it works."

Rose feared that Gus might be making this up just to soothe her, but soothe her it did. "I thought you were the only cat who can talk," she said suspiciously.

"The narrowness of your perspective is endearing. Most cats do not speak *English*, as I do," said Gus. "But all cats speak *Felinsch*. You can't hear it, but it is being spoken."

Rose was too happy learning about the Caterwaul to feel embarrassed. If she couldn't get out of this dreadful prison of a factory, at least her family would know she was safe. "How will you get word to other cats?" she asked. "Where are you going to find one in this place?"

"I shall have to leave this place, obviously."

"But how are you going to get out of here?"

Gus hopped onto the window ledge and looked down. Then he moved over to the glass wall that overlooked the test kitchen. "Down there!" he said. "Do you see that hose?"

Rose peered out onto the darkened floor of the test kitchen and saw that there was, indeed, a floppy white fire hose coiled on one side of the wall.

"You want me to dangle the hose out the window, and you'll climb down it?" she asked.

"No!" Gus exclaimed. "I'm not climbing down a hose! I'd break a claw. You are going to tie the hose to the strap of your backpack, and gently lower the backpack to the ground with me in it!"

A short time after Gus laid out the plan, Rose found herself peering over the ledge of the tiny window, watching him hop out of the backpack and slink off into the darkness, his tail held high.

She wished he hadn't left. Gus usually slept with her little sister, Leigh, but his night-time purring was so loud and guttural that Rose could always hear it across the room like the calm lapping of the nighttime ocean. There was no need for a white noise machine with Gus in the house.

Maybe I should try to climb down the hose, too, Rose thought.

But the building she was in was awfully tall, and the entrance to the compound was far away. Which way should she go once she got out – *if* she got out? She didn't even know where the compound was located. Was home to the south? The west? All she had to do to win her freedom was to perfect a few recipes. How hard could that be? Maybe she could even make it happen in less than five days.

Rose pulled the hose up through the window, brought it back down to the dark kitchen, and threaded it back around its hook, praying that none of the bakers would wake.

Her stomach grumbled. She was in a kitchen, wasn't she? There must be *some*thing here to fill her belly. But a quick search turned up only the ingredients for sweet treats, and she didn't want dessert for dinner. She was briefly tempted when, in one corner of the dimly lit kitchen, she came upon a pyramid of individually wrapped Dinky Cakes. There must have been a hundred in the pile.

But the more she looked at how identically flawless they were, the more she realized she didn't want to eat one. There was something deeply eerie about such machine-made perfection, something that made Rose think of Mr Butter and shiver with disgust.

She climbed back up to her room, crawled into bed, and went to sleep hungry.

Chapter 4

THE MOONY PYE OF INSATIABILITY

ROSE WAS AWAKENED the following morning by an unpleasant greenish-yellow light that filtered through the glass walls of the bedroom.

She stumbled out of bed. "Wake up, Gus," she said automatically. Rising up from below was a sound of banging metal – the bakers bustling around the kitchen and frantically scrubbing all of the metal surfaces, which, if she wasn't mistaken, were still sparkling clean from the night before.

Gus didn't answer. And then she remembered: he'd gone out to pass a message along to the Caterwaul. She sneaked a look out of the window, but there was no sign of the grey Scottish Fold on the asphalt below. He hadn't yet returned.

Somehow, Gus's absence made Rose feel all the more sad and alone.

She turned her attention to the kitchen. Peering through one of the glass walls of her room, Rose saw Melanie, Felanie, and Gene scrubbing the basin of an enormous deep fryer, one big enough for three adults to swim in comfortably. Jasmine and Ning were wiping down the fronts of the ovens.

"Whistle while you work!" commanded Marge, smiling broadly as she darted back and forth between them.

And on cue, all of the bakers began to whistle cheerful tunes. Periodically they'd stop and clap in unison, and then they'd take up the song once more. Rose looked from face to face, and all of them wore an identical wide smile: teeth slightly parted, lips stretched. Why would people who were living in a factory be smiling so hard?

Rose selected the smallest chef's coat and the smallest chef's trousers. Since the trousers were so large, she wore her own shorts underneath them as a secret reminder of home.

She felt weird – like a child playing dress-up, instead of a proper Food-Like Consumer Product Director. Still, she had never actually worn a chef's toque before, and she felt the puffy white cap endowed her with a certain power, almost like a wizard's hat.

Rose stepped delicately down the spiral steel staircase, careful not to trip over the cuffs of her trousers, which were too long.

"Ahhhhh!" Marge cried. "The Director is coming! Ready yourselves!"

Melanie and Felanie ran to meet Rose at the bottom of the staircase, and with a bow and extended arms, led her to a prep table. It was an enormous, empty stainless steel expanse, as big as a church door. Ning and Jasmine brought her a tray with coffee, a copy of the *Wall Street Journal*, and a scone with butter and jam.

Rose was about to take a bite when she realized the six bakers were staring at her, the same smiles plastered on their faces.

"You don't have to smile for my benefit," said Rose.

Instantaneously, the bakers dropped their smiles into identical grim frowns.

"You don't have to frown, either," Rose said.

Some of the bakers went back to smiling, others smiled and then frowned, but all of them looked confused.

"You guys!" Rose said, exasperated. "Smile if you want to! Or frown if you want to! Or don't have any expression at all. It doesn't matter to me. Honest."

The bakers looked at one another and relaxed. A few smiled easily, and the one named Ning wagged his eyebrows. For once, their faces looked normal, like the faces of regular people.

"That's better," Rose said. She bit into the scone and winced – it was so dry that it sucked all the moisture from her mouth. She grabbed the mug of coffee and took a big sip, then made herself swallow. So much for breakfast. "I'm twelve. You should be giving me milk. Or juice. Not coffee."

"Oh!" said the curly-haired one named Gene. "My bad." He frowned again.

"It's OK," Rose said, pushing the plate away. "We should get to work, anyway. Marge, what are we supposed to do first?"

"Here," said Marge, handing Rose a colourful box labelled MOONY PYE! with the signature Mostess cow grinning in the corner. "This is the first FLCP on our list: Moony Pyes. Sales have gone down over the years, so we've been tinkering with a new recipe, but it's unfinished. This is what we have so far, left to us from the former directrice."

The description on the side of the box read, MOONY PYE! A MARSHMALLOW AND SUGAR COOKIE SANDWICH, COVERED IN DELICIOUS CHOCOLATY FROSTING! The top of the box had a moon-shaped cutout in the cardboard, which was sealed with cellophane. Rose opened the box and pulled out the Moony Pye. Immediately, flakes of chocolate frosting coated her fingers.

She held the Mooney Pye in both hands and dove in.

It tasted like... wax. Like a waxy reminder of what chocolate was supposed to taste like. And under that taste? Stale sugar cookies. Then her teeth and tongue reached the marshmallow center, which tasted like... clay.

She spat the mouthful of Moony Pye into the garbage and wiped her tongue with her hand.

"Ugh!" she exclaimed. "I'm sorry, but that is *terrible*."

And yet, as she wiped the last bits of chocolate coating from her lips, she found herself craving another bite. There was something about that Moony Pye that made Rose want to dive in for more. "Weird," she said. "It was awful, but I still kind of want to eat it."

"I love them," Marge said gravely, that creepy smile returning to her face. "But I could love them even more.

That's where you come in, Rose. It is for *you* to make them *better*." At the word "better," she clasped her hands together.

"Better?" Rose said, flabbergasted. How was she supposed to make this *thing* better when it wasn't even good to start with?

"Our previous director of the FLCP Development Kitchen," said Marge, "she liked to be called the *Directrice* – was in the middle of tweaking the recipe. But tragically, she never finished!" Marge took a rubber-banded stack of recipe cards from her pocket and handed the top one to Rose. A recipe had been handwritten on it in a beautiful cursive using a rich purple ink. "This is as much as she was able to do."

In the corner of the card was an embossed picture of a rolling pin, with beams of light radiating out from the center. It looked familiar, but Rose couldn't think where she'd seen that radiant rolling pin before.

But the handwriting she recognized immediately: Lily. As she suspected, the "Directrice" and her wicked aunt were one and the same.

The recipe on the card was divided into three sections.

1. Sugar Cookies

2½ cups flour, 1 tsp baking soda, 1 cup butter, 1½ cups white sugar, 2 eggs, 1 tsp vanilla. Bake at 375 for 8–10 min.

Nothing special there, Rose thought. Nothing unusual, either. Nothing that would cause the Moony Pye to taste so *wrong.*

Dark Chocolate Icing

Melt 2½ lbs of semisweet chocolate with 2 cups milk and 1 cup paraffin wax.

Gross! Rose thought. Paraffin wax in the coating instead of butter. No wonder it was so shiny. But still, that didn't explain the peculiar taste. The third section, though, made Rose gasp.

*MARSHMALLOW CREAM: For the townsfolk of Delhaney Square did boil three fists of **water** with three fists of **sugar**, then did cool this mixture and pour it over whipped whites of twelve **chicken's eggs**, then did* *whip them further until a marshmallow cream had nearly emerged.*

*She did add four acorns of the **MOON'S CHEESE**.*

Rose put down the card and stared at Marge, speechless. This Marshmallow Cream recipe had been taken from the *Bliss Cookery Booke*! She'd seen it there herself.

But in the *Bliss Cookery Booke*, the Marshmallow Cream had the magical effect of making a person perfectly buoyant in the ocean, and the magical ingredient was the breath of a mermaid – not Moon's Cheese, whatever that was. Purdy had made the marshmallows once when the family took a trip to the coast, so none of the kids would be in danger of drowning.

Not only had the Bliss recipe been stolen – it had been tampered with as well.

"This is from my family's *Cookery Booke*!" Rose said, shocked.

"It couldn't be!" Marge fretted, pressing a stubby hand over her heart.

"Where did you get this?" Rose demanded. Either Lily

had copied out of the *Cookery Booke* and left a copy here, or...

Marge ran her fingertips over the surface of the card like it was a precious object. "This recipe was created by our previous director, our dear Directrice. It was *her* work, *her* inspiration, *her* astonishing-at-all-times genius, *her*—"

"Wait!" Rose called out. Marge's out-of-control praise was familiar. Rose's sister, Leigh, had suffered a similar fate after eating one of Lily's concoctions. "Was this Directrice called... Lily?"

The bakers looked at one another in confusion. "She was called Directrice, of course!" Marge answered. "If she had any other name, we certainly didn't know it."

"Perhaps it was 'Glorious One,'" Felanie suggested with a sigh.

"Or 'Most Beautiful,'" Melanie added softly.

Rose stared at the card, befuddled. The *Bliss Cookery Booke* was supposed to be impervious to attempts to copy it. Unravelling the binding would destroy the recipes, and photocopying didn't work. Had Lily copied out a bunch of recipes before returning the *Booke*? If so, why weren't the recipes working? She tapped her finger against the card. Maybe it had to do with these weird ingredients Lily had substituted.

"What the heck is Moon's Cheese?" Rose asked.

Marge snapped her fingers, and Jasmine and Ning reached into the refrigerator and brought forth a small jar of gloppy white stuff.

Instead of a blue mason jar, the Moon's Cheese was sitting in a square red jar with chicken wire embedded in the glass. Rose had seen a jar like that somewhere before but didn't remember where.

Rose reached in and poked at the Moon's Cheese with her finger. There wasn't a whole lot in the jar, just a thin layer in the bottom. It was denser than any cheese she'd ever seen – almost like a drying wad of mud.

She glanced back at the recipe card. She knew instinctively that four acorns of this stuff, whatever it was, was *way* too much for the Marshmallow Cream. No wonder it had tasted like a chalky rock. She absentmindedly took a red pen to the recipe card, crossed out *four acorns* and scribbled *one acorn*.

"I don't know what factory you guys got this cheese from," said Rose, shaking her head, "but you only need a little bit of it for the marshmallows. I think I know how to fix this."

"Oh, heavenly day!" Marge exclaimed, her eyes as wide as saucers.

All of the bakers leaned together and gazed at Rose unblinking, their smiles returned, all of them beaming down on her.

"Guys!" Rose said. "Stop it already! You're seriously creeping me out."

Later, without saying a word, Gene set a tray of orange juice and toast in front of Rose. He winked and joined the rest of the bakers as they set to work.

Ning and Jasmine started on the sugar cookies, while Gene and the twins prepared a chocolate ganache for the coating with butter, not paraffin. Lastly, Rose and Marge worked together on the Marshmallow Cream.

First Marge beat a dozen egg whites while Rose made a simple syrup. Then Rose poured the cooled syrup over the egg whites while Marge whipped, until they were almost marshmallowy. "Moon Cheese time," Rose said.

Rose attempted to remove just one acorn of the Moon's Cheese from the red jar with a measuring spoon, but the spoon got stuck inside. "I need to thin this out," she said. She poured a bit of water into the jar and tried to stir, but the Moon's Cheese stayed as dense as ever. As much as she dug into it with her spoon, the cheese wouldn't budge.

"What *is* this stuff?"

Just then, a stack of empty metal mixing bowls fell from the prep table and landed right on Marge's foot. All the other bakers stared on in horror as Marge grabbed her foot and howled.

"Owwww!!!!!! Ow ow ow owwwwwww!!!!!!!"

Rose was about to run to Marge's aid when she noticed that the Moon's Cheese had suddenly melted, as if by magic. It had taken on the consistency of a perfect cream cheese frosting.

"Ohhhh," Rose said quietly.

"What?" Marge asked, wincing in pain.

"I… never mind." It was too silly to say out loud. Had Marge's wailing somehow melted the cheese? She scribbled *wail/crying? maybe?* on the card near the mention of Moon's Cheese.

Rose stirred one acorn of the softened Moon's Cheese into the Marshmallow Cream, then sandwiched the mixture in between two completed sugar cookies. Finally, she instructed Gene to pour the chocolate ganache over the entire thing.

After the ganache cooled, Rose cut the Moony Pye into pieces and passed them around to the other bakers.

Ning took a bite with his fork and shouted for joy. "Celestial!"

Melanie and Felanie tasted it, and tears started rolling down their cheeks. "How have you done this?" they whispered at the same time.

Marge took a big bite and her eyes flashed a strange shade of purple. "It's like nothing I've ever eaten," she insisted. She licked her lips, running her tongue around them once, twice, and a third time. "I must have more."

"No, I need more!" shouted Gene, rubbing his mole vigorously. He and Jasmine shoved each other, reaching for the final bite.

Rose grabbed the plate away before anyone could reach it. "Guys! That's no way to behave!"

"We're sorry, Directrice!" Ning cried.

"We are not worthy of your attention!" Melanie and Felanie said together, bowing their heads in embarrassment.

"Of course you are right," Marge said. "The final bite must go to the genius who leads our kitchen, Rosemary Bliss!"

These six are loony, Rose thought. Then she took her

fork and stabbed the remaining piece of Moony Pye. The whole Moony Pye was transformed, and the texture of the Marshmallow Cream itself was perfect: soft, dense, moist. She let the pie melt in her mouth.

Her feet began to tingle.

Then the tingling spread throughout her body – her arms, hands, legs, toes, and even the tip of her tongue were full of a fizzy, *alive* sort of feeling. She wanted another bite, but there was nothing left on the plate, not even the tiniest piece. The bakers had already siphoned off the final crumbs, bending down and pressing their lips against the ceramic, making loud slurping noises.

"I can't believe we only made one!" Rose said, her mind swimming with visions of the heavenly Marshmallow Cream. "I could eat a dozen of those things!"

She looked at the six bakers and they stared back at her. All she could think about was the particular texture of that bite of Moony Pye. She poured herself a glass of milk and gulped it down, but even after her mouth was clear, a perfect Moony Pye remained in her mind. It seemed to hang in the air in front of her no matter what she looked at, a devilishly good treat like a magical new moon in the sky.

She tried to count to ten in Spanish, but ended up

thinking *uno Moony Pye, dos Moony Pyes, tres Moony Pyes*...
She tried to remember the name of her first-grade
teacher, *Mrs Ginger... Pye?* That couldn't be right. All she
could think of was Pye.

"We must make more of them," Rose announced,
salivating at the thought, then got hold of herself. "So...
Mr Butter can see that we fixed the recipe."

All of the bakers started chortling. "Oh, Mr Butter
doesn't eat sweets!" said Marge. "He's never once
touched them. Never! He subsists on a diet of plain
boiled potatoes." She planted her thumb against her
round chest and said, "I am the taster who determines
if a recipe has been perfected, and I say that it has!"

Marge fixed the amended recipe card to the surface
of the stainless steel fridge with a magnet, then turned
to the team of bakers. "Make a dozen Moony Pyes!
Right away!"

That night, after the bakers had finished icing the Moony
Pyes and stored them in the fridge, and Marge had
warned her fellow bakers off from devouring them,
wielding a rolling pin and promising to hurt anyone
who disobeyed, Rose retired to her little room above
the test kitchen. A fat, round Moony Pye – *moon*, rather

– had risen over the sea of factory buildings and cast a bright light on everything, and faint starlight poured in through the small, square window.

She still couldn't stop thinking about the Moony Pyes. *What if I snuck down to the kitchen and had just one?* she asked herself. *Or two? Or five?*

"Rose!" wailed a voice. It sounded like it was coming from outside.

Rose peered over the ledge of the tiny window and saw something small and grey pacing back and forth at the bottom of the building, with green eyes that shimmered in the dark.

"Gus?"

"Who else? Are you expecting another feline visitor? Are you seeing another cat behind my back—"

"Gus!" Rose cried out. "You're back!"

"Yes, yes, I've returned. Rosemary Bliss, Rosemary Bliss, let down your hose!"

Rose gathered the fire hose from the dark test kitchen, tied it to her backpack, and lowered it to the pavement. "Thank you!" Gus called as he jumped into the backpack.

She hoisted him up, thinking, *Gus can sneak down and get a Moony Pye for me.*

When the backpack reached the window ledge, Gus leaped through the air and landed squarely in Rose's lap, where she hugged him until he nearly stopped breathing.

"Rose!" he gagged. "I know you've missed me, but please, be careful. My ribs aren't made of iron."

Rose kissed Gus on the head and loosened her grip. "I'm sorry. I'm just so happy to have you back. When you weren't there this morning, I almost worried you'd invented the story about the Caterwaul just to have an excuse to get out of here."

Gus gasped. "How could you even think such a thing! You silly kitten."

"So..." Rose stared into his bright-green eyes. "Did you find another cat?"

"Of course I did," Gus said, licking his paw with feline nonchalance. "Across the great black sea of asphalt, I travelled. The rising sun did not stop me, nor did hunger. No, I was single-minded in my determination. But the fence I found was too high even for a cat of my famous agility to leap over. I had no choice but to wait."

"And a cat came by the fence?" Rose asked.

"Don't rush me," Gus said with a twitch of his whiskers. "A tale, like a tail, should be long and strong and interesting. Now where was I?"

"Fence," Rose said. "Waiting."

"Oh yes! The night had passed, and I waited there all day in the hot sun. With each passing hour, my energy waned. I needed a fat piece of tuna, or a can of chicken. But I could not forsake my duty!

"Finally, as I was beginning to doze off into what might have been my final rest, a lynx appeared from the surrounding grasslands."

"Grasslands?" Rose repeated.

The cat made a tiny shrug. "He stepped out of a bush, if you must know."

"Gus, did he agree to pass on the message?"

"Eventually."

"And that's the end of your story?" Rose said.

Gus turned several tight circles on the bed before settling down. "Minus the part where I came back. It was much easier once I knew where I was going, of course."

"Thank you," Rose said. "At least my parents will know where I am." But the cat was already asleep.

Rose tucked herself into bed and tried to ignore the train engine sound of Gus's purring.

She tried to think about what her family might be doing at that moment – crying at the police station, no doubt – but her thoughts drifted once again to the

Moony Pye. She didn't want to gloat, but it was pretty impressive, the way she'd adjusted the recipe to make a Marshmallow Cream so decadently delicious, so spellbindingly scrumptious, that even she couldn't stop thinking about it. It was sheer kitchen sorcery of a sort even her mum would have admired.

Magic! Suddenly, she thought of how Marge's shrieks of pain seemed to soften the Moon's Cheese. There seemed to be a connection there, but hard as she tried to puzzle it out, it slipped out of reach.

Gus awoke and whined, "Please, cease your sobbing. I can't sleep."

"I'm not crying!" Rose retorted.

"Then who is?" Gus asked. "My folded ears detect the sounds of distress."

Rose left her bed and looked out over the starlit darkness of the test kitchen. Sitting on a stool at one of the prep tables was Marge, her face and hands smeared brown with melted chocolate.

"No more!" Marge wailed. "What will I do? I've eaten them all. There are no more!"

Chapter 5

IN AN APRICOT JAM

"MARGE?" SAID ROSE, tiptoeing down the steel spiral staircase and into the test kitchen. "Are you OK?"

"Moony Pyes!" wailed the Head Baker. "I need more Moony Pyes!"

"Why don't you put on a light so I don't trip," Rose said, "and then we'll talk about Moony Pyes."

Sniffling, Marge rolled off her stool and waddled over to the wall, where she switched on a single overhead lamp. It left most of the kitchen dark except for the area around the prep table. Marge's fingers were coated in chocolate and cookie crumbs, and soon everything she touched – the light switch, her mouth, her apron, her hair, and underneath her eyes – was coated as well.

Rose sat at the table and patted Marge on her round shoulder. "Now, Marge, what happened to the dozen

Moony Pyes that we made before everyone went to bed?"

"Absolutely gone," Marge answered with a smack of her lips. "One hundred per cent in my stomach right now. Ate them. All twelve. Took about three minutes." Marge drummed her sticky fingers on the table. "I tried to make more, but I couldn't get the Moon's Cheese to melt like you did! You truly are a rare genius, and I will serve you forever if you'll just make me a few dozen more Moony Pyes."

Rose eyed the Moon's Cheese in its jar. What was left had solidified into a dense stony layer. Rose didn't know if she could get it to melt again.

"I feared this would happen," said Marge. She stared at Rose, her eyes enormous, teary disks.

Rose furrowed her brow. "Feared *what* would happen?"

"That Mr Butter would find a way to make Mostess treats so perfect that they'd… enslave people who ate them! They always had a secret ingredient in them that made you want to eat more," said Marge, patting her belly, "but now… wow. Who will be able to eat anything else? One bite and you're hooked. America really is in trouble."

"Hold on," said Rose, placing a hand on Marge's broad

damp wrist. "Mr Butter is trying to create baked goods that you actually *can't* stop eating?"

"The only thing that will stop the hunger..." Marge began, glancing around.

"Is another Moony Pye," Rose finished.

"Yes! But I've said too much!" Marge leaned forward and said, "We're not allowed to talk about it."

"What if I told you I'd make more Moony Pyes?" said Rose. "*Then* would you tell me?"

Marge nodded and immediately launched into a gossipy whisper. "Once the recipes are perfected, the new Moony Pyes will go into factory-wide production and be shipped everywhere. There will be so many Moony Pyes! Just imagine!" She gazed blankly at the empty cupboard.

Rose snapped her fingers. "Stay with me, Marge."

With a gulp, Marge continued. "And people will eat and eat and eat them, and then all of the country will be ensnared. They'll *have* to keep buying Mostess treats – starting with the Moony Pye that you perfected into the most divine form of enslavement ever imagined!"

"Wait!" said Rose. "That's not what I did! I just fixed the proportions in some marshmallow cream!"

"Yes," said Marge. "A marshmallow cream *of mass*

destruction!" She let out a tiny burp. "Yum!" Marge's gaze returned to the almost-empty jar of Moon's Cheese. "Don't you think you ought to preheat the oven, if you're going to make more?"

"Sure." Rose sighed as she moved to the row of ovens. She'd have to make a fresh batch to show Mr Butter – otherwise he'd never let her leave the factory. "Why did the Directrice want to help Mostess, anyway?" What was in it for Lily?

"The Directrice – may her cakes never fall! May her pie crusts always be the flakiest! – worked for Mr Butter, and Mr Butter works for—" Marge stopped herself. "I can't say any more!" she cried, shoving a fistful of flour into her mouth. She plumped down onto a stool and sat silently.

"Marge!" Rose said sharply. "If you want any of the Moony Pyes I'm about to make, you better keep talking!"

Marge spat the flour into the sink. Her face dusted in white, she blurted, "Mr Butter works for the International Society of the Rolling Pin!"

Rose had heard that name before, but where? "The International what?"

"The International Society of the Rolling Pin," explained Marge fearfully, glancing around the kitchen to make sure no one else was listening. "The dark order of bakers who rule the world through what we eat. Obesity? Their evil work. Diabetes? One of their secret plans. Cavities? Never known until they got busy. They've caused kids to drop out of school, incomes to fall, and nations to go to war." Marge blinked at Rose. "Shouldn't you be preparing the Marshmallow Cream?"

"In a moment," Rose said. "But how do these Rolling Pin guys connect up with Mostess?"

"Mr Butter and Mr Kerr work for the Society, and they're using Mostess to create a nation of Dinky-addicted zombies."

Rose thought there could be no one worse than her scheming, self-serving Aunt Lily, who was the worst kind of kitchen magician. She used the recipes and spells in the *Bliss Cookery Booke* to make people adore her and to make herself rich and famous. But what Mr Butter and the Mostess Corporation were doing was far, far worse: they were trying to enslave an entire nation.

It was a horrible vision – a country full of obese, Moony-Pye–eyed drones who ate only Mostess Snack Cakes. Mr Butter and his Society had to be stopped, and Rose knew she was the only person who could do it.

"Marge," Rose said, squeezing the older woman's

hand, "I am a baker." Saying it, Rose felt it to be true. She *was* a baker – and a kitchen magician – down to her bones. "I come from a long line of bakers, who try to improve the lives of people through our... *special* baked goods. That Moony Pye recipe today, it reminded me a lot of one of the recipes in my secret family cookbook. Now, are you sure that that Directrice didn't use a book?"

Marge looked guilt-stricken once more. "She *did* use a book," she whispered. "Not a whole book, more a book*let*. A skinny book. A book of old paper and smudgy writing. One night I glimpsed her through the windows up in that room, flipping its delicate pages, reading the recipes aloud to herself." Marge mimed tiptoeing. "I tried to get closer to see what it was, but I was walking in the dark and bumped into a stack of metal bowls. Such a clatter!"

"What did she do then?"

"She fussed about with the dresser and then came downstairs and told me to go to sleep."

Rose's heart thumped in her chest. "I'll be right back," she said and hurried up to her room.

"What's wrong with that chocolate-covered woman?" asked Gus, yawning.

"She's addicted to Moony Pyes," Rose muttered, distracted. "Because I fixed the recipe for Mr Butter, who is trying to enslave America on behalf of the International Society of the Rolling Pin, which is evil."

As she talked, she opened each drawer in the dresser, checked under the clothing, and felt the bottom. Nothing. "I think they might be using magic, but I don't know what kind. Other than that, Marge is *fine.*"

"Rolling pins," Gus grumbled, licking at his left paw and dragging it forward across his ear. "Balthazar used to talk about that in his sleep. 'Beware the Rolling Pin!' he'd cry. I always thought he was having nightmares because he baked too much."

"Apparently, there was more to it than that." Rose peeked behind the dresser, then leaned her shoulder against the side and pushed it away from the wall. "Ah ha!" she said.

Wedged in the space behind the dresser was a ribbon-bound stack of grey papers, thickly coated in dust. Rose cleaned them off and stared at the papers, her stomach churning. She knew exactly what they were, and where they were from.

"What is it?" Gus yawned.

"It's *Albatross's Apocrypha,*" Rose said faintly. Just as she'd suspected. She turned the sheets over and found a horrible inscription in purple ink across the back:

Property of Lily Le Fay,
Novice
International Society of the Rolling Pin

That's where she'd heard of the International Society of the Rolling Pin: Lily had left the same inscription in the back of the *Bliss Cookery Booke*, in the pocket where the *Apocrypha* was usually kept. The family had only discovered Lily's note after she'd returned the *Booke* and disappeared. Balthazar had warned Rose then of the dangers of the International Society of the Rolling Pin, but Rose had still been too much in shock to quite hear him.

They'd thought Lily had taken the *Apocrypha* that night, but maybe it hadn't been in the back of the *Booke* at all. Maybe Lily had hidden the *Apocrypha* here so that she'd still have some recipes in the unlikely event Rose won the Gala.

Rose smiled to herself. Her aunt Lily had worried about losing to Rose, even with the *Cookery Booke* in her possession.

Then, after she lost, Lily must have been too ashamed to return to the Mostess Corporation. She'd left her work here undone, not even bothering to come back for the *Apocrypha*.

"Aunt Lily," Rose muttered.

Gus looked around the room with slitted eyes, his newly cleaned claws extended. "Where?"

"She worked here, at Mostess. Sometime long before they kidnapped us." Crouching against the wall next to her tiny dresser, Rose turned to the first recipe in *Albatross's Apocrypha*, something called Lack-a-Wit Black-Bottom Cupcakes. Invented in 1717 by Albatross Bliss in order to ruin his brother's wedding on the tiny Scottish island of Tyree, the cupcakes were clearly sinister and required drops of Tears from a Warlock's Eye.

She'd used the Tears of a Warlock's Eye before. She remembered the sickening sight of that preserved eyeball floating around inside a mason jar that had been reinforced with chicken wire.

"Chicken wire!" she said.

"What?" grumbled the cat, mid-lick. He'd finished cleaning his left ear and was working on the right.

"In our secret cellar, back home," Rose said, "all the

really nasty ingredients were in green jars reinforced with chicken wire!"

"So?"

"The Moon's Cheese was in a red jar reinforced with chicken wire!"

"Green and red," mumbled Gus. "Put them together and you get Christmas."

Rose gently flipped through the *Apocrypha*'s pages, which were cracked and creased with age. In the corner of one, something caught Rose's eye: an engraving of a half-moon, with a tiny man digging into the surface with a shovel. The recipe read as follows:

PERENNIAL PATRONS' PASTRY CREAM:

For the magical assurance of Customer Loyalty

It was in 1745 in the Romanian town of Dragomiresti that Albatross Bliss's distant cousin Bogdan Tempestu did notice his bakery's popularity waning after he had begun to substitute sawdust for flour in order to increase his profits. He did create this pastry cream and inject it into all of his fruit tarts, after which his patrons did become violently addicted to his pastries.*

Sir Tempestu did stir in a copper saucepan two fists of the freshest **cow's milk** *with one fist of* **white sugar**. *He did stir in the yolks of six* **chicken's eggs** *and three acorns of* **white flour**. *When the mixture had almost cooled, he bid his caged wolf, Dracul, to* **howl at one jar of the Moon's Cheese**, *then did stir four acorns of the melted* **Moon's Cheese** *into the pastry cream.*

"This must be the recipe that Lily was adapting from," Rose said. "Instead of using the Moon's Cheese in pastry cream, she stuck it in Marshmallow Cream. But she got the proportions all wrong."

So Moon's Cheese wasn't some kind of processed factory cheese after all – it was a Bliss family magical ingredient. But it wasn't a gentle ingredient, like the first wind of autumn, one that could be stored in a regular blue mason jar. The Moon's Cheese required a reinforced container, something suitable for an ingredient that could only be activated by the howl of a wolf.

Or a baker with a stubbed toe.

In the margins was a note written in Lily's unmistakable calligraphy: *Tried to insert four acorns Moon's Cheese into Marshmallow Cream. Texture all wrong. Had no howling wolf* – had to microwave instead. *Cheese was chunky and rancid. Yuck-o!*

Rose smiled in spite of herself. She had done what Lily could not – adjust the amount of Moon's Cheese, recognizing that four acorns would be too much for Marshmallow Cream. And it was just a stroke of sheer luck that Marge's howling had triggered the Moon's Cheese to melt.

Rose read the remainder of the recipe:

The townsfolk of Dragomiresti, thence addicted to Sir Tempestu's pastries, did demand more and more, until he could no longer meet their demand, and they did descend upon his bakery in a starved furor, clawing him to death and setting the bakery on fire. Only the wolf Dracul survived.

As Rose read, Marge's head poked through the floor. She had ascended Rose's private staircase. She was sweating and scratching her arms. "I need my Moony Pyes! MOOONNNNYYYYYY PYE-PYESSSSSSSS! If I don't get that sweet marshmallow in my belly NOW, I'm going to claw out somebody's EYESSSSSSSS!"

Gus froze in terror, pretending to be a Scottish Fold statue.

Thanks for the help, Rose thought at him. Then she smiled at Marge's wild-eyed face. "OK, Marge," she said. "Why don't you go and bake two dozen sugar cookies according to the recipe, and prepare the chocolate coating, and I'll make the Marshmallow Cream."

Marge nodded, then immediately vanished, her feet clomping down the stairs sounding like a whole troop of bakers.

Gus hopped atop the dresser. "Is she gone? My goodness. What a loon. A loon for a Moony Pye."

"*Everyone* in the *country* is going to be acting like that if Mostess puts that recipe into production," Rose said to Gus. "This could be bad. *Really* bad."

"I think you ought to just worry about fixing *her* first," Gus said, pointing a puffed grey paw at the window. Below, Marge was skipping around the kitchen, shaking ingredients into bowls and dashing to set them all in a row on a prep table.

"How?"

"If I remember correctly from overhearing Balthazar's mutterings during translation," Gus said, "antidotes are always there. Just look on the back of the page."

Rose flipped over the page and saw, in extremely fine print, another recipe:

DRAGOMIRESTI'S APRICOT JAM: To cease the effects
of the PERENNIAL PATRONS' PASTRY CREAM

The good baker Nicolai Bliss did fix an apricot jam that he injected into Bogdan Tempestu's fruit tarts, after the townsfolk had murdered Bogdan Tempestu and set fire to his bakery and other portions of the town. The jam had the miraculous effect of causing the townsfolk to yearn, instead of for Tempestu's pastry cream, for apricots. After rebuilding their beloved town, the people of Dragomiresti became Romania's prime exporter of apricots.

*Sir Bliss did stir in a copper saucepan two fists of **fresh apricots** with one fist of **white sugar**. He did then add ONE **tale of one who has known the most fiery love, TOLD BY THE LOVER**, then stirred, and cooled the preserves.*

"This is worse than useless," Rose moaned. "Who has known the most fiery love? I sure haven't." The most torrid exchange that she and Devin Stetson had ever had was when he accidentally touched her hand while giving her change at Stetson's Doughnuts and Automotive Repair.

"I have," said Gus with a gentle lick of his lips. "Grab a jar."

To the soft sound of the snores that came from the Bakers' Quarters, they laboured through the night. At one point, Rose found her stomach grumbling and nearly crying out *Feed me!* but then she found a package of the cookies that had been left out for her on her first night. KATHY KEEGAN KRISPIES, it read. She took one out and had a nibble and was surprised to discover that she liked the taste. Could use some milk, but this little cookie was better than anything she'd eaten made in the Mostess factory. She gobbled down two and that took care of her hunger.

In a storage closet in the prep kitchen, Rose found an empty red mason jar. She coated it inside with a fine film of almond butter and brought it over to Gus, who proceeded to recount – into the jar, of course – the story of his first love affair.

"Her name was Isabella," he began, "and she was an Italian Manx with brindled fur that was mesmerizing. That feline temptress turned many a tom's head, but left only her claw marks on their hearts. I espied her one afternoon lying in the sun astride the bricks of a

Roman church, and I fell head over paws in love. I would make her love me even if it killed me." Pausing dramatically to scratch at his neck, he added, "And it very nearly *did*."

Gus's tale involved a voyage to America, a wealthy but brutish Siamese to whom Isabella was engaged, and plenty of stolen glances on a moonlit poop deck. When the story was over, Rose just stared.

"Wow, Gus. Whatever happened to Isabella?"

"Oh, we lived together for a time. But it was not to be. A Manx and a Fold can never get along. We're both too stubborn, too proud. But it was beautiful while it lasted. Our love was like a pizza oven: full of flame during the day, but cold and unused at night. Loving Isabella made me the heartsick Scottish Fold you see before you today."

Rose snapped the mason jar closed and, tucking it underneath her arm, dashed over to the metal counter where the bowl of apricot preserves sat – sad and goopy and still. Rose stood, staring down into the orange mass, then carefully opened the red mason jar and let the essence of Gus's fiery love for Isabella seep into the dish.

And then she waited.

"Oh gosh!" Marge cried out as she raced around the kitchen preparing the sugar cookies, her cheeks flapping as she ran.

"What's wrong?" Rose asked, looking over at Marge, who was wiping wisps of hair off her forehead.

"Nothing!" Marge cried out. "I'm just so excited! Baking gives me such a rush! I feel like... a little girl on Christmas morning about to open up all the presents – and all I want is a new Barbie, and I just *know* there's a new Barbie hiding in one of those boxes, somewhere..." Marge stopped in the middle of the kitchen, holding three eggs and a cup of sugar. Her lower lip began to tremble. "Only there never was a Barbie. Not for me, Rose. Not for me."

"Oh, um, I'm sorry about that, Marge," Rose said, glancing back at the bowl of apricot preserves.

When she did, her eyes nearly popped out of her head.

The preserves were no longer mushy and still. Gus's fiery love had thickened them and turned them bright red. The mixture was heating up in the bowl, bubbling and hissing, bubbles nearly rising over the sides of the bowl.

Pop!

The preserves looked angry. They began to swirl in tiny circles, faster and faster like a miniature tornado. Within seconds, the preserves took on the shape of a gigantic red heart. Rose glanced over at Marge, who was busy stuffing a tray of sugar cookies in the oven.

Soon the heart morphed from red to orange to yellow, like one enormous flame – and then, as quickly as they had erupted, the preserves seemed to calm and drop back inside the metal bowl in one loud *gloop*.

"Whoa," Rose whispered, staring at Gus. He only smiled and gave a gentle purr.

When it looked safe to touch, Rose grabbed the bowl with an oven mitt and stuck it inside the refrigerator to cool. *That Isabella must have been some cat*, she thought to herself.

"That looks awfully *orange* for marshmallow cream!" Marge noted suspiciously. The windows of the kitchen had gone from pitch-black to a warm grey: the long night was nearly over.

"Do you want the Moony Pyes or not?" Rose asked, exasperated. "Because I can just throw this mixture out and—"

"Noooooooooo!" Marge cried. "Please don't stop, Master Directrice Rose!"

Finally, just as a fine blush of sunrise bled through the high panes of the Development Kitchen windows, Rose sandwiched the Dragomiresti's Apricot Jam between Marge's sugar cookies, coated the sandwich in chocolate, and presented the antidote Moony-Pye-in-Disguise to Marge on a white plate.

In every respect, it looked like the Marshmallow Cream Moony Pyes that Rose had made the day before. Still, Marge sniffed it skeptically, her nostrils flaring in and out. "It doesn't *smell* like a Moony Pye!" she said. "I want a REAL Moony Pye!"

"It's the same thing, Marge. JUST EAT IT."

"No!" Marge crossed her arms.

"Yes!" Rose said.

Marge clamped her lips shut and violently shook her head, so Rose did what she had to do: She stomped on Marge's foot.

"Owwww!!!!!! Ow ow ow owwwwwww!!!!!!!" Marge howled.

And while she was howling, Rose stuffed the antidote Moony Pye into Marge's open mouth.

Overcome with her need for a Moony Pye, Marge

chewed and swallowed. She wiped her mouth free of chocolate and then let loose an enormous belch – a belch so strong that it blew Rose's hair back like a fan and rattled the glass in the windows.

"Oh my goodness!" Marge exclaimed. Her eyes flashed orange with a sudden clarity. "What happened to me? It's like I was gaga for Moony Pyes! And they aren't even *good!*" Marge ran her tongue around the inside of her lips and belched again, more like a tiny little hiccup this time. "I could sure go for some apricots, though."

"Welcome back," said Rose, smiling. Her hard work – and Gus's memory – had paid off. "I made you an antidote to the Moony Pyes. You may crave apricots for a while, but otherwise you'll be OK."

Suddenly, Marge enfolded Rose in her flour-coated arms, and though it was hard for Rose to breathe, the hug felt good. Somehow it reminded her of her mother – which made Rose miss her family all the more.

"You… you *saved* me!" Marge gasped and dropped Rose, backing away in panic. "Wait! If they know that you changed the recipe, they'll never let you go home!"

Oh no, Rose thought. *That's not good.*

Then an idea came to her. "We won't tell them about

the antidote," Rose said. "As far as they know, there aren't any Moony Pyes left because you ate them all. You're proof that the recipe works. Mr Butter will have to be satisfied with that."

"But I no longer crave Moony Pyes!" Marge made a face. "I ate a dozen of those things. I think I'm going to be sick."

"They won't *know* that you're cured," Rose said. "Just be… loony."

"You want me to lie to Mr Butter? Pretend I'm still in a pickle over those Pyes?" Marge said. "Why, I have never lied in my life." She placed her hands firmly on her wide hips and blew a stray wisp of hair away from her face.

"Not even once?" Rose asked.

Marge thought for a second, then cringed. "Oh goodness! I just lied about never lying! I *have* lied. Once. As a young girl, to my mother. She did my hair in braids before a Sadie Hawkins dance and asked whether I liked them, I said *yes* even though I really didn't! I hated them!" Marge sucked in a long breath of air. "I'm a terrible person."

"No, you're not," Rose said, placing a comforting hand on Marge's shoulder. "There's nothing wrong with a tiny white lie."

Marge blinked. "There isn't?"

"Not if it's going to help someone," Rose said. "And if you tell Mr Butter that you're obsessed with Moony Pyes, he'll think I did what he asked. Then there's only four recipes left and he'll let me go home. To my family."

Marge nodded dutifully. "I shall accept the challenge," she said, speaking in a strange sort of British accent. "It will be a *role*. A portrayal such as the stage has never seen. The performance of a lifetime!"

"Sure," Rose said, cutting a piece of another antidote Moony Pye and eating it as well. She couldn't be too careful.

Gus trotted down the staircase from Rose's room and leaped onto the table. "I thought you'd want to know: they're on their way! I saw them through the window."

Marge stared at Gus, dumbfounded. "Is one of the side effects of the antidote Moony Pye that I hallucinate talking cats? It's fine if it is; I always wanted a talking cat, I just want to be prepared for it."

Rose immediately shot Gus a glare that said, *Why did you speak in front of her?*

Oh well – she'd have to tell Marge the truth now.

"No, this cat actually does talk," Rose admitted. "But don't tell anyone, not even the other bakers."

Marge gleefully swept Gus into the air, holding him aloft like a doll. She pressed her face into his belly and rubbed it back and forth, making cootchie-coo noises. "How is this possible, young cat?"

"I am a very *old* cat, one who ate a magical biscuit when he was young," said Gus. "Please put me down."

Marge set him on the table and rubbed the underside of Gus's chin. "What a naughty kitty you were."

Just then, red lights flashed from every corner of the room, and an insistent buzzing siren began to wail, on and on, like the world's loudest alarm clock.

Marge gulped. "They're here."

Chapter 6

CHEESY HOME VIDEOS

AS THE GOLF cart with Mr Butter and Mr Kerr appeared through the floor, the five other master bakers marched out from their quarters at the back of the test kitchen.

Rose glanced up at the clock on the wall. It was seven a.m. She and Marge had baked all night. This was officially the morning of the third day she'd been at the Mostess compound. "Best not let him see you," Rose whispered to Gus, who skulked off behind one of the ovens.

"It is a new day!" said Mr Butter as he slid from the passenger seat of the golf cart and moseyed over to the prep table. "How comes along recipe number one – the Moony Pye?" (He actually said *Mooooony Pye*.)

"They're, um, perfect," Rose said, stifling a yawn.

"They're perfected. The best Moony Pye the world has ever seen!"

Mr Butter gestured at the empty prep table. "Funny, Miss Bliss, but I don't *see* any Moony Pyes. Where are they?"

"We don't have any left," Rose answered. It was the truth.

"I don't understand." Mr Butter scratched his bulbous bald head with exaggerated care. "I thought you wanted to get home to your family as soon as your little feet could carry you. But we agreed that you wouldn't leave until you perfected those Moony Pyes. So where are they?"

It was then that Marge emerged from behind the rest of the bakers with her arms spread wide. Her cheeks were covered in chocolate, her lips were covered in chocolate, even her eyelids were flecked with chocolate. Chocolate coated her tongue and sat in the spaces between her teeth. Her formerly white apron was dotted with sugar cookie crumbs, and each of her fingers was topped off by a white cap of hardened Marshmallow Cream.

Apparently, this was what Marge considered *getting into costume*.

"The Moony Pyes are gone!" she thundered in an

operatic vibrato. "There are no more – because I ate them all!" Marge clasped her hands together and swayed on her feet as if she were preparing to launch into a Shakespearean monologue. "They were the finest things I have ever shoved down my throat! I can't stop eating them! *Yum yum yum yum yum yuummmm!*" Now Marge was actually singing, in a high falsetto. "I will die if I can't have another right now! Fire me if you must, but I regret nothing!"

Nervously, Rose glanced at Mr Butter. His expression was hard to read, mostly because, well, his face was so strange. Was he buying it?

After a few seconds, Mr Butter turned to Mr Kerr with a sour look, which dissolved into an unnaturally wide smile. "This is really something," he said quietly. "This is really remarkable. Didn't I tell you she could do it, Mr Kerr?"

"Actually," answered Mr Kerr, "if I remember correctly, I told *you* she could do it. *Cook* not *book.*"

Mr Butter cleared his throat and squinted, his eyes looking extra glossy behind his spectacles. "Miss Bliss, you've done yourself very proud. We'll go into production on the new Moony Pyes immediately. May I have the new recipe card?"

Rose stiffened. The recipe card was still tacked to the front of the fridge. If Mr Butter had it, he could begin production on the dangerous Moony Pyes, the kind that had ripped the village of Dragomiresti to shreds.

"Oh, there it is," he said before Rose could think of a response. Mr Butter floated over to the fridge and snatched it up. "Interesting," he said, reading over Rose's notes.

Rose turned frantically to the red mason jar of Moon's Cheese. *It's almost empty!* she privately rejoiced. *They can't make more because it's almost empty!*

"I'm *so* sorry, Mr Butter," Rose said, "but I actually used up the last of the Moon's Cheese making those Pyes. There's no more. I'm afraid you'll have to halt production."

Mr Butter let a sneaky little laugh out between the tiny spaces in his closed grin. "Rose, my dear," he said, "we here at the Mostess Corporation never *ever* run out of ingredients. Do you think I'd let a little thing like an empty jar of Moon's Cheese stand in the way of Americans everywhere enjoying the taste of your perfect Moony Pyes? I don't think so. Follow me."

Rose couldn't move. All that work creating an

antidote, and she'd let the evil recipe fall right into the hands of this evil man.

"Come along." He walked to the golf cart and beckoned with his pointy finger.

Rose saw a grey head disappear into her backpack, hooked her arm through it, and then climbed into the golf cart.

"Oh, and Marge?" Mr Butter said to the frazzled, chocolate-covered Head Baker. "Marge, honey, clean up yourself and this kitchen. You know how I hate a mess."

Mr Kerr drove Mr Butter and Rose between the warehouses for what felt like miles. The rising sun threw its golden colour on everything, and Rose felt a bit of hope worm its way through her despair. It was a beautiful morning, and Mr Butter hadn't put the recipe into production *yet*.

At first, they passed grey box after grey box, like the test kitchen warehouse, but after a while different sorts of buildings began to appear. There was a sleek office building where Rose could see men in the windows scribbling away at drafting boards – the front entrance was in the shape of a giant Mostess cow.

"Those are our graphic artists," said Mr Butter. "They

weren't the ones who originally came up with the cow, of course. We've hired all new ones. We're working on some other packaging ideas, something... more modern."

They passed another office building covered in billboards with Mostess slogans splashed across the front. MAKE THE MOSTESS OF YOUR DAY – EAT A DINKY CAKE! and LAUGH AWAY THE DAY WITH A TEE-HEE!

"With the right marketing," explained Mr Butter, "you can make a person do something they don't even want to do – such as eat a Dinky Cake. It's like... *magic*! But it's magic that makes money!"

Rose gritted her teeth and stayed silent. She should never have helped with the Moony Pye recipe. Then again, Mr Butter hadn't given her much of a choice. She briefly wished her mum were there – Purdy Bliss would know what to do.

But on second thought, Rose was happy her mum didn't have to see what Rose had done. Her disappointment would have been too much to bear.

"Ah, here we are," said Mr Butter as the golf cart pulled up in front of a building shaped like a wedding cake. "The Mostess pantry, if you will."

It was a stack of round floors with tinted windows,

each floor progressively smaller than the one below it. Atop the highest, smallest story was a giant statue of a smiling cow. Mr Kerr drove the golf cart into an enormous revolving door, which rotated until the golf cart was safely inside the lobby.

Rose thought she had stepped into the future – or someone's nightmare of the future. Instead of something that looked like the Bliss Bakery pantry, only larger, there were, she saw, men in white lab coats standing at a giant control board in front of an enormous wall of dark-red mason jars. The wall was at least five stories tall, with a rolling ladder that ran along the top – to access the jars from the upper levels, Rose figured.

"This is what we refer to as the laboratory," said Mr Butter proudly. "It is where we store all of our ingredients."

"Isn't it more of a warehouse, then?" Rose asked. "You store things in a warehouse. You create things in a lab."

Mr Butter waved away her comment. "You say poe-*tay*-toe, I say poh-*tah*-toe. We also do experiments here – how to get the recipes just right, this and that, and more. Plus, laboratory sounds much fancier than warehouse, doesn't it?"

Rose couldn't disagree with that. Instead of arguing with Mr Butter, she turned her attention back to the wall of jars: there were too many of them to count, but Rose estimated that it must have been at least one thousand. It was hard to see inside the jars, but their contents were bobbing and glowing and growling and screeching.

"Doubtless you've realized by now, Rose, that ours is no ordinary factory," said Mr Butter. "You probably thought yours was the only kitchen equipped with magical mason jars, but no. We, like you, use *special* ingredients."

So Lily had betrayed all the family secrets. Rose had figured as much, but it was still mortifying to hear it said so plainly by Mr Butter.

"Yes, we too use magic," Mr Butter said, rubbing the top of his perfectly bald head, "but unlike the Bliss family, we maximize the effects of the magic through the power of technology."

Mr Butter moved to the giant control board and picked up a megaphone. "Mr Mechanico! We need more Moon's Cheese. Enough to produce ten million Moony Pyes!"

Just then, a lavender-coloured robot whose shape

could only be described as octopus-esque floated through the air and hovered above Rose's head. Its mechanical arms writhed and clinked as it moved, like eight strings of metal cans. "At your servissssss," the thing whispered through a silver-mesh metal grill.

"Here is the recipe," Mr Butter said, holding out the card with Rose's notes on it. One of Mr Mechanico's segmented arms clanked and telescoped, reaching down toward Mr Butter. With a strange slurping noise, the card stuck to one of hundreds of tiny suction cups underneath the mechanical tentacle. The robot curled the tentacle under its belly and appeared to swallow the recipe card whole.

"Received," said Mr Mechanico. His voice was higher than Rose would expect from a flying octopus robot. It sounded frighteningly real, like a human voice.

"Where are they going to get all that Moon's Cheese?" Rose asked. "What *is* Moon's Cheese, anyway? I mean, I know it's a magical ingredient, but what *is* it?"

Mr Butter slapped Mr Kerr on the shoulder and laughed. "'What is Moon's Cheese?' she asks! She never heard about Moon's Cheese! Oh, these poor country bakers. Why don't you explain, Mr Kerr?"

Mr Kerr knelt down next to Rose on one massive

knee. His head was as thick as her entire body. "The moon," he said in his deep voice, "is made of *cheese*."

Rose tried not to giggle. "Mr Kerr, with all due respect, I believe the moon is made of rock."

"Nope! It's *cheese*," said Mr Kerr. "A green cheese, actually."

Gus curled his whiskers with his paw. Rose could tell that he also disagreed.

"It isn't *actually* cheese," Mr Butter said, correcting Mr Kerr. "Not in a made-from-curdled-cow's-milk sort of way. Rather, it's a cheese-like substance with powerful magical properties. These magical properties have been known to descendants of Filbert and Albatross Bliss for quite some time, due to the occasional piece of broken moon rock crashing onto Earth. But no one has had the technology to harness the magical properties of Moon's Cheese on a grand scale – until now, that is.

"Mr Mechanico," continued Mr Butter. "Why don't you show Miss Bliss the cheese video."

Mr Mechanico reached over to the control board with one of his tentacles and pulled a red lever. The giant closet of red mason jars parted down the middle, revealing a movie screen as tall as the building itself.

Mr Mechanico pressed a series of buttons, and a video started to play of a trio of octopus-shaped robots making grilled cheese sandwiches over an open campfire. A faint soundtrack of classical music played softly.

"No," said Mr Butter, exasperated. "The other one."

Another series of pushed buttons and a new video came on the screen – this time it was of another octopus-shaped robot dipping a crouton into a pot of fondue.

"The *other* one, Mechanico!"

A third video clicked onto the screen – a view of the moon through the windshield of an approaching spaceship. The moon grew larger in the image as the ship drew closer to the moon's surface, and Rose could see that it wasn't the dull-grey rock she'd expected. Instead, it seemed to jiggle like a vast greyish-white sea of Jell-O.

Then the view changed to a camera mounted under the ship. As the craft flew close to the surface, something extended from its belly – a massive robotic arm with a scoop on the end as big as a school bus. It plunged beneath the surface and pulled up a wedge of thick white cheese.

"You see, Rosemary Bliss," said Mr Butter, "there's plenty of Moon's Cheese to be had – more than enough to feed every person in the nation one of your marvelous Moony Pyes."

"Great," Rose said, feeling sick to her stomach. "That's just great."

"Marvellous," Gus muttered under his breath, dripping with sarcasm.

"Yes," said Mr Kerr, unaware that it was the cat, not Rose, who had spoken. "It *is* marvellous."

"But that was old footage from our last cheese run. Where are we now with the current launch, Mechanico?" asked Mr Butter.

"All systems go," answered Mr Mechanico, and he reached down to the control board and pulled a green lever.

At first, nothing seemed to happen.

Then, on the enormous video screen, Rose saw the cake-shaped building from the outside. From its top, swirls of white smoke curled into the air. "What's that?" she asked.

"A launch pad," Mr Butter replied.

"For what?" Rose asked.

Mr Butter eyed Rose with faint disdain. "For the rocket

ship. Which we are now launching. Which will go to the moon. And fetch us more cheese." His broad, thin smile reappeared. "Easy. As. Pie."

Rose clutched Gus in her arms. The mason jars began to rattle on the shelves, and there was a whirlwind of noise. The smoke on the screen thickened, and the rattling grew fiercer and fiercer and then—

All of a sudden, it stopped.

For a moment, Rose thought she could make out a tiny rocket ship soaring into the dark-blue sky on the video screen, but she wasn't completely sure.

"There it goes," said Mr Butter with an elated sigh. He pinched his own cheeks and smacked his nonexistent lips together. "We should be all cheesed up in two weeks or so."

Rose's heart sank. With her help, there'd be no stopping the unholy alliance of the Mostess Snack Corporation and the International Society of the Rolling Pin.

"Come along, Rose," said Mr Butter. "That's not even the main attraction. There's still more!"

"More?" Rose repeated weakly. "Isn't that enough?"

Mr Butter wagged a stick-thin finger. "There's something else I need to show you. Something very important." He folded himself back into the front seat of the golf cart, then scowled. "Don't look so down in the mouth! We'll have your Moony Pyes out there in the world lickety-split!"

That's what I'm afraid of, Rose thought to herself. But she got into the back of the cart without another word.

It wasn't even noon yet, but Rose could see heat waves piping up from the road as Mr Kerr pulled up in front of another building. This one was in the shape of a giant pastry bag, plumped up at the bottom but narrowing to a fluted glass tip at the very top.

"You're going to like this one, Rose," said Mr Butter as Mr Kerr parked outside the towering glass doors.

"If you say so," Rose muttered, following Mr Butter and Mr Kerr through the building's grand lobby. In place of flower arrangements, there were bouquets of candies and cookies. "This looks almost like a hotel," she said.

"That's because it *is* a hotel," said Mr Kerr.

"And people say children aren't observant!" said Mr Butter.

"A hotel for who?" Rose asked. "The families of the bakers?"

"Certainly not," said Mr Butter. "This is a hotel for guests to the compound."

They boarded a glass elevator on the far wall of the lobby. "To the top!" Mr Butter announced, fishing a key from his pocket. It was a silvery miniature rolling pin with teeth and notches carved into it. He slid it into a waiting keyhole, turned it, and then pressed the highest button.

The glass box immediately began to rise, slowly at first but gaining speed. One wall looked down upon the hotel lobby, but the other looked out upon the world. Rose could see the whole expanse of the Mostess compound, the rocket launchpad atop the warehouse building that Mr Butter had called a laboratory, the desert of grey warehouses, the jungle of marketing buildings and ingredient laboratories, and acres of delivery trucks parked in rows.

At the farthest corner of the compound, she spied a curiosity, something completely out of place in the whole industrial mess: a small red cottage, with a brick chimney and a dilapidated front porch, sitting on a bit of grass the size of her own backyard back in Calamity Falls. It was as if Mr Butter had cut something from the pages of a fairy tale and planted it in the corner of his space-age empire.

"What's that?" Rose asked, pointing toward the cottage. "That little shack back there?"

Mr Kerr looked nervously at Mr Butter. "What? I don't see anything."

"It's nothing," Mr Butter said stiffly, adjusting his glasses. "Been so long since I've been over at that corner of the compound, I forget what's there."

"But does someone live there?" Rose asked.

"I said, never mind!" Mr Butter hissed, his eyes bulging and wild. He clenched his fists tightly, as though he were upset, and Rose didn't ask any more questions.

The elevator dinged at floor 34.

"We're here." Mr Butter smiled and smoothed out the creases in his trousers. "Aren't surprises exciting?" He seemed overcome with glee, completely recovered from his sudden anger about the strange little cottage.

The doors opened on a plush corridor, carpeted in gold-and-red-patterned carpet and lit by golden wall sconces. Soft music tinkled faintly in the air, accompanying them as they knocked on the door of room 3405.

Rose yawned. Baking all night had left her too

exhausted to worry about what Mr Butter had behind the door. At this point, what could one more surprise from him matter? He couldn't be any more evil than he already was.

And then the door flew open, revealing Purdy, Albert, and Balthazar, looking as surprised as Rose felt.

"Mom. Dad. Grandpa." Rose stood in the doorway, unsure what to do.

"Go on," Mr Butter said. "Talk to your family. We'll give you a moment of privacy." With a sharp push, he shoved her inside and pulled the door shut.

Rose's shock gave way to sweet relief as her family surged forward and surrounded her, embracing her in turns and together so that she could barely catch her breath. "I can't believe you're here!" Rose cried, dropping her backpack to the floor and hugging them back. "I thought I'd never see you again!"

Gus crawled out of her backpack. "You *dropped* me," he said.

"We were so worried!" said Purdy, hugging her daughter so tightly that Rose could barely breathe. "We had the police searching. Everyone was a mess. Then Jacques came running in from the backyard saying that he'd had a conversation with the neighbour's Persian cat, and the cat had heard a story about the Bliss girl of Calamity Falls being held at the Mostess Snack Cake Corporation."

"The Caterwaul!" Gus proclaimed. "I told you, dear Rose. Never doubt the organizational skills of a herd of cats."

"At first we thought Jacques was just being French," said Balthazar.

From his pocket came a small voice, "Oh, you are a rude man to insult my people in such a way after how loyally I have served you!"

"Sorry, Jacques," Balthazar muttered. "But even you'd admit that you are one gullible mouse."

A soft *"Oui"* came from his pocket.

"We decided it was our only lead," Albert continued. "The police weren't having any luck tracking you down, so we all piled in the van and drove two hours, and here we are. We left your siblings safe at home with Mrs Carlson."

"Mr Butter has been very nice to us," said Purdy, whose hair was so dishevelled with heat and worry that it looked like an angora rabbit. "But he hasn't quite explained why you're here."

"Rose has been wonderful," said Mr Butter from

behind them, as he swung open the door again and stepped inside the room. "Giving of herself and her talents. Aiding us in our time of need. Doing the work that only she can do." He cleared his throat. "Speaking of which, it's back to the test kitchen for her. The day is wasting away!"

"No!" Rose snapped. "I'm going home with my parents now, thank you very much."

"Oh, actually, *no* one is going home," said Mr Butter. "Everyone will receive these luxurious, free accommodations until Rose finishes formulating her recipes."

"And what recipes are these?" said Purdy.

Rose looked over her parents' shoulders at Mr Kerr, who smiled at her and drew a finger across his throat.

"Um," Rose said. "Just some recipes. For Mostess treats."

"May I have a word with you outside, Rosemary Bliss?" Mr Butter said, ushering her out into the hall again with a shallow bow and a swish of his arm.

Mr Kerr held back Rose's parents while she and Mr Butter went back out into the plush hallway. On the soft, soft carpet, Mr Butter said, "It's a curious thing, Rose. When these fine folks showed up at our door, I first considered telling them I had no idea who you were and sending them back home. But then I realized that their presence gave me a unique tactical advantage."

"Tactical advantage?" Rose repeated with a gulp.

"I have in my captivity," said Mr Butter, "the one thing that Rosemary Bliss cares most about in the world: her family. Now, if you fail to perfect the remaining recipes, I have the power to take that family away."

"But they can help me!" said Rose. "We're all magical bakers!"

"I don't think so," said Mr Butter sourly. "I want enough brainpower in that kitchen to fix the recipes – not enough to outsmart me and sabotage the company."

"I knew it," said Rose. "What happened to all that junk you told me about trying to brighten people's lives with baked goods? I believed you. I would have helped you! I would have helped you make better snack cakes!"

"I want *more* than better snack cakes," said Mr Butter with a snarl. The lines of his face seemed to deepen, and the corners of his barely visible lips turned down. "It's not enough to have a better snack cake. I have bigger plans, a grander vision." He spread his arms wide.

"Mostess Snack Cakes need to be so good people will *kill* for them."

Something dark flashed in his eyes, and Mr Butter pointed a crooked finger directly at Rose. "And you're going to make them that *way* – or else."

Chapter 7

THE BUNNY AND THE HAG

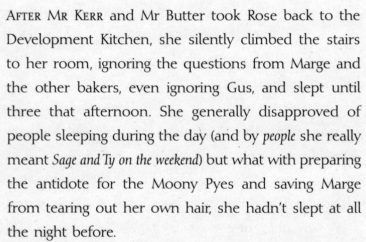

AFTER MR KERR and Mr Butter took Rose back to the Development Kitchen, she silently climbed the stairs to her room, ignoring the questions from Marge and the other bakers, even ignoring Gus, and slept until three that afternoon. She generally disapproved of people sleeping during the day (and by *people* she really meant *Sage and Ty on the weekend*) but what with preparing the antidote for the Moony Pyes and saving Marge from tearing out her own hair, she hadn't slept at all the night before.

And she was upset at seeing her parents held captive.

It was bad enough that Rose was being forced to help the evil Mostess Corporation take over the country – but the fact that her family was now in danger because of her was too much to bear. If Rose didn't do exactly what Mr Butter wanted, exactly how he wanted her to do it, who knew what he would do to her parents and to Balthazar?

She was groggy and confused when she finally woke up, and her pillow was wet with drool. As she rubbed her face and sat up, she remembered everything. She had to rescue her parents *and* stop the Mostess Corporation *and* somehow fix Calamity Falls.

Rose shook her head. It was too much to think about.

Just then, the sound of Marge's voice from the test kitchen reached Rose's ears.

"Rose!" Marge was calling out in a sharp, loud voice. "Please come down and get started! These Glo-Balls won't fix themselves!"

Through the glass window of her bedroom, Rose could see Marge holding up a tray of Glo-Balls, which were tiny puffs of chocolate cake covered in coconut that glowed in different colors: neon blue, neon green, neon orange, and neon pink. Rose thought they looked more like signs in the window of a seedy diner than things people should eat.

"I don't want to," said Rose, looking around at the

glass walls of her room, which felt more like a prison every second.

Just then, Gus jumped down from the windowsill. "Well, well, well," said the cat, swishing his tail. "Look who's awake."

Rose folded her arm across her eyes to block out the world. "I don't want to fix the recipes, Gus. I don't want to help Mr Butter and his Rolling Pin people. I want them to let Mom and Dad and Balthazar out, and I want to go home."

"Ugh." Gus sighed. "You're just like Moses."

"Moses?" Rose asked. "Like, Bible Moses? From the Old Testament? How?"

Gus sat on Rose's chest, and his heavy, furry warmth felt like a balm on Rose's worried heart. "Moses was a Hebrew slave born in Egypt," the cat explained. "But his mother sent him down a river in a basket, and he was found by the pharaoh's wife and raised as a son of the pharaoh instead."

"How is that like me?" Rose asked. She loved the cat – honest she did – but sometimes she tired of how long it took him to say anything.

"Hold on, Rose," said the cat, pressing a paw to her lips. "Moses was next in line to become the pharaoh, and he was thrilled, I tell you, *thrilled* – until he learned that he was in actuality a Hebrew slave."

"Again," said Rose, "feel free to wind your way back to how this relates to me."

"Patience!" Gus protested, holding out one of his paws. "Now, of course, being a Hebrew slave himself, Moses wanted to free the rest of the slaves. So he wandered into the desert. And he came back to the pharaoh's court a long while later, begging the pharaoh to free the slaves, and he had to go to all sorts of trouble to do it. There were frogs and locusts and boils and the Red Sea split in two and a forty-year journey, and frankly the whole thing was a big mess." Gus twitched his nose and scratched behind his ear. "Do you see my point?"

Rose furrowed her brow. "Slavery is the greatest evil of civilization, justice is hard-won, and cats are long-winded?"

"Yes," Gus said, baring his sharp teeth. "All that is true. But my point is this: Don't you think it would have been easier for Moses if instead he had just worked *within the system*? Isn't it easier to free the slaves after you yourself have *become the pharaoh*?"

Rose sighed and curled into a ball, dislodging the

cat, who scrambled atop her hip. "I am not a pharaoh, and this is not Egypt, and I don't see what this has to do with me."

Gus stalked forward and sat on Rose's head, which he did when he wanted to truly make a point. "If you want to take down the Mostess Corporation, you have two options. You can try to rescue your family and leave, like Moses, risking your own life and the lives of everyone in your family. *Or*, you can pretend to cooperate while planning your attack, making the recipes Mr Butter wants *and* their antidotes, then sneak up from behind and ruin their entire operation." He paused. "Which sounds like the better plan to you?"

"The second," said Rose, removing the cat from her head and placing him at her side. She sat up. "I've got to do it."

Gus put a paw on Rose's forehead. "You must, it's true. You don't have a choice. Not if you want to keep your family safe."

"Rose, please!" Marge shouted up. Her voice sounded worried and thin. "The Glo-Balls!"

Rose looked to Gus and grumbled. "OK, let's go make some evil Glo-Balls."

"And?" said Gus.

Rose turned up a corner of her mouth. "*And* the antidote."

Rose and the bakers stood over the prep table and stared down at the tray of chocolate Glo-Balls, which were the exact same colours of the highlighters Rose used at school.

"Man, do I want one of these," said Gene, salivating. "They look way better than those Moony Pyes."

"Moony Pyes are gross," said Felanie with a shudder.

"Grosser than gross," said Melanie. "They're... *grewse*."

Rose looked to Marge, confused, and rolled up the white sleeves of her baker's uniform. "They're not still under the Moony Pye spell?"

Marge pointed proudly toward the stove. "I made them some Dragomiresti's Apricot Jam! We all had scones with apricot jam for breakfast, and now we're feeling a lot less Moony, if you know what I mean."

"Though I *am* craving apricots," said Ning, patting his round stomach. "Sweet, delicious apricots!"

"It's a trade-off, Ning," said Marge. "Go with it."

"But even more than that, I'm wanting some of these here Glo-Balls," Ning said.

"Me too," said Jasmine. She blinked, and her eyes

seemed to grow. "Something about the way they *glow*... I really want them."

Rose noticed that she, too, felt a strong urge to eat a Glo-Ball, even though she knew they were just dressed-up pieces of brown junk. Still, up close, the coconut-covered pastries seemed irresistible. The colours were so bright – the blues so blue, the greens so green – that each Glo-Ball looked like an enormous neon jewel.

"*Pretty,*" Felanie said underneath her breath.

"As the, erm, Directrice," Rose said, "I will sample the Glo-Ball."

"*Lucky,*" Melanie whispered.

Rose reached toward the neon-coloured balls and popped a piece of an orange one in her mouth. The frosting tasted like shredded tissue paper, the chocolate cake tasted like gluey ash, and the creamy filling tasted like frothy, warmed-over saliva. And it was all sickeningly sweet.

"Ugh!" said Rose, spitting it into the sink. "I hate it," she said, perplexed. "I really hate it." She rinsed her mouth, then rinsed it again. "But I want to eat another one right now. Maybe."

"That's why the recipe needs work," said Marge. "It's not *perfectly* addictive."

Rose shuddered at the thought of what might happen if they were. "OK," she said. "Show me how you guys make these."

Gus sat on Rose's shoulder as she watched the bakers re-create Lily's Glo-Ball recipe.

Marge held out another of Lily's creamy-coloured, beautifully copied-out recipe cards and hollered out orders. Jasmine made the fluffy balls of chocolate cake, while Gene, the Vice President of Fillings, pulled a fire hose from the wall and attached a long metal wand to the end. It looked like an enormous hypodermic needle.

"What are you doing with that fire hose, Gene?" asked Rose.

"Fire hose?" Puzzled, Gene looked at the object in his hand. "Oh man," he said. "You thought this was a fire hose? No, this is a Preservation Nozzle."

Rose saw that the hose was connected to a churning tank of a thick clearish substance that looked a lot like mucus, which she hadn't noticed before. *Yech.*

As if he'd done this a couple of thousand times before – which he probably had, Rose thought – Gene brought the hose to the tray of hot chocolate cake balls and injected each one with a small dose of the churning white goop.

"*That's* the filling that goes into the Glo-Balls?" Rose's stomach did a gentle flip. "That weird snot?"

"No no, those are the preservatives," Gene explained. "It's an FLCP must. A dollop of this ensures that those Glo-Balls won't go bad until after the earth has been inherited by zombies and cockroaches. Keeps them tasting as good as the day they were made – even a thousand years from now." He smiled proudly.

Rose thought of the Prohibition-era Dinky Cake sitting under the display jar in the main production facility.

"Some things just shouldn't be possible," she said to Gus, who sat next to her on the spotless stainless-steel prep table. He nodded in agreement.

After Gene had filled all of the Glo-Balls with their preservative snot, Ning and Felanie prepared four separate bowls of plain white vanilla frosting. Then they produced a red mason jar that contained a large black beetle. The beetle was turning circles inside the jar, as if looking for the exit. It looked more gross than magical; but then again, so did the Moon's Cheese.

"What is *that*?" Rose asked.

"The Blinding Beetle," said Marge, handing out black

welding helmets to Rose and the rest of the bakers. "You'll want to put these on."

Rose had seen helmets like these on the faces of construction workers joining steel beams with white-hot sparks outside the Calamity Falls Library. They looked a little heavy-duty and out of place for a bakery.

She pulled hers over her head. It was like someone had turned out the lights. "I can't see anything," Rose said, "and I can barely breathe. Is this really necessary?"

"Yes," said Ning, opening the jar and dumping the Blinding Beetle into the mixing bowl.

Rose stood in the pitch dark, listening to her own breath, until suddenly the beetle began to glow like a firecracker, running around the sides of the bowl and spraying a trail of crackling orange sparks from its wings. It sounded like the sparklers that she, Sage, and Ty would light in the backyard on July fourth – all hisses and crackles and pops.

Ning spooned it over to the next bowl, where it began to glow neon green, shooting streams of green sparks. And then another bowl where it was an electric pink smudge in the dark. And then a final bowl, where it burned orbits of metallic blue. Even through the welder's mask, the glow was almost too bright to look at. Trails of light snaked across Rose's vision, so that she had to blink and look away.

When the beetle had gone dark again, Ning trapped it and dropped it back into the red jar, then snapped on the lid.

Rose took off her mask, wiping beads of sweat from her forehead, and saw that the four bowls of frosting were now neon orange, green, pink, and blue. Inside the mason jar, the unassuming black beetle crawled about looking exhausted.

"My my," said Marge, who was blinking rapidly. "My my."

"Interesting," Rose said, flipping through the *Apocrypha*. She searched for any mention of the Blinding Beetle, and at last landed on this page:

It was in 1832 in the Thai village of Songkram that the visiting British trader Deveril Shank, a descendent of Albatross Bliss, did discover the Blinding Beetle in the wild jungles of Southeast Asia. He did use the magical sparks produced by the Blinding Beetle to colour the frosting of a poisoned cake that he fed to the royal family of Songkram, who had threatened to expel him. The royal family ate the cake, even though it was poisoned, because they were so entranced by the icing.

"That's awful!" said Marge, who had been leaning over Rose's shoulder and reading the *Apocrypha*, too.

"I know," Rose said.

Marge glanced back down at the recipe card that had been left to her by Lily. "I never saw the original recipe, only the version that our former Directrice gave to us." She sucked in a large, dramatic breath and shook her head. "Albatross Bliss *poisoned* people! What is wrong with your family?"

"They aren't my family," said Rose, feeling slightly defensive – only there wasn't enough time to explain the Bliss family tree, and how a never-settled feud between two brothers – good-hearted Filbert and dark-hearted Albatross – led to two kinds of kitchen magic. There was helpful magic worked by Rose's mother (and by Rose, too, she reminded herself). And there was the dark magic Albatross and his descendants performed.

"But never mind that. Even though these are awful" – Rose pointed at the various bowls in front of her – "they're nowhere near awful enough."

"What do you mean?" said Gus, hopping up onto the table. He shivered and all his hair stood on end. "I really *hate* bugs."

"This recipe only makes the Glo-Balls irresistible from the outside," Rose explained. "They need to be irresistible from the *inside*."

Just then, Gene waddled over to the group. Rose ran her finger across her mouth, as though she was zipping up a zipper, and motioned for Gus to be quiet.

"She really knows her stuff!" said Gene, patting Rose on the back.

"Indeed!" Melanie and Felanie said simultaneously, staring into one of the frosting bowls.

Rose beamed as she flipped through the pages of the *Apocrypha* and found this recipe, which seemed *perfectly* awful.

FAMINE CAKE:
For the terror of the towns

It was in 1742 in the Irish Town of Ballybay that the nefarious Albatross descendant Callum O'Frame did bake tiny cakes that, when eaten, did cause the folk of Ballybay to feel a great emptiness in their bellies. They did eat as much food as they could, but nothing did cure the hunger. They ate up all of their own food, then did rove about the land in search of food, murdering their neighbours for boiled potatoes and shepherd's pie. The Ballybayans did transform into ravenous beasts.

Sir Callum O'Frame did mix two fists of **flour** with one fist of **chocolate powder** and one fist of **white sugar**. He did add one staff of **cow's butter** with two **chicken's eggs** and one fist of **milk**, one acorn of **vanilla**, and the **howl of a Hag o' the Mist**, which surpassed even the howling stomachs of the villagers.

"So, if we make this recipe, then we'll become beasts?" Marge asked. She pulled off her chef's toque, which was no longer white, exactly – it was dirtied with bits of food colouring and brown sugar. "I don't want to become a howling hag."

"This'll cure you," said Rose, pointing to the fine print on the back of the page.

BUNNY BUNS: To cease the effects of the
FAMINE CAKE
The travelling baker Seamus Bliss did witness the murderous starvation of the perfectly well-fed Ballybay villagers and

did fix for them sweet buns that did cause them to feel
perfectly satiated whenever they touched the fur of a pure
and sweet rabbit.

*Sir Bliss did mix three fists of **flour** with one acorn of*
*the **yeast**, one fist **cow's milk**, one **chicken's egg**,*
*and one fist of **sugar**. He did add the **blessing of the***
***Benedictine Bunny**.*

Thereafter, the townsfolk did wear preserved rabbit's feet
around their necks – garnered from rabbits who had died
of natural causes, of course – so that they would always
be touching the fur of a pure and sweet rabbit.

"Wow!" Gene exclaimed, his eyebrows spiking nearly
to the top of his head. "Maybe that's the origin of
rabbit's-foot key rings! I love those! I have a whole box
of 'em under my bed!"

"But where are we going to get the Benedictine
Bunny?" Rose wondered aloud. "Let alone a Hag o' the
Mist?"

While the bakers stood around and thought, Gus
hopped into Rose's arms and whispered into her ear.
"It looked like they have every possible ingredient in

that cake-shaped warehouse," he said softly. "The one with the robots. I'm sure they'd give you the Hag o' the Mist. The Benedictine Bunny, on the other hand, might cause some suspicion. You'd probably have to steal that one."

"Good idea," Rose whispered into the cat's ear. She let Gus hop down onto the floor, and then repeated his idea word for word.

"I'll go," said Gene after Rose had finished speaking. He puffed out his chest. "I used to do some heavy-duty shoplifting when I was a teenager, before I straightened myself out and found baking. I'm sure I could make that Benedictine Bunny disappear like a rabbit in a top hat."

"Gene, my friend, we've all done things we aren't proud of," said Marge, patting him on the back. "I once stole a horse from a racetrack. It's a long story." She grinned broadly. "Point is, I'll be your wing-woman."

"No!" Felanie cried out. "It's too dangerous!"

"Steal a bunny?" Melanie asked. "It's too sweet a thing to steal!" She turned to Jasmine, who was breaking up a chocolate bar and feeding the pieces to Ning. "Did you hear this, Jasmine? Marge and Gene are going to steal a bunny!"

"Hmm?" Jasmine said, looking up.

"Never mind all that," Marge said. She walked right up to Jasmine and took two pieces of chocolate out of her hand. With one of them, she drew dark lines underneath her eyes – like a football player would do. With the other piece, she did the same thing for Gene.

"There," Marge said. "Now we're basically unrecognizable. Come on, Gene." She popped the nubs of chocolate into her mouth and winked at Rose. "Duty calls."

Rose and Gus and the rest of the bakers stayed behind in the test kitchen preparing two versions of the revised Glo-Balls chocolate cake recipe: one for the Hag o' the Mist's howl, and one for the Benedictine Bunny's blessing. They made giant portions of the batter in two metal mixing vats the size of timpani drums that Jasmine wheeled out from a storage closet.

"Poor bunny," Melanie kept muttering. "Poor, poor bunny."

Poor, poor me, Rose thought. If it hadn't been for Felanie, Ning, and Jasmine pitching in, she would have ruined both batches of mix. No matter how much she tried to focus on the recipe, she kept making mistakes. She kept seeing her parents and Balthazar in that hotel room, surrounded by Mostess treats. And she kept hearing Mr Butter say, "Or else!" What would he do to them if she failed?

"Maybe you should do cleanup on this recipe?" Jasmine gently suggested, handing her a bowl filled to the brim with goopy implements.

"Good idea," Rose said.

Just as she was washing the thin chocolate cake batter off of a giant mixing spoon, Marge and Gene returned. They looked a bit tired, but happy grins were stretched across their faces. The chocolate lines under their eyes must have sweated off, leaving their cheeks a bit muddy-looking. But one thing was clear: they were excited.

"How'd it go?" Rose asked.

Marge was pushing a cart that held two red mason jars. One was four feet tall and two feet wide. Through the translucent red glass, Rose could see a ghostly old woman lurking inside. The other jar was the standard size and contained an adorable cream-colored bunny wearing a black-and-white collar.

"Success!" Marge cried, pumping her fist in the air.

The other bakers crowded around the cart, oohing and ahhing at the mason jars. While they were distracted,

Rose crouched down and had a brief conversation with Gus, who'd been tugging at her apron with an extended claw.

"I'd be careful with that Hag o' the Mist," Gus whispered as Gene strained to push the jar toward the prep table. "I hear they're very... unruly."

"What is she?" Rose asked, squinting at the ghostly woman in the jar. She had stringy grey hair, wrinkled white skin, and a long, pointed nose. Rose couldn't tell whether the Hag was staring past Rose or straight at her. It was unnerving, to say the least.

"Hag o' the Mist," Gus began, clearing his throat, "is mostly a Welsh phenomenon. They are creatures of hollowness, made of mist. They're said to prey on the hearts of the innocent. They howl because of the terrible emptiness in their bellies and the terrible ache in their hearts, an ache that can never be filled, no matter how many souls they eat."

"That doesn't sound good," Rose said, then stood up. She repeated this new information to the group.

"Sounds like my ex-husband," said Marge with a low moan.

Rose covered one vat of chocolate batter and slid the other vat forward.

Opening the large jar containing the Hag, Marge said, "It's all yours, Haggy!"

The Hag burst from the jar, growing to full size in moments. She was as large as the bakers, though nowhere near as fat. Her black eyes darted around the room. She raised her claw-like hands to the ceiling and let out an ear-splitting howl.

The stand mixers rattled and the linoleum floor tiles curled at the edges. Crumbles of plaster fell from the ceiling. Rose plugged her ears with her thumbs, but the Hag's unholy shriek seared her eardrums like a hot poker.

Prodded by the scream, the chocolate batter rippled up from the mixing bowl and began to revolve in the air, spinning itself into a giant tilting sphere. It spun wider and wider, creating a hollow shell, the chocolate turning at such an intense speed that it barely looked like it was moving at all.

A moment later, the Hag hiccupped and stopped howling.

Wow, Rose thought. *That was ten million times worse than Marge's shrieks. And I thought those were bad.*

At the same moment, the batter stopped spinning, and in the blink of an eye, it settled back into the bowl with a loud *sploosh*. A stink of rot and the particularly nasty breath of a cafeteria full of hungry people rose from the bowl.

"Yech!" Ning said, fanning the air from his face.

The Hag o' the Mist sniffed around the room, searching for something, and her black, empty eyes fastened on Rose.

An innocent heart, Rose realized. *She wants to devour my heart.* "Grab the jar!" Rose cried. "Help!"

Chapter 8

GORGING ON GLO-BALLS

Rose hid behind the six bakers as Marge turned the mouth of the jar toward the Hag.

"Keep it away from me!" Rose called out. She closed her eyes but all she could see were the beady black irises of the Hag. Focused on her. Wanting to devour her.

"Don't worry, Rose," Marge said. "We'll protect you!"

"Just try it, Haggy," cried Felanie, crooking a finger. *"Just try."*

"Yeah, come and get it," Melanie purred. "Get. It."

The Hag o' the Mist growled so long and so deeply that the floor rumbled. All the hair on Rose's head seemed to stand at attention as the Hag surged toward her.

But the bakers never moved. They stood their ground

and thrust out the mason jar, snapping the Hag out of the air in front of Rose at the very last second. Felanie snapped the lid shut, and Melanie locked the clasp, trapping the Hag, who smacked her face on the bottom so hard that she dissipated into mist again.

"Phew," said Rose with a shiver. "That was close."

Gus raised his head from behind the bowl of one of the big stand mixers. All of his hair was standing on end, as though he'd been charged with static electricity. "Is that thing trapped again?" he asked softly.

"All locked up," Rose said, relieved.

The bakers set the jar in a corner of the room. As they all watched, it rattled for a few seconds, then went still. "Phew," said Ning. "That thing was scarier than my own grandmother."

Once everyone had settled, Melanie and Felanie began spooning the altered chocolate batter into little Glo-Ball-shaped cake tins. Meanwhile, Marge uncovered the other vat of chocolate. "Now for the antidote," she said.

Rose pulled over the other mason jar. "Anything I need to worry about with this one?" she asked the cat.

Gus shrugged. "That it is too dumb to help, perhaps? It's a rabbit, after all."

Rose unclasped the lid of the second jar and drew out the Benedictine Bunny. She stood holding him, stroking his silky fur.

His eyes, like the Hag o' the Mist's, were pitch-black, yet instead of a hollow coldness, they radiated warmth and innocence and light. He was the sweetest thing she'd ever seen, and Rose was overcome with a desire to cradle the Bunny in her arms forever. All of the bakers stopped their work and stared, entranced by a feeling of utter peace and calm.

"Wowie zowie," Jasmine said. "That is the most beautiful bunny I've ever seen."

"It has—" Ning struggled to finish his sentence. "An otherworldly tenderness!"

"It's fluffy!" Melanie whispered.

Everyone was so busy staring at the Benedictine Bunny that they didn't see the Hag o' the Mist sniffing frantically within her jar, her empty eyes boring through the scarlet glass and straight at the innocent bunny.

Rose dandled the bunny near the chocolate batter. "Now what?" she whispered, not wanting to disturb the perfect creature.

"You're in luck," said Gus. "I'm familiar with basic conversational Rabbitsch. I'll ask him to bless the batter."

Gus purred a series of long and short purrs, something like Morse code. The Bunny seemed to smile and nod, then he hopped over to the edge of the prep table and sat on his hind legs, raising his soft paws in the air. He closed his eyes and uttered a series of squeaks, which sounded to Rose like the sweetest music she'd ever heard.

Behind her, the red jar containing the Hag o' the Mist began to rattle. It shook and shook and then clattered to the floor. The glass cracked and a tiny chip tumbled out. The Hag o' the Mist squeezed triumphantly through the tiny hole in the glass and, with a howl, rushed at the Benedictine Bunny.

The Bunny continued his incantation, oblivious.

Rose covered her ears and threw herself in front of the Hag, but the misty white figure passed right through her. Jasmine jumped in front of the Bunny, but the Hag shot through her, too, like a nearly invisible arrow.

"The Bunny!" Melanie cried.

"What?" Felanie called out over the Hag's howl.

"THE BUNNY!"

The Hag stopped short right in front of the Benedictine Bunny and opened her mouth, wider and wider, until it was a round black pit as big as the rest of her body.

She began to inhale with a sound like an industrial vacuum.

The Bunny slowly slid across the cold steel of the prep table toward the Hag's mouth.

"No!" Rose screamed. "Stop!"

Gus leaped atop the table and grabbed the Bunny's cottontail, hitching himself to the edge of the table with his paws, but the Hag was too strong. Gus, too, slowly slid forward.

Rose looked frantically around the room and her eyes settled on the tank of preservatives. "Gene!" she shouted. "The hose!"

Gene's eyes widened in understanding. Quickly, he grabbed the long needlelike nozzle and tossed it to Rose, who caught it and shoved it into the Hag's wide-open mouth.

Then Rose squeezed the trigger.

As the mucousy preservative shot into the Hag, her blank black eyes widened—

With fright, Rose realized. The Hag was scared.

The gloppy preservative seemed to congeal inside the mist, creating a solid figure of grey terror. The Hag grew more and more solid, finally sinking to the ground under her own weight, until finally she burst in an explosion of grey gunk that coated the walls, ceiling, and all of the stainless steel appliances. Marge covered the second vat of chocolate batter just in time to protect it.

"Eww!" cried Felanie. "Disgusting!"

The Bunny finished his blessing and opened his eyes, a clueless smile on his face. Then he sat back on his haunches and twitched his nose.

"Thank God," Melanie said. "Thank God the Bunny is safe."

Gus sighed and looked to Rose. "Looks like they're going to need a new Hag."

By five thirty that evening, the Benedictine Bunny was back safe in its jar and the two different versions of Glo-Balls sat in trays on the prep table, frosted with four kinds of neon frosting.

Rose lifted the tray of antidote Glo-Balls. "I'm going to hide these somewhere in the kitchen," she said to the team of bakers. "If the sinister Glo-Balls work like they're supposed to, you'll be so desperate for more that you'll search the entire kitchen until you find them. That will be the test. Now don't look!"

The bakers obediently closed their eyes while Rose

hid the antidote Glo-Balls underneath an overturned metal bowl on the farthest prep table. When she was done, she climbed the staircase to her room and left the bakers hovering over the tray of dangerous Glo-Balls.

"Dig in!" she shouted.

It was a Glo-Ball massacre.

The bakers fell upon the tray of neon Glo-Balls, pushing one another out of the way, and shoved one Glo-Ball after another into their mouths until their cheeks were so plumped out they looked like chipmunks. Smears of filling and flecks of neon frosting and coconut decorated their faces like confetti.

"I feel sick just watching them," said Gus.

"You're one to talk," said Rose. "I've seen what you do to cans of tuna."

"That, my dear, is a connoisseur savouring a fine meal. This… This is a frenzy."

For her own sanity, Rose was glad the Glo-Balls were out of reach. If they were anywhere near as addictive as the Moony Pyes, she'd be in trouble with even a taste.

After the chewing stopped, Marge and the rest of the bakers lay on the floor digesting, smacking their lips.

Then the rolling began.

Marge clutched at her belly. "I'm starving!" she wailed. "I need more Glo-Balls! My stomach is a black hole that nothing can fill!"

Ning huffed himself to his feet and waddled around the kitchen, crying out, "I call dibs! First I fill the emptiness in my tummy, and then we'll talk about yours, Marge." He looked in and under everything he found – cabincts, bowls, paper towels. "I know that the Directrice made more of those wondrous, sweet Glo-Balls – where are they?"

Jasmine and Gene were too full to stand, so they crawled along the floor, sniffing the tiles and underneath the stainless steel appliances like bloodhounds.

Melanie and Felanie merely contented themselves with licking the crumbs off the baking sheets, blubbering all the while. "No more! No more! Oh, why are there no more?"

Rose watched the bakers in horror. If these Glo-Balls were unleashed on the country, there'd be no stopping the Mostess Corporation. The false feeling of starvation that the Glo-Balls created would lead to people looting stores, willing to do anything necessary to get more Mostess goods. Anything that Mr Butter – or the

International Society of the Rolling Pin – wanted them to do.

"This is terrible," Rose said.

"Seems the Hag o' the Mist has done her worst," Gus whispered.

"I hope those antidote Glo-Balls work," said Rose. "Come on, Benedictine Bunny – don't let us down."

Jasmine knocked her head hard against the prep table where Rose had hidden the antidote Glo-Balls. The prep table tipped over and fell to the ground, spilling the hidden Glo-Balls across the floor. They rolled across the tiles, a dozen balls of bright color, and the six bakers gasped and froze in place.

"They're *mine!*" Marge screamed, leaping atop another prep table and sliding down its length.

"Over my fat body!" Gene cried, rolling himself forward.

Melanie and Felanie just roared incomprehensibly and scrambled across the floor, crying and laughing at the same time.

Everyone met in a headbutting crash atop the antidote Glo-Balls, and the screaming and shouting was such that Rose had to cover her ears and turn away. She looked to be sure that each baker got at least one

Glo-Ball, then waited for the antidote to take effect and for her sweet-natured team to come back from whatever evil place the sinister Glo-Balls had taken them.

And then? The fighting stopped.

The bakers looked at one another while they wiped their faces of crumbs and licked the last flecks of frosting off their fingers.

Marge was the first to speak. "I need more," she whispered. "If you little piggies hadn't eaten it all, there would be more for me!" Then she lunged.

"You're the piggy!" Ning shouted, throwing himself at Marge. Soon Jasmine was pummeling Ning with a pair of eggbeaters, Gene was smacking Felanie with a sheet pan, and Melanie was pulling people's aprons over their heads and beating them with a wooden spoon.

Rose turned to Gus in terror. "What happened?" she cried. "I followed the recipe just as written! Why are they still going crazy?"

She took out the card and reread it quickly. "Oh no," she said, and read aloud: *"Thereafter, the townsfolk did wear preserved rabbit's feet around their necks... so that they would always be touching the fur of a pure and sweet rabbit."*

"It's never going to work if they all have to hold on to that spaced-out rabbit," Gus said. "There's not enough rabbit to go around."

Rose shook her head. "Gene said he has a box of rabbit's-foot key rings, remember? Those should work. I have to get them!"

Rose began down the stairs, but Gus galloped out in front of her and blocked her path. "No," he said. "It's too dangerous. They'll rip you to shreds." He crouched down low, saying, "This is a job that only a cat can do. Allow me."

He turned and flowed down the steps like a furry grey streak, darted around the edges of the room, and disappeared into the Bakers' Quarters.

Five minutes later, by which time Rose began to fear that the bakers might actually hurt one another, Gus zoomed out from their quarters, toting six rabbit's-foot key rings in his mouth. He ran straight into the wrestling knot of bakers.

"The cat has more Glo-Balls!" Rose shouted. "The cat has Glo-Balls!"

For a moment, nothing happened – the bakers just continued their slow-motion tussle on the floor. But then, slowly, the heaving and shoving eased until the six bakers untangled themselves and lay scattered across the tiling, panting heavily, each clutching a rabbit's foot in their frosting-coated fingers. Gene belched loudly enough to rattle the pans on a nearby prep table, and suddenly all the bakers were moaning aloud.

The cat sat in the empty centre of the floor, examining the smears of frosting on his fur. "Rose, you're going to have to clean this poisonous stuff off me. I wouldn't want to lose control of my claws. No telling who'd get hurt."

"I will never eat again," said Marge. "This is it. This is the last time."

Suddenly, the red lights in the corners of the room flashed, and the siren wailed. "Mr Butter is coming!" Rose shouted, dashing down the steps to the kitchen floor. "Everybody, remember: you are still addicted to the Glo-Balls! You have to pretend."

"I can't!" Jasmine groaned. "I can't even *pretend* to want to eat!"

The bakers rolled on the floor like seals basking on rocks in the sun.

"Guys, please!" Rose cried. "If Mr Butter sees you moaning about how you'll never eat another Glo-Ball, he might hurt my parents! And my grandpa! Please, get up!"

Just then, the trapdoor slid aside as the elevator reached the floor. Two figures were there, but they weren't sitting in a golf cart.

"What gives, *hermana*?"

Rose's brothers, Ty and Sage, were standing on the elevator platform.

Chapter 9

TWO BROTHERS, WITH SPRINKLES

ROSE BOUNDED OVER to Ty and Sage and clung to them, and they patted her awkwardly on the head. The three of them hadn't shared a group hug in a while – or ever, for that matter. It was weird but wonderful, and Rose blinked back tears.

"What are you doing here?" she asked. "Did you get Mum and Dad out? Where's Leigh?"

Ty's spiky red hair stood tall like the proud coxcomb of a rooster. Sage's freckled, pudgy cheeks were like glowing orbs. The boys stood with their arms crossed proudly across their matching white T-shirts. Rose thought they looked like angels. She had never been gladder to see two people in her life.

"Who are these fine young men?" Marge asked. She

burped, then clapped a hand over her lips. "Excuse me," she said. "I've... eaten one too many Glo-Balls."

Sage nodded at the bloated Head Baker. "It happens to the best of us," he said.

"Marge, these are my brothers," said Rose. "Thyme and Sage. And these," Rose continued, indicating the bakers scattered across the floor, "are the Mostess Corporation Head Bakers. Now," she said. "How did you get here?"

"I drove us here!" Ty said proudly, raising a hand as though to stifle applause. "In Mrs Carlson's car. With my licence."

"She didn't want us to go," Sage said, "so we had to wait until she was watching her stories."

"She likes that one about that bigwig doctor in the military," Ty said. *"Hospital General."*

"Anyway, Mum and Dad had gone to get you after Jacques told us where you were," said Sage. "They didn't want us to come along, but when they didn't call to check in, we figured something was wrong."

"Mrs Carlson drives a thirty-year-old station wagon," Ty said. "It was a challenge to handle, I have to say. But I was able to master its controls with only a few mishaps."

Sage whispered, "We backed up into a delivery truck at a gas station."

"It was strategic," Ty insisted. "It was part of my plan! You see, it was a Mostess delivery truck."

Sage smiled. "The driver was superfriendly. He let me check out the cab of his truck while he got Ty's insurance information. And then we followed him here."

"We got here this morning and waited outside the gates until a different truck blocked the guard box," Ty said, "then we walked through on the other side."

"It was easy," said Sage. "The guards were gorging themselves on this pile of chocolate-covered cookie-marshmallow things and didn't even notice us."

"Oh dear," said Marge. "Sounds like they're giving your new Moony Pyes to the guards, Rose."

"But how did you know I was in this building?" Rose asked.

"I found a map," Sage said. He reached back and fished something out of his jeans pocket – a ratty square of paper. "It was in the truck driver's glove compartment."

Once he'd unfolded it, she saw a map of the entire Mostess compound. Each of the buildings was labelled – MOONY PYE FACTORY #3, MOSTESS LABORATORY, THE PASTRY

BAG HOTEL, and more. Toward the centre, circled, was DEVELOPMENT KITCHENS.

"Jacques said that cat who brought the message from Gus had said something about development kitchens, so we came straight here," Sage said, folding up the map with a flourish and returning it to his pocket.

Rose hugged the two of them again.

"All right already!" Ty said, throwing up his arms. "Careful you don't mess up the hair!"

"But what are you doing here?" asked Sage. "And where's Mom and Dad?"

Rose explained everything to her brothers – her own kidnapping, how their parents and great-great-great-grandfather had been taken hostage, and the plans of Mr Butter and the International Society of the Rolling Pin to enslave the world through the power of sweets. "It's all because of Lily," Rose said at the end, taking the grey booklet from within her coat. "She used the *Apocrypha* to perfect the recipes."

"So she came here after Paris?" Sage asked. "Is she here now?"

"No, she was here before Paris. She hid the *Apocrypha* here and never came back for it after she lost the *Booke* in the Gala. Too ashamed, I guess."

"I'm very disappointed in *Tía* Lily," Ty said, clucking his tongue. "If only she'd finished her work here, you wouldn't be held prisoner."

"Ty, that's not the point!" Rose said, exasperated. "Everyone in America is in serious trouble of becoming a Mostess Snack Cake–eating zombie unless we can find a way to stop these people."

"We should probably go bust out Mum and Dad," said Sage. "They'll know what to do."

"Let's just wait for the police," said Rose, relieved. Her brothers were here. They were going to help her rescue her parents – *somehow*. It had been a crazy couple of days, but now it was over.

"Police?" asked Ty. "Are they here, too?"

Rose smacked his arm. "Didn't you guys call the police?"

"And tell them *what?*" Ty said. "That a mouse with a French accent told us where you were?"

"And what, *précisément*, is wrong with that?" came a squeaky French voice.

Jacques scampered out from a pocket of Sage's khaki cargo shorts and took a seat in the mess of red curls atop his head. Gus gave him a regal nod.

At the sight of the rodent, the bakers all screamed.

"Mouse!" Marge cried.

"Kill it!" yelled Jasmine.

"Bash that boy over the head with a frying pan, Gene!" said Ning.

Gene heaved himself onto his feet and waddled over toward a cast-iron skillet that was sitting on a metal shelf.

"No!" Rose shouted. "Stop! This is not a mouse! This is Jacques!"

Jacques peeked out from the shrubbery of Sage's curls.

"Don't bash me over the head with a frying pan!" Sage cried.

"No one is bashing anyone with anything," said Rose, rushing over to Gene and calming him down. "Gene, this is our friend Jacques. He is a mouse, but he's a... good mouse."

Just then, the red corner lights flashed, and the siren sounded. Mr Butter's Southern drawl piped in over a loudspeaker. "Hello, bakers! We're coming up now. There better be some marvellous Glo-Ball action up there!"

The trapdoor slid open as the top of the golf cart emerged through the floor.

Rose shoved her brothers toward the Bakers'

Quarters, shooing them in the direction of the stairs like flies. "They're coming! Hide!"

"Pretend you're still crazy for Glo-Balls!" Rose hissed to the bakers. "Hands with rabbit's feet in apron pockets!"

Rose pulled each of the bakers to his or her feet. "Tidy yourselves up!" she called out, and Melanie, Felanie, Jasmine, Gene, and Ning all wiped the front of their aprons, fixed their chef hats, and tried their very best to straighten their trousers. But it was no use: They were still complete messes, covered with flour, frosting, and smears of chocolate.

Gene winked.

Messes, maybe, but happy ones. Rose smiled at him and took her place at the head of the line. She hoped Ty and Sage were smart enough to shut the door to the Bakers' Quarters behind them.

The seam in the floor opened up, and the golf cart rose up level with the kitchen. Mr Butter emerged from the passenger side, with Mr Kerr driving, as usual. "How are those beautiful little Glo-Balls bouncing along?" he asked. "Hmmm?"

"I'd tell you to see for yourself," said Rose, hooking her thumb at the bakers, "but these amateurs you've assigned me have eaten every last one of them." Behind her, the bakers swatted weakly at one another.

"I need more!" Marge cried. "My stomach is a bottomless pit!"

"My stomach is even more bottomless!" Ning growled.

"Mine's the bottomless-est!" Melanie shouted.

"Most bottomless, you mean," Felanie said to her.

"I mean what I said, and I say what I mean," Melanie hollered, "and I mean to eat ALL the Glo-Balls!"

"They already ate a dozen each," Rose whispered to Mr Butter, smiling like she was his right-hand woman. "I thought that would be enough, but I underestimated how many they could put away."

"I'd say the recipe works!" Mr Butter cooed, clapping his hands. Rose stiffened as he moved toward the two giant vats of leftover chocolate batter. "But certainly you can make more," he said, "as I see that there are two of these."

"One was a mistake!" Rose explained. "It took some testing to get the proportions of ingredients correctly balanced. It's the tub on the left that's full of the good stuff."

Mr Butter dipped his finger into the vat the Hag had poisoned, then licked off the chocolate batter. "Oh my!"

he said. "Oh dear! Mmmmm, this is so... I do believe I need a bit more to taste." He extended another finger and then, at the last moment, dunked both his hands into the batter up to his wrists. "And I don't even like sweets! In fact, I detest them!"

As he raised his goop-covered hands to his mouth to lick them again, Mr Kerr shouted, "Stop right there!"

Shocked, Mr Butter froze, his eyes blinking. "Who would dare tell me what to do?"

Mr Kerr ran to the sink and grabbed a tub of soapy water. He brought it to Mr Butter and said, "Sir, I recommend that you wash your hands, sir."

"But I want to taste more of this delectable confection!"

"Butter," coughed Mr Kerr. "That's not for you. Remember?"

Mr Butter's eyes went wide and he instantly plunged his hands into the bin of soapy water. He scrubbed at them until they were free of batter and then, for good measure, plunged his face into the tub and scrubbed at his mouth and lips. When he raised himself back up, trails of suds ran off his big bald head.

"That was a close call!" he said, spitting out streams of soapy dishwater. "My tiny taste is enough for me to declare that this batter is divine! Good work, Miss Rosemary Bliss."

Mr Butter paced around the kitchen, and behind his glasses his beady eyes went wide again. "Your talents are extraordinary, Miss Bliss. I am almost tempted to say you've made these recipes too good, but then I remember why we are here. Why, the things I can do with these Glo-Balls are—"

He stopped and raised a finger, then shrieked, "Mouse!"

Chapter 10

LITTLE HOUSE ON THE TARMAC

ROSE GASPED AS she spotted Jacques cowering in a corner.

Mr Butter grabbed a frying pan and was dashing forward to smash it onto Jacques, when Gene pointed at the tall man and shouted, "He's got Glo-Balls!"

Immediately, all the bakers tackled Mr Butter, and Jacques scampered out of sight.

"Get off of me, you dolts!" Mr Butter shouted. "I don't have any Glo-Balls!" Mr Kerr rushed forward, flinging the bakers aside like they were nothing more than empty aprons. He set Mr Butter back on his feet, and the bald man brushed at his suit, irritation obvious in each gesture. "I was speaking *about* Glo-Balls; I didn't say I *had* any."

"Oh, sorry," Gene said, sheepishly dropping his chin. He turned to Rose and shrugged.

"I'd better not see another mouse in this kitchen," Mr Butter said, wiping his smudged glasses. "I know you can't avoid making a mess in here, what with all the fighting over the delicious Mostess treats, and that's terrific. But you know how much I prize cleanliness as well. So let's make sure all those crumbs get swept up."

"Absolutely," Rose said. "I'm *so* sorry, Mr Butter. It won't happen again!"

Mr Butter looked around and saw the cracked red mason jar that had held the Hag o' the Mist. "I suppose you'll need another Hag o' the Mist, then?"

Rose shrugged. "I'm sorry, sir. She... got out of hand."

"They always do!" Mr Butter laughed. "We'll send a team to Wales and trap a few more. No problem."

"Mr Butter," said Mr Kerr, tapping his watch. "We're on a tight schedule. They'll be here soon."

Mr Butter made a pouty face. "Ah, well. I'd love to stay and chat, but we've got to toodle," he said, following Mr Kerr back to the golf cart and folding his skinny frame back into the passenger seat. "Oh, and Rose!"

"Yes?" she said tentatively.

"You're doing such a wonderful job, why don't we

see if we can't speed up our rate of recipe perfection, shall we? I bet you can work out the kinks for recipe number three, Dinky Doodle Doughnuts, by later this evening!" He glanced down at his watch. "Why, it's not even seven! The night is young!"

"I don't know…" Rose began.

"I'm sure your parents would really appreciate it," he added, grinning, as the golf cart descended out of sight. "I'll be back to check on you before bedtime. Ta ta!"

The doors in the floor whispered shut and everyone in the room sighed and slumped down.

"Great job, you guys," Rose said to the bakers, who let loose a collective groan of indigestion.

Suddenly, two figures emerged from the enormous tub of sprinkles sitting by the wall. One of the figure's heads was covered with sprinkle-covered spikes – Ty. The other was Sage. Both were completely coated head to toe in party-coloured sprinkles. They wiped sprinkles away from the space where their eyes would be, then blinked at everyone in the room.

"Why didn't you guys just hide in the Bakers' Quarters like I told you?" Rose asked as Ty and Sage struggled out of the vat, dripping like swamp things.

"There wasn't time," said Ty.

"It wasn't so bad hiding in sprinkles," Sage said. "You can breathe through them so long as you don't open your mouth too wide. But you can't really breathe through your nose." He put a finger against one nostril and blew a clump of sprinkles out of the other.

"Eew, Sage!" Rose said. "Come on. We have to go get Mum and Dad and Balthazar and get out of here." Rose ladled some of the Hag-filled Glo-Ball batter into a muffin tin and shoved it into the blazing oven.

"What's that for?" said Ty, licking the sprinkles from his fingers.

"*That*," Rose said, "is gonna get us a car."

Rose and her brothers rode the elevator to the ground floor. During the lift's slow descent, Sage and Ty had warned her about the two guards at the entrance.

"They weren't there before," Rose said. It shouldn't have surprised her that Mr Butter had placed a guard on the test kitchens, but it still sort of did. How could she trust him to actually let her and her parents leave once the five recipes were done?

"The guards are not that smart," Ty said.

"How'd you get past them?" Rose asked.

"Using Jacques," he said, opening the pocket of his khaki shorts.

The little mouse raised his grey head and said, "*Oui*, it is true that I risked my life to create a diversion. I stood at the corner and serenaded them with my flute—"

Rose could picture it – the thin, ghostly music drifting down the asphalt alleyways between the warehouses, the guards wandering off toward the music like rats after the Pied Piper of Hamelin.

"But they did not see Jacques," the mouse continued. "Such big music, they think, must come from a big person! *C'est un truc! What a trick!* No one thinks to look for a mouse. But even the smallest of creatures can contain the mightiest of talents!"

"It's true, Jacques," Rose said with a smile.

"It is the least I could do," the mouse said, bowing. He'd come along in case the kids needed to send a message to Gus, who'd stayed behind with the bakers. "I need to gather my energies," the cat had explained.

Sage had replied, "You're just going to take a nap."

"You say *tomato*," the cat had purred, stretching, "and I say *siesta*."

Now, the mouse ducked his head back into the pocket as they arrived at the ground floor. The big door to the outside rose up in front of them. Two people in dark uniforms stood on either side of the entrance, a man and a woman. Beyond the open doorway was an empty golf cart.

"Hey, you two!" Rose yelled, waving with one hand. In the other hand was a bowl full of Glo-Balls. "Over here!"

The man, who was tall and blond and looked like a weatherman Rose had seen on TV, came over, smiling in a completely fake way. "Young lady, you are not supposed to leave the building! It's dangerous out there!" He inched toward Rose and Ty and Sage, his eyes fixed on the bowl of little chocolate cakes in her arm.

Rose handed him a Glo-Ball, still warm from the oven. "We just had extra and we thought we probably shouldn't let them go to waste."

"This isn't a proper Glo-Ball!" he said, examining the confection. "Where's the neon frosting?"

"We were just experimenting with the *cake* part of the recipe. Try it," said Rose.

The man popped the hot cake in his mouth and

chewed. "Whoa!" he said. "This is incredible!" He chewed some more. With each move of his jaw, his eyes glazed over until it seemed like there was a milky white film covering his irises.

"You too," Rose said, extending the bowl to the female guard.

The woman said, "Don't mind if I do!" She reached for a cake and took a bite. "Ah-may-zing!" she declared, letting her tongue hang out of her mouth. "Just how many you got there?"

"Yes," the man said, stepping forward, "I see you have some more in that bowl."

Rose raised her arms, extending the bowl toward the two, but tripped and flung it at the last second. The perfectly round Glo-Ball cakes flew through the air, onto the pavement, and began to roll away.

"Oh no! The Glo-Balls!" the man cried, running frantically after them.

"No you don't!" the woman said, leaping out and tackling him in the doorway. "Those are mine!" She scrambled across him and after the balls, while he hung on to her leg, sobbing hysterically, *"Mine, mine, mine!"*

Rose and her brothers tiptoed over to the golf cart and plopped into the seats.

"Piece of cake," Sage said with a grin.

Rose just rolled her eyes and consulted the map. "This is where we're going," she said, pointing to the pastry-bag-shaped hotel.

"I'll drive," said Ty, patting the pocket that held his driver's licence.

Rose led Ty and Sage into the lobby of the grand hotel with its bouquets of candy and cookies. "May I help you?" said the concierge, a skinny teenager who didn't look much older than Ty.

"No, thank you," said Rose.

"Are these your guests, Miss Bliss?" said the concierge.

"These two?" Rose said, pointing to Ty and Sage. "Um. These are fans of mine. They're from an organization that helps children who have... weird voices. The children get to spend a day with their favourite celebrity. Did Mr Butter not tell you? I'm just taking them around the compound for the day."

"I see," said the concierge. "Of course. Feel free to show them around."

"What do you say, boys?" said Rose.

Ty and Sage groaned and sputtered in strange guttural voices. "Thernk yew!"

"That was real nice, Rose," muttered Sage as the three walked away toward the elevator bank. "Real nice."

"I'm sorry. It's the only thing I could think of," said Rose as she stepped into the elevator and pressed 34.

"Key required," said a robotic voice. "Please insert key."

Rose stared at the panel of the elevator and saw, next to the button that said 34, a small indentation in the metal, in the shape of a rolling pin. *Figures*, she thought.

"Oh man," said Ty, frowning. "Where are we gonna get the key, *hermana*?"

Rose couldn't remember Mr Butter having used a key in the elevator. But she could recall the way he bristled when she had pointed to the tiny red cottage in the corner of the compound.

"I don't know for sure where we're gonna get the key," she said, "but I have an idea."

After half an hour's driving, they finally stopped the golf cart in front of the little red cottage in the corner of the compound.

The house looked like it had been plucked from another era: a white picket fence surrounded a green lawn, and a flag swayed above the porch in time to the soft jangle of wind chimes. Two empty rocking chairs sat on the wide porch, just waiting for a lazy day.

"What is this place?" Sage asked.

Rose pointed to the stencilling on the old-fashioned mailbox: THE BUTTER FAMILY. "I think this is where Mr Butter grew up," she said.

She led Ty and Sage through the white gate, up a brick walkway lined with flowers, across the porch, and through the front door. The green shutters were pulled closed over the windows of the darkened living room, but the rug was painted with ribbons of late-afternoon light. Next to a dusty player piano was a worn corduroy easy chair, with a basket of half-finished knitting at the foot.

"It's like a museum," Sage whispered.

"The most boring museum in the world," Ty said.

Over the mantel was a faded photograph in a frame. A father and a mother wearing chef's hats stood flanking a little boy, who was pudgy and round, with a crew cut. "Who is that?" Ty asked.

"It must be Mr Butter," said Rose.

"That skinny, bald alien dude?" asked Sage. "Looks like someone bought a treadmill."

"Do you really think the key is in here, *hermana*?" Ty asked.

"I don't know," Rose said. "But there's got to be *something* in here worth finding. Mr Butter freaked out when I asked him about this house."

"I wonder why it's still here?" Ty said. "If I had the kind of money he must have, I'd build a huge house. One big enough for me, Katy Perry, and all her band members."

Rose led her brothers up a narrow, creaky wooden staircase. Next to a bathroom with floral wallpaper and cracked sconces was a bedroom painted in light blue. A nautical comforter lay over a twin bed, and model airplanes hung from the ceiling.

On a wooden desk sat a few dried-up jars of paint, a barrage of half-painted WWI models, and a book bound in brown leather. JOURNAL read the front cover.

"Jackpot!" Sage cried, grabbing the book.

"You can't read that!" said Rose. "That's spying!"

"Rose," said Ty, putting a hand on his sister's shoulder. "The man *kidnapped* you, not to mention our parents. I think we're pretty much allowed to read his journal."

Fair enough, Rose thought, opening the journal to the first page. The letters were large and wobbly.

The Journal of Jameson Butter III, age ten.

Day 1
I found this old journal today in Mr Sansibel's garbage can. I'm not one for writing, but Mama says it's a shame to let things go to waste, so I will write what happens every day. Today, Grandpapa baked his Dinkies, and Mama and Papa worked in the front of the bakery, and everyone in town came to eat one. Another home run for the Mostess Bakery! I got pinched in the nose again by Raymond Kerr at school and I came home and told Mama about it and she fed me a Dinky Cake.

"Real juicy," said Ty sarcastically. "Where's the stuff about girls?"

Rose flipped a few pages.

Day 45
Raymond Kerr and the rest of the Pine Ridge Crew stole my overalls while I was at the swimming hole and gave them to Polly Rainer, and she screamed and dropped them and

said cooties. When I got out, they were covered in mud and leaves and I had to walk home with mud inside my overalls. When I got home, Mama scolded me for bringing dirt into the bakery. When I told her what happened, she fed me three Dinky Cakes and told me to calm down.

"Seems like he was eating a lot of Dinky Cakes," said Rose.

"You know who I bet likes Dinky Cakes?" Ty asked.

Sage shrugged. "Who?"

Ty's eyes seemed to twinkle. "Katy Perry."

Day 162

My overalls no longer fit me. Mama took me to the store to buy me bigger overalls, and who was there, of course, but Raymond Kerr. He called me Lardo and pinched my nose. I shed a tear and reached out for Mama, but instead of petting me on the head or giving me a hug, she shoved a Dinky Cake into my mouth.

"Fine," said Ty. "Looks like all the Dinky Cakes caught up to him anyway."

He sighed. "Let's skip ahead. Raymond Kerr is a jerk. We get the point."

"Wow, he really wasn't much of a diary writer," Rose said, reading the dates. "He passes over whole years in just a couple of lines." She pointed to a series of entries that read simply: *Age 13 – HORRIBLE. Age 14 – Never mind! Age 15 – I got taller. That's something, I guess. But mostly? HORRIBLE.*

She turned a few more pages.

Day 2,920

It is my eighteenth birthday today. Papa has asked what I'd like as a present and I told him that I would like him and Grandpapa to retire so that I can take over the chain of bakeries that Grandpapa has built up over the years. Papa and Grandpapa are happy with sixteen bakeries, but they don't have any vision. Maybe because they still eat our baked goods and are still fat and round like I used to be. Last week I received a letter in the post from something called the International Society of the Rolling Pin. Apparently, I am a descendant of a great baker named Albatross Bliss. I will join this Society and use the knowledge they give me to build a huge corporation. The people I hire will all be as short and round as I was as a boy, and I will become so important and make so much money that I can make Raymond Kerr work for me and

*have him do my bidding. Ha ha ha! One day, the world
will be at the mercy of the Mostess Bakery.*

That is my dream.

"That's it," said Sage, closing the journal. "That's the end. Geez."

"Wow," Ty said. "I can't believe that Mr Butter is a descendant of Albatross Bliss. That makes him sort of like—"

"Don't say it, Ty," Rose said, cutting off her older brother.

"*Family*," Sage said softly.

"So, wait – has he been using magic the whole time?" Ty asked.

"I don't think so," said Rose. "He probably wanted to, but he didn't have the know-how. He just had those industrial strength preservatives," she added, thinking of the historical Dinky Cake. "Then Aunt Lily joined up with him, and she used the *Apocrypha* to make the Mostess recipes dangerous."

The grim truth settled over the room. Rose glanced at the far wall, where a tiny ticking cuckoo clock had begun to chime. It was nine o'clock! Mr Butter said he would be back later – and later was… now.

"Guys!" Rose cried out, peering through one of the windows. She felt a strange grumbling in the pit of her stomach. "We didn't find a hotel key, so we need to perfect the Dinky Doodle Doughnuts *tonight* or our parents are toast!"

Chapter 11

DINKY DOODLE DOUGHNUTS OF ZOMBIFICATION

ROSE, TY, AND Sage returned to the test kitchen to find that the bakers had graciously cleaned up, and the kitchen was once again spotless.

The giant vats of batter were covered and set off to the side, and the bakers were chatting among themselves, crowded around one of the steel prep tables. Ning and Jasmine were drinking espresso, while Melanie and Felanie were brushing each other's hair. In the corner, Gus was napping, curled into a tight grey ball atop a pile of flour sacks.

Marge saw them first. "There you are! Did you kids get your parents?"

Ty and Sage shook their heads *No*.

"There's a key to the elevator, and we couldn't find it," Rose said. "But Mr Butter said we had to perfect the Dinky Doodle Doughnuts before bedtime. So here we are."

Something soft butted against her shin, and she looked down and saw the folded ears and fuzzy grey head of the cat. Rose dropped to her knees and gave him a gentle stroke behind the ears. "Are you all right?" she whispered.

"Of course," the cat replied. "Bored by these ninnies, but fine." He stood and stretched. "Due to the urgency of our situation here, I abandoned the idea of napping and instead threw myself into our joint endeavour."

"What?" Rose said.

"I read through the *Apocrypha*. And I believe I have already located the necessary recipe, Rose."

Rose gave Gus a quick kiss between his wrinkled ears. "Oh good." Then she stood, wiped her knees, and rolled up the white cuffs of her baker's uniform, which had unrolled and fallen below her wrists.

"Here are the Directrice's Dinky Doodle Doughnuts," said Marge, handing Rose two packages of six mini doughnuts. Some were covered in white powdered sugar that looked to Rose like chalk dust from a blackboard, and some were covered in a waxy chocolate glaze. All of the doughnuts were hard and puck-like.

"And here is the recipe." Marge held out a creamy-coloured recipe card that bore Lily's familiar purple-ink calligraphy. The only magical direction listed on the card was to *fold in the voice of Drimini.*

Before anyone could stop him, Sage grabbed a doughnut and took a bite. He immediately spat it out. "It's like biting on a rock," he complained. "Except not as tasty."

Rose gave her younger brother a pat on the shoulder, then turned to Marge. "So, what's wrong with them, other than that they have the texture of concrete?"

"Nothing," said Marge. She wiped a sweaty palm across her forehead. "I've tried them. Dozens of them! I get no magical feeling whatsoever."

Rose tapped the card. "Where is this ingredient, this Drimini thing?"

"The Directrice used this." Marge showed Rose a red mason jar, which did indeed appear empty. "Maybe that's why the doughnuts do nothing. The jar is empty."

"It's getting late," Sage said. "I'm tired."

"You can't be tired," Rose told her younger brother. "We still have a lot to do."

Meanwhile, Gus hopped onto one of the prep tables and sat on the *Apocrypha*, and flipped it open to a recipe. "This was Lily's inspiration," he said.

For the pulling of strings

It was in 1932 in the Italian village of Montecastello that the nefarious Albatross descendant Vesuvio D'Astuto did bake a basket of popovers that he did serve at the fourth birthday of the boy who lived next door, Arlecchio. Arlecchio and all of his young friends did eat the popovers, whereupon they became puppets, controlled by the person who bade them "pop to my voice" – the nefarious Vesuvio D'Astuto, who did instruct the boys to pick the pockets of the rich and deliver the spoils to him.

Rose scanned down to find the magic ingredient:

*Sir D'Astuto did imbue his batter with the **soothing voice of Grigory Drimini**, the famous hypnotist.*

Rose compared the recipe with Lily's recipe card. "Why didn't it work?" she asked.

"Maybe this is the wrong Grigory Drimini?" said Sage.

Rose opened the jar and held it to her ear. She heard a lilting tenor singing an aria. She squinted at the label. It was almost impossible to make out, but she was sure that the faded print read GRIGORY DRIMINI, MUSICIAN.

"Good thinking, Sage," said Rose. "Marge, do you have any *other* empty jars?"

Twenty minutes later, after the correct red mason jar had been located and the voice of the great hypnotist Grigory Drimini had been added to the batter for the Dinky Doodle Doughnuts, Rose pulled a tray from the oven and fed a half dozen doughnuts to the bakers.

Immediately, the bakers' eyes glazed over, and they stood perfectly still, waiting.

"Tell them to do something," said Sage. Then his eyes widened with delight. "Make them dance. Make them do it Gangnam Style!"

Rose didn't want to take advantage of the bakers, but it *had* been a long day, and well... a little dancing never hurt anybody, right?

"Pop to my voice!" Rose said to the bakers, and the six straightened up and gazed blank-eyed at her. "Um, put your arms out straight."

Immediately, the bakers lifted their arms straight into the air, as if Rose's voice were a set of invisible puppet strings.

"Nice, *mi hermana*," Ty said, clearly impressed.

Rose had to think for a second before she remembered

the next move. "Cross your hands at the wrists," she said, and the bakers did as they were told. "Now pretend you're riding an invisible horse, tugging at the reins."

The bakers moved their hands up and down. Some moved their entire arms, some moved only their hands.

"You forgot the leg moves!" Sage protested, squatting up and down.

"This is terrible," said Rose.

"I know," said Ty, frowning. "They are the worst dancers in history. They have no rhythm. Worse than Dad."

"Come on!" Sage said. "There's more to the dance than that!" He raised his right hand into the air and twirled his fist like he was spinning an invisible lasso.

"No," said Rose, "that's not what I mean. It's terrible that Mr Butter is trying to turn everyone in the country into an army of zombies who just want to eat Mostess Snack Cakes!"

Ty scratched his head. "Yeah," he said after a few seconds. "That's bad, too."

The bakers quietly continued rocking their hands back and forth.

"That's enough," Rose said. "Everyone stop!" The bakers froze in place, their arms extended.

Rose leaned down and whispered into Gus's ear. "Gus, what is the antidote ingredient?"

Gus flipped the page and placed his paw toward the bottom.

"Ah!" said Rose, turning to Sage and Ty. "We need something called the Capsules of Time."

Rose turned to zombie-Marge, who stood at attention with her arms extended. "Marge, do you have any mason jars with Capsules of Time here in the kitchen?"

"No, we have none," Marge said, her voice flat, her eyes as cloudy as marbles.

"OK, I know where to get these capsules," said Rose. "Maybe they have a key to the hotel there as well. Ty and Sage and I are going out. You all stay here." She looked at the motionless bakers. "Drop your arms and relax." They did as they were told but still didn't seem quite normal.

To Gus and Jacques, Rose said, "You guys are in charge."

Gus and Jacques looked at each other mischievously. Or rather, as mischievous as a Scottish Fold cat and a French mouse could look.

"Don't make them do anything silly," said Rose. "They're completely in your power."

* * *

A thunderstorm rolled in as Ty drove Sage and Rose toward the cake-shaped multitiered laboratory and warehouse that housed all of the red mason jars.

Ty pulled his shirt up over his head to protect his marvelous spiked hair from the rain. Sage and Rose huddled together under the roof of the golf cart as the evening sky gave way to deep purple storm clouds, with the occasional white flash of lightning and a barrage of fat, cold raindrops.

They sped past the darkened marketing offices and the abandoned graphic design building and slowed as they approached the laboratory/warehouse. The alleyways were filled with parked cars, long rows of gleaming black limousines, and sleek red sports cars.

"What's going on?" Sage asked.

"It's supposed to be a warehouse for magical ingredients," Rose said as she saw that the outside of the laboratory was fully illuminated, like the exterior of a museum at night. "I'm not really sure why all these people are here."

A red carpet now led from the street up to the front entrance, where hundreds of men and women in chef's toques, aprons, and pristine white cooking outfits were filing through the front door.

Above, two giant banners sported the glowing rolling pin logo that Rose recognized from Lily's recipe cards. Another cream-coloured banner spanned the entire width of the second tier of the building. It read ANNUAL CONFERENCE.

"Whoa!" Rose whispered. "It must be a meeting of the International Society of the Rolling Pin!"

"Isn't Aunt Lily one of them?" said Ty. "Do you think she'll be there? Ugh. I shudder at the thought of her, despite how stunning she is."

"I don't think she'll come back here," said Rose. "She didn't return after she lost the Gala, and that's why they kidnapped me. And even if she does show up, we have no choice. We need Capsules of Time to make the bakers stop being zombies, and we need the key to floor 34 at the hotel. I think both are in there."

"Come on, dude," said Sage. "Don't you want to hear their evil plans?"

"I don't know if I do," said Ty, crossing his arms and staring up at the dark, cloudy sky. "But I sure don't want to stay out here in the thunderstorm, so I guess I have no choice. This rain is really harshing my hair."

Rose and her brothers pulled on chef's toques and tried to blend in with the crowd of hundreds who had wormed their way through the front doors and into the lobby.

The laboratory was decorated with lavish arrangements of candy and cupcakes and a giant device that made doughnuts. While the audience watched, rings of dough were deep-fried, scooped out of the oil by robotic hands, rolled down a chute, and sprayed with chocolate, sprinkles, or powdered sugar, before finally dropping down a slide onto a platter.

A stage and podium had been set up in front of the control board. Mr Mechanico and the men in the hard hats were nowhere to be seen, but the five-story-high cabinet of red mason jars glittered in the bright lights.

Rose pulled Ty and Sage through the crowd toward the circular ramp that spiraled upward around the central courtyard. The ramp was darkened, and the three of them were able to creep up to the second tier without being noticed. They tiptoed up and around until they were near the top of the building, looking down on the crowd in the lobby.

Below, a tall woman wearing a purple sequined gown and white satin gloves took the stage. She had long, wavy hair that was perfectly black, save for two streaks of white on either side of her face. She reached beneath the podium and pulled out a rolling pin made of glimmering gold. Immediately, a hush fell over the crowd.

A giant black video screen descended from the ceiling. On it were the words INTERNATIONAL SOCIETY OF THE ROLLING PIN.

"Good evening," said the woman. She had a deep voice with a thick accent that made each of her vowels stretch like kneaded toffee. "I am Eva Sarkissian, your president!"

Everyone erupted into applause.

"Thank you," Eva Sarkissian continued. "We decided to hold our annual meeting here at the Mostess headquarters because the Mostess Snack Cake Corporation has done the most in the past calendar year to advance the interests of our organization."

The crowd clapped and cheered.

"The Mostess Corporation, under the leadership of distinguished Society member Jameson Butter, has made great strides in the arena of irresistible sweets for adults, children, senior citizens... even newborn babies! Who is responsible for tooth decay?"

"We are!" the crowd cheered.

"Obesity?

"We are!"

"Sugar rushes?" Eva asked.

"We are! We are! We are!" A mixture of applause and gentle weeping broke out in the crowd. Some of the men bowed, and the women curtsied.

"In the history of the United States, no one has done more to advance our cause than Mr Jameson Butter," Eva Sarkissian said. "Thanks to the secret support of his Mostess Corporation, we have at last succeeded in getting Congress to pass the Big Bakery Discrimination Act!"

Rose gasped in horror. "Of course the Society is behind that insane law!"

"Shhh," Ty whispered.

"Thanks to this law," Eva continued, "our competition is out of business. Our agents – such as the Mostess Corporation – no longer have to compete with small bakeries for the taste buds of the American people."

The crowd roared its approval.

"Correction," Eva said tenderly, cutting them off. "*Almost* all of our competition is out of business. A *single* other thousand-plus employee bakery remains, and it is the only thing standing in the way of Mostess's – and our – total magical sovereignty over this nation. I am speaking, of course, of the insidious Kathy Keegan Corporation."

A loud chorus of boos floated up from the audience as a cartoon drawing of Kathy Keegan popped up on the video screen. She was depicted as a spritely woman with red cheeks and short blonde hair. She held a piping-hot pie and wore a blue apron.

"No one knows what the real Ms Keegan looks like," said Eva, "but we know her products, don't we? They boast that Keegan Kakes are made using only natural ingredients, made by a network of smaller bakeries. Her customers are loyal, her cakes are wholesome." The boos nearly drowned Eva out, but she silenced the room with a sharp rap of the rolling pin. "In other words, Kathy Keegan must be eliminated."

"I thought Kathy Keegan was just another big industrial factory," Rose whispered to her brothers. "I didn't know she employed small bakeries to make her stuff."

Eva raised the Golden Rolling Pin. "Here to discuss the problem of Kathy Keegan and her devilish wholesomeness is our proud host, Mr Jameson Butter."

Mr Butter took the podium, and Eva handed him the Golden Rolling Pin. The audience applauded.

"As you are aware, we have spent the past six months perfecting our five key recipes," Mr Butter said, adjusting his white silk handkerchief in the pocket of his impeccably starched black tuxedo jacket. "For all too brief a time, Mostess employed the talented and beautiful Lily Le Fay, one of the only masters of the dark recipes contained in the fabled *Bliss Cookery Booke*. Unfortunately, after her surprising loss at the Gala des Gâteaux Grands this year, she chose not to return to our employ." He cleared his throat. "She disappeared and took with her the magical expertise we so desperately needed.

"But there was another baker at the Gala who caught our eye, one with a true understanding of the principles of kitchen magic. She was kind enough to come join us in our work. Thanks to her efforts, in three days, we will have achieved the impossible! Five perfectly addictive recipes! And thanks to the Big Bakery Discrimination Act, there will be no other baked goods on the market! Nothing and no one will be able to stop us!"

"*Brava!*" shouted a man who looked suspiciously like a famous opera singer.

"No one, that is, except for Kathy Keegan." Mr Butter

coughed, pushing his glasses further up the skinny bridge of his nose. "But we have a plan to take care of her, too. Kathy Keegan has already accepted an invitation to visit our factory in three days' time for a joint press conference. There we will each try the other's baked goods as an act of friendship… and our first customer for our perfected recipes will be none other than Kathy Keegan herself!"

The room twittered with confused murmurs.

"Once she has eaten these treats," Mr Butter explained, "she'll become a Mostess-obsessed zombie! And then we will take over her business and destroy it!"

The audience erupted into wild applause.

"Oh no!" Rose said to her brothers in a harsh whisper. "We have to warn Kathy Keegan!"

"I thought you said she wasn't real!" said Ty, whispering just as harshly. "And you told us you wouldn't do her commercial because the Kathy Keegan Corporation was run by a group of businessmen!"

"I guess I was wrong," said Rose. "If she's real, we have to save her, or there'll be no one left to fight against Mostess."

Mr Butter handed the Golden Rolling Pin back to Eva Sarkissian, who smoothed the folds of her sequined gown.

"Now, Jameson has generously invited us all on a tour of this laboratory facility this evening, where he has recently acquired all of the magical ingredients used in *Albatross's Apocrypha*. If you'll all make your way up the ramp toward the top of the building, the tour will commence."

Cheerful chatter filled the room as the crowd filed up the curving ramp, toward where Rose, Ty, and Sage were crouched on the second floor. Mr Butter and Eva Sarkissian led the pack.

"We have to get out of here!" said Sage.

"Where?" Ty wheezed.

"The only way to go is up," said Rose, leading her brothers farther up the spiral ramp.

They ran as fast as they could, until they finally reached the top floor, where the ramp opened up onto a short hallway with three doors. One was a bathroom, one was marked LABORATORY: EMPLOYEES ONLY, and the other had a sign that read DOUGHNUT HOLES.

"What do you think this is?" said Ty.

"It can't be what it says it is," Rose said, placing her hand on the knob. "Who'd save doughnut holes?"

She wrenched open the door and was thrown back against the wall by a torrent of sweet, deep-fried balls of dough. If not for her hand holding tight to the knob, and Ty holding tight to her other hand, and Sage clutching Ty's leg, the three of them would have been swept away.

Thousands upon thousands of little balls of vanilla and chocolate and fruit-flavoured dough came tumbling out from behind the door, an endless stream as high as the doorway and as wide. There were plain doughnut holes and glazed doughnut holes and holes that were bright with powdered sugar. They flooded out the open door and bumped down the ramp with a long, low rumble, like raging whitewater rapids.

"Hold on!" Rose cried as she felt Ty's grip loosening. His hand slid and he caught the strings of her apron.

After a good five minutes, the rush of doughnut holes had thinned to just an ankle-high trickle, and they were able to get back to their feet.

"I didn't expect so many," said Rose. "And why would they just be piled behind a door?"

"Who cares why they're here," Sage cried out. "They're here!"

He reached for a powdered doughnut hole and popped it into his mouth at the very same time that Rose said, "Sage, don't eat those!"

"Why can't he have one, *hermana*?" Ty asked.

"Because," Rose said, "they're probably old. Years and years."

"Hmm," Sage said between chews. He licked his lips. "They taste like they were made yesterday!"

"The power of preservatives," said Rose as Sage stuffed a couple dozen of the doughnut holes into the pockets of his khaki shorts.

"Sage!" Rose said, thinking of the tank of preservatives back in the test kitchen. "Stop! You don't want to eat those!"

"I'm starving," said Sage, continuing to munch on the doughnut holes. "We haven't eaten a proper meal in days. You know what Mrs Carlson's cooking is like!"

"*Es la verdad, hermana*," Ty said, shrugging. "That means, it's true, sister."

By that time, the tsunami of doughnut holes had rolled down to where Mr Butter, Eva Sarkissian, and the rest of the Society of the Rolling Pin were making their way up the ramp. They heard the doughnut holes before they spotted them – "What is that noise?" sang the opera singer – but by then it was too late. They were engulfed.

The crowd was too thick and the ramp was too

narrow. The doughnut holes filled the space from wall to wall at chest height. *"Mama mia!"* sang the opera man, until he was overwhelmed by the flood. The Society members disappeared under the doughnut hole deluge, screaming and shouting as they were all pushed and rolled back down the ramp.

From the top floor, Rose, Ty, and Sage peeked down and watched as the raging river of guests and doughnut holes flooded out across the ground floor. "So embarrassing!" someone cried. "So delicious!" someone else shouted back, his mouth full.

"Come on," Rose said, thinking again of her parents. "We have no time to lose." She pulled her brothers through the door marked LABORATORY: EMPLOYEES ONLY. "We have to find those Capsules of Time before Mr Butter finds us."

Chapter 12

ON THE WINGS OF SQUIRRELS

ROSE SHOVED TY and Sage inside the dark laboratory, which fortunately was unlocked, then followed, bolting the door behind her. The only light in the room came from the dim glow of the various red buttons on the control board, and from an occasional crackle of lightning, visible through a skylight far overhead.

Rose could hear the incessant pounding of the rain on the roof and the humming of the control room. She could barely make out the imposing, deep-sea form of the octopus-like Mr Mechanico, who appeared out of nowhere, his eyes glowing a dim red.

The robot floated toward Rose and her brothers. "Directrice Bliss," he said. "Good evening." He rippled all eight of his segmented arms, which clicked and clacked in sequence like rows of stainless steel dominoes.

"What *is* that thing?" Sage asked.

"I could say the same of you," Mr Mechanico replied. "I am Mr Mechanico. I am in charge of Red Mason Jar Acquisition and Organization here at the Central Laboratory. And who might you two be?"

Sage cleared his throat and adopted a clipped, guttural German accent. "We are the German ambassadors to the International Society of the Rolling Pin, of course. I requested that Directrice Bliss give us a private tour of this laboratory."

"Of course," said Mr Mechanico, his glowing eyes taking in Ty's spiked hair and Sage's cargo shorts. "I was confused because you are both dressed like low-level employees at a country club." Mr Mechanico turned to Rose. "Directrice Bliss – how may I help you this evening?"

Rose was on the verge of asking for "Capsules of Time," when Mr Mechanico said, "You are perfecting the Dinky Doodle Doughnuts, are you not?"

"That is correct," Rose replied, thinking furiously. Mr Mechanico knew way too much about the recipes she was working on; if Rose asked for the Capsules of Time straight out, he might suspect that she was concocting an antidote. Best to distract him.

"I have come up with a bold change to the recipe," she told the robot.

"Yesssss?" he said in his monotone voice, floating lower. "Tell me which ingredient you require, and I will fetch it for you. As well as help you calculate the correct proportions for your recipes."

"I need…," Rose said, thinking furiously. Where would she find a big enough distraction for the robot assistant? The dark room flashed electric blue from the crackle of the thunderstorm outside. "Lightning, Mr Mechanico. I need lightning."

"A bold choice, indeed." The robot's red eyes seemed to glow even redder. "This will not be a problem. I can get you some fresh lightning right now." He raised his eight arms and the tips glowed at the same time as an ear-splitting whistle sounded from a steel mesh speaker grill under his eyes. "Time to get to work!" he said.

Slots in the wall opened, and five other octopus-like robots drifted into the room and set to work. Surprised that Mr Mechanico didn't question her further, Rose strolled over to the rows of red mason jars, her hands behind her back, reading the labels as quickly as possible. BASILISK GAZE. HEART OF A COMET. INCHWORM OF LOVE. TOEJAM OF DESTRUCTION.

Eew, Rose thought after reading the last one. Definitely *not* what she was looking for.

"You have such a big collection!" she called over her shoulder.

"The greatest in all the world." Mr Mechanico floated away to a control board, making a series of tiny clicks and clacks as he moved. It was packed with large, glowing labelled buttons. One read ROCKET LAUNCH. DEFENESTRATION PORTAL read a second. ARMED RESET and COUNTDOWN read a third and fourth. Around him, the other robots hovered just over the floor, as if held up by invisible strings.

"There are too many of them, *hermana,*" Ty whispered, grabbing her arm. "If they turn on us, we're—"

"Shhh!" Rose said, pulling herself free. "I've got a plan. Sort of." She continued along the row of jars. Where were the Capsules of Time?

BLEAKEST TIME, read another jar, in which sat a tiny little man as big as her fist, who appeared to be weeping into his hands. SOARING SQUIRRELS read the next jars, each of which held little balls of fur. KRAKEN SCALES seemed to be in the next, though all she could see was a massive clawed fist flexing again and again. It seemed to rise right through the bottom of the jar. Rose shivered and moved on.

Meanwhile, Mr Mechanico pressed a fifth button on the control panel, this one marked ELECTRICITY HARVEST. Rose stopped in her tracks as the room filled with a screeching noise: thirteen long metal rods telescoped down into the room from a ring around the skylight, just as thirteen antennae extended from the roof into the thundering sky.

Mr Mechanico and the other five octopus robots gathered red mason jars – two to each robot, except for Mr Mechanico, who held three. They floated into a loose circle around the convergence of the thirteen antennae and raised the open mouths of the jars. "This may take some time," he said.

"This is, um, very kind of you," said Rose. Ty shot her a glance, as if to say, *What does lightning have to do with Capsules of Time?*

"It is no problem whatsoever," said Mr Mechanico. "We happened to be running low on lightning."

"Whoa!" Ty said, stepping back and pointing a finger at Rose. "Your hair! It's standing straight up!"

"It is?" Rose said. Ty's hair looked perfectly normal

– then again, Ty's hair always stood straight up. But as Rose checked her reflection in the darkened skylight, she saw that her hair was standing straight on end, like the fluff surrounding a dandelion. *Weird.*

Sage was poking around a set of metal file cabinets in the perimeter of the room. He'd pulled out a pair of firm white gloves dotted with patches of metal at the joints. The gloves stretched to encompass the wearer's entire forearm, and the word MASTER was emblazoned across the arm in bold black letters.

"What's this?" he said, then reached to shut the drawer – when suddenly there was a bright spark of light. "Ow!" Sage tumbled backward. "That file cabinet shocked me!"

"It is just a little static electricity," said Mr Mechanico. "Nothing to worry about, Ambassador. It always happens when we do a lightning harvest."

"Erm, yes." Sage patted his own chest. "Ambassador. That is me." He gave a throaty laugh, tucked the gloves into a pocket, then dragged his feet as he walked toward his siblings. He gleefully reached toward Rose and put his finger an inch away from her arm. A bright-blue ribbon of electricity arced from Sage's finger to Rose's shoulder.

"Ow!" she cried, backing away. "Cut that out!"

"Lighten up, *hermana*. I mean, *Schwester*," said Ty, remembering to stay as German as possible. "It's just static electricity."

Sage rubbed his feet on the blue industrial carpet, then aimed his electric finger in Ty's direction. A tiny bolt of lightning zapped from his finger and landed inside the forest of Ty's spiked hair.

"Ow!" Ty cried, falling to the ground. "Watch the hair!"

Sage cackled like a young wizard, rubbed his feet again, and aimed his electrified finger in the direction of Mr Mechanico and the other mechanical octopi. Mr Mechanico saw what was happening just as the bolt of light arced from Sage's finger.

"No!" Mr Mechanico said sternly. "Not while we're gathering the lightning. It generates a dangerous level of electricity—"

But it was too late.

The ribbon of blue electricity crackled from Sage's finger to the circle of robots, enwrapping Mr Mechanico like a bright-blue net, then leaping off in a series of arcs to each of the other five.

"Stop!" Mr Mechanico cried, his voice getting higher

and higher. "Stop! Stop! Stop! Stop!" until it was just a tiny squeak.

The six robots fell gently backward, still holding the red mason jars, and landed on the floor in a pile of twisted, smoking metal. They let out a loud, collective hiss – like a teapot just taken off the stove.

"Sage!" Rose cried. "You broke the robots!"

"Whoops. I guess I did. But wait!" he gasped. "Not necessarily!"

Sage dug the strange white gloves out of his pocket. "Maybe *these* control the robots!"

He slipped one of the gloves over his arms and moved his hands slowly in an upward motion, as if he were a conductor preparing for the downbeat of a symphony. "Rise from the dead!" he intoned in a creepy voice. "Rise up, my robotic army!"

Sage moved his arms in wild circles, but the robots just continued to smoke and crackle, frayed wires exploding from their tentacles like bones from a broken arm.

"Doesn't seem to be working, bro," Ty said.

"So they don't do anything at all," Sage said. He peeled off the gloves, wadded them into a ball, and stuffed them into the side pocket of his shorts.

Suddenly, there came an urgent knock from the other side of the door. "Mr Mechanico?" shouted a voice. Rose recognized the Southern drawl as that of Mr Butter. "Did you let open the doughnut hole portal?"

Rose and her brothers froze, staring at the bolted laboratory door.

Mr Butter pounded harder. "Mr Mechanico!" he insisted. "Why did you lock this door? You know you're not supposed to do that!"

"We have to get out of here," whispered Rose.

"But we didn't find any Capsules of Time!" Ty said, panicked. "Isn't that why we came here?"

"Yes, but it's too late," said Rose. "We have to leave. *Now.*"

"How?" asked Sage. "The only way out is the door. The one that Mr Butter is pounding on."

"Not the *only* way," said Rose with a determined grimace.

She pushed the button on the main control board labelled DEFENESTRATION PORTAL, and, as she'd hoped, the large panoramic window that spanned the front of the room, like the dashboard of a starship, parted down the middle. A cold, wet wind blew into the room, chasing away the stink of electricity from the burned-out robots.

Rose handed each of her brothers a red mason jar that held what looked like a chipmunk.

"What are these?" said Sage.

"Soaring Squirrels," Rose answered, gingerly scooping her own Soaring Squirrel from the jar and heading toward the window.

"Wait, *hermana*," said Ty. "You want us to jump out that window and fly on the wings of this little rodent? It's the size of a deck of playing cards! Flying squirrels don't meet FAA regulations, last time I checked. They're not *licensed*," he added, patting the pocket with his driver's licence.

"They're not *flying* squirrels," said Rose, "they're *soaring* squirrels. There's a big difference. I think you'll find that the wingspan of these little guys is bigger than you'd guess."

Mr Butter rammed into the door, possibly with his shoulder. "Mr Mechanico!" he screamed. "What on earth is going on?"

"There's no time," said Rose, brushing her hair out of her eyes. "You guys have to trust me. Mum told me about this one time when she and Dad were in the Amazon, and they had to climb a tree to escape an anaconda, and they hitched a ride with some Soaring

Squirrels. I have to admit I always thought they'd be a little bigger, but it doesn't matter. Right now they're our only option."

"OK, *hermana*," Ty said. "Whatever you say."

Sage nodded in agreement.

The three of them swung their legs over the ledge and sat on it. Rose's heart pounded as she contemplated the danger of leaping out the window of a six-story building holding nothing but a tiny ball of fur. She couldn't even see the ground, it was so far away. As the rain soaked her hair and pelted her face, she began to wonder whether this actually *was* a good plan after all. She wasn't going to get them all killed – was she?

"How do we use these things?" Sage asked, holding his squirrel so tightly that only its tiny alarmed head was visible. It chirruped. "Where do we hold on?"

"I don't know," Rose said. She opened her hands and the squirrel stretched itself like a person awakening from a long nap. Around its neck was a thick ruffle of loose fur. Rose tugged at it and the squirrel didn't seem to mind at all. She dug her fingers into the fur and it chirruped and seemed to nod. "The neck ruffle," she said.

Suddenly, the tiny Soaring Squirrel unfurled its

forelegs. They seemed to go on and on, and with a loud *fwap* they unfurled into a pair of giant wings – as white and as wide as the sail of a pirate ship. The squirrel took to the air, Rose astride its tiny back, her knees snug against the base of the wings. Rain lashed her face, but she didn't mind, because she was flying.

"Yaaaaaah!" she cried, holding on for dear life as the squirrel glided gently over the dark, wet expanse of the Mostess compound. She was cold and wet but right now she didn't care – she was *flying*.

Rose glanced behind her and saw Ty and Sage soaring through the air, as well.

"Woohoo!" Sage cried. "I want to bring this little guy home!"

"Ahhhh!" Ty wailed. "I want to GO home!"

Rose noticed her squirrel wandering in the direction of the electric fence to her right, so she tugged on the left side of the ruffle, and the squirrel banked and veered in the opposite direction.

"Follow me!" Rose shouted back to her brothers.

Even through the rain, the signs on each of the boxy grey warehouses were easy to read from the air. Rose steered toward the building labelled TEST KITCHEN.

Gradually, Rose's Soaring Squirrel lost altitude and

slowly coasted to the pavement between the buildings, Ty and Sage sinking to the ground right behind her. It was still raining, but now they were all so soaked that a little more water hardly mattered.

As soon as her squirrel landed, Rose hopped off its back, and, freed from her weight, the squirrel gently flapped its massive wings and rose up into the air again.

"Thank you," Rose said quietly to it, but she couldn't tell from its tiny face whether it heard or understood her, and then it was beating its wings toward the distant electric fence. Soon it was just a darker piece of shadow in the rainy night.

Ty's squirrel followed close behind it, and Sage's would have flown off, too, if only Sage hadn't been clinging so fervently to its neck ruff.

"No!" he cried, wiping water off his forehead. "Don't go! You'd be the most amazing pet in the universe! You could give me rides to school!"

The squirrel opened its tiny jowls and hissed at Sage, and as it did, its mouth grew larger, and its fangs bigger and more menacing. Sage let go in a hurry. Then the squirrel shrank back to its normal size, chirruped happily, flapped its wings, and soared away.

Ty patted his brother on his wet head. "If you love

something, bro, you've got to set it free. Otherwise it will bite your hand off."

Sage shivered and watched the squirrel disappear. "We could have had so much fun together!"

"We *could* have rescued our parents and gotten out of here," Ty said.

"I don't think so. My squirrel could barely carry me, let alone me and Great-Gramps Balthazar," Sage said, shivering and turning toward the door. "Anyway, it's *cold* out here. I'm pretty sure I have hypothermia."

Inside the test kitchen, Rose threw on an extra chef's jacket.

She and her brothers were still damp from the rain, but it was time to work until Mr Butter returned. She was tired and everyone was hungry, but there was no time to do anything except bake the antidote to the Dinky Doodle Doughnuts.

Only – apparently, none of the other bakers felt the same amount of pressure that she did.

"Hello?" she said, but the bakers, still under the zombie influence of the Dinky Doodle Doughnuts, paid her no mind. Gus and Jacques had put them to work, and the Scottish Fold cat and the brown field mouse sat on one of the prep tables in their own miniature lawn chairs, drinking little glasses of iced tea. Gene was fanning them with cookie sheets, while Melanie and Felanie rubbed their furry feet. Ning and Jasmine massaged their scalps, while Marge read out loud from a novel called *Twilight*.

"Nice, you two," Rose said to Gus and Jacques. "Making these poor zombified bakers into your personal servants. I would expect this from you, Gus – but, Jacques?"

Jacques stretched his pink paws behind his head and heaved a relaxed sigh. "What can I say? I have a taste for the finer things."

Ty whispered in Rose's ear, "Do you have to cure the bakers just yet? I have this knot in my back and I think those blonde twins could really help me out."

"No way, Ty!" Rose scowled. "I'm curing them right this minute! Once I figure out how."

Rose plowed through the *Apocrypha* searching for an anti-zombification recipe that didn't involve the elusive Capsules of Time. Meanwhile, Ty beckoned Melanie and Felanie away from the cat and mouse and bade them rub the knot in his back.

"As you wish," they said in a flat monotone.

"Thank you so much, ladies," he said. "This means the world. I've been so tense lately."

Sage gave his older brother a look of disgust as he unloaded two dozen preserved doughnut holes from his khaki shorts. He popped one into his mouth, then set the rest on a cookie sheet on one of the prep tables. "Ugh, I can't eat another one of these," he said. "I'm too full. Bakers. Pop to my voice! Get rid of these, please."

Immediately, Melanie and Felanie stopped rubbing Ty's shoulder and ambled over to the prep table with the rest of the bakers, who were haphazardly shoving the doughnuts holes into their mouths.

"Don't make them eat those!" Rose said, but it was too late. The bakers had plowed through the pile of black-and-white doughnut holes, tossing them into their mouths as if their gullets were garbage disposals. "It's not fair, Sage. They can't help themselves. They don't know they're eating nasty old doughnut holes. They're zombies."

"Who's a zombie?" Marge asked, shaking her head. She smacked her lips a few times. "I need a glass of milk."

"I didn't give you permission to stop rubbing my

feet," Gus said to Ning. "Pop to my voice! I need a refill on my drink."

"Refill it yourself!" said Ning, indignant.

"Jasmine," Rose cried, "pop to my voice! Do ten jumping jacks!"

"Why should I?" said the woman, blinking and rubbing her eyes like she had just woken up from a very long nap, as colour seemed to seep back into her cheeks. "Pop yourself!"

Marge chuckled, clearly her regular non-zombie self. Rose threw her arms around the Head Baker's chubby shoulders. "You're back!"

"Where did I go?" Marge asked.

"You were a zombie," said Rose. "You did whatever we told you to do. You read *Twilight* to a cat!"

Marge sighed. "Wouldn't be the first time."

"I don't understand!" Rose said to her brothers. "What cured them?"

"It was me," Sage said proudly. "I fed them the old doughnut holes, and they were miraculously cured. Looks like I have the magic touch."

"Sage, I love you," Rose said, "but no. There must have been something *in* those doughnut holes."

"These old things?" said Marge, tossing another doughnut hole into her mouth.

Rose stared at Marge, then burst out, "Of course! Those OLD things! The doughnut holes are Capsules of Time. They're preserved bits of the past." They may have been dried up and tasteless, but thanks to all the preservatives in them, the doughnut holes had a wonderful magic all their own – each was a sugared, tiny bit of a sweet yesterday.

"Lucky I had the good sense to bring some along with me in my pocket," said Sage.

At that moment, the sirens wailed and the red corner lights flashed. Rose glanced at the clock on the wall. It was after eleven p.m. "Butter's back," said Rose, suddenly feeling the exhaustion of the entire day from the tips of her fingers to her toes. "Bakers, you know the drill. Just act like brainless zombies and do everything I say. Got it?"

Marge blanked out her face. "Yes, master," she said.

"...and then, the doughnuts rolled down the ramp and engulfed all of my guests!" Mr Butter ranted, pacing back and forth on the linoleum floor of the test kitchen. He hadn't quieted down since barging out of the elevator in an explosion of anxious energy. "The entire International Society of the Rolling Pin was overtaken in a doughnut hole flash flood!" Flecks of doughnut dotted his tuxedo and the top of his bald head.

"That's... horrible," Rose said carefully.

"And you know nothing about this?" Mr Butter said, pausing to squint down at her. "Why are you so damp?"

"Sweat, sir," Rose said, wishing she'd toweled off from the rain. "I've been in here baking and working up a storm all evening."

"I see," he said. "I've come here because I can think of only one person on the Mostess compound who would do such nefarious things. Releasing a room full of old doughnut holes onto a distinguished group of Society members? Destroying my most-trusted aide, Mr Mechanico? Only one person is so clever, so sly, so... independent. That person is you, Rosemary Bliss." He extended one long finger and squeegeed some water off her head. "Sweat, eh?"

"Someone *broke* Mr Mechanico?" Rose asked, feigning incredulity.

"Yes!" Mr Butter wailed. "That robot was a dear friend. He reminded me of my mother. They were both... cold.

Metallic." Mr Butter's glasses began to fog. "I found him comforting."

"Maybe he can be fixed," said Rose.

"Perhaps." Mr Butter shrugged sadly. "I don't even know what happened to him!"

"Well, I have some good news!" Rose said. "I've perfected the Dinky Doughnuts recipe! Right, bakers?"

The six bakers stood in a line like toy soldiers and nodded yes, their eyes glazed and shiny like a freshly coated Dinky Doughnut.

"That is wonderful, yes," said Mr Butter, distracted. He turned to Mr Kerr. "See? It wasn't her. Rose is loyal. She's been here all evening. Because she knows that if she had anything at all to do with tonight's fiasco, that would mean the end of her beloved family." He cracked his knuckles. "You do understand that, don't you, Rose?"

"Of course," said Rose, smiling stiffly.

"This means that we have an intruder on this compound, one who may still be at large," said Mr Butter. "Mr Kerr? You will find this intruder and squash him, yes?"

"Like a bug." Mr Kerr brushed doughnut crumbs from his velour jumpsuit.

Suddenly, there was a clatter of metal from the Bakers' Quarters, where Ty and Sage were hiding with Gus and Jacques. The room quieted completely.

"Who's back there?" asked Mr Kerr.

No no no, Rose thought. *He's going to find Ty and Sage!*

But then Gus skidded out from behind the door, stopping on the floor in front of Mr Kerr and licking his paw.

"It's just Rose's filthy cat," said Mr Butter. "Mangy creature. Shoo! Shoo, I say!"

Gus shot past them and hid underneath one of the prep tables. Mr Butter shook his head. "First mice and now cats. We're going to have to have the exterminator come through here. I *hate* small things." He suddenly smiled at Rose. "Except for you, Rosemary Bliss. You are small, but we won't have *you* exterminated – or your cat, as long as he behaves."

"Gee, thanks," Rose said, the smile still frozen on her face.

"Carry on, here." Mr Butter glanced at the clock. "I'd recommend getting some sleep. You'll need it if you're to keep to schedule."

"We have two more days," Rose said, "and that should be enough time to—"

But Mr Butter shook his head. "I'm afraid I had to make some changes. It is true, you have only two recipes left to perfect: King Things and Dinkies, but now you have only one day to finish them. They must be done by the end of the day tomorrow, if you please, before this mysterious saboteur is able to cause any more mayhem here at Mostess."

"But that's not enough time!" Rose protested.

"It will have to be." Mr Butter turned to leave, then spotted the few remaining doughnut holes on the cookie sheet. "Doughnut holes!" he shouted. "Where did you get those?"

"Um… leftovers from the Dinky Doodle Doughnuts we just made!" Rose said quickly. "Just scraps. Freshly baked."

"I suppose that makes sense." Mr Butter's fingers twitched as he eyed the doughnuts with what looked like disgust – but just as easily might have been longing. "OK, I must return to my guests. Mind that you and your team stay in here so that Mr Kerr doesn't mistake you for the culprits behind tonight's attack. I'd hate for him to accidentally hurt you."

Mr Kerr threw her a menacing look, then slid behind the wheel of the golf cart. As Mr Butter climbed in beside him, Rose glimpsed a thick bundle of dozens of keys dangling from his belt.

The moment Mr Butter and Mr Kerr disappeared into the floor, the bakers let out sighs of relief.

"Phew!" said Gene. "It's hard to stand up straight for that long. Exercise is tough!"

"Let's all try and get some sleep," Rose said to Marge and the bakers. "We have a long day ahead of us tomorrow." But all Rose could think about was that key ring on Mr Butter's belt.

The key to the hotel elevator has to be one of those, she thought to herself. *If I can get those, I can rescue my parents and Balthazar, and we can all get out of here.*

Chapter 13

KING THINGS OF REVULSION

ROSE WAS AWOKEN the next morning by Sage, who bounced onto her bed, crying, "Surprise! Rose, wake up! We did the King Things for you!"

"What do you mean, you did them for me?" she asked, worried by the sight of her younger brother with his wild ginger curls dusted in flour and his fingers and face coated in sticky chocolate.

"We did it! Ty and me and Marge. We took Lily's recipe card and looked at the original recipe in the *Apocrypha*, and we fixed it!" He paused to lick a finger. "We think."

Rose took a deep breath and looked down over the test kitchen, which was scattered with dirty bowls of flour and spilled canisters of cocoa and a dozen eggshells.

Ty was standing over a tray of freshly baked

chocolate-covered logs. He waved up to Rose, wearing a look of extreme pride. The bakers were frantically cleaning up the mess her brothers had made. "Thank you, Sage."

"It's no problem, sis," her brother said. "We're all in this together, you know?"

"I know," Rose said. "And I'm really grateful for that."

She smiled at Sage and hugged him. Thank God he and Ty had come for her – she had no idea what she would have done without them. It was a good feeling knowing that the three of them were in this together. And Leigh, too, in spirit.

"Look what we did!" Ty said, gesturing to the tray of King Things as Rose came down the stairs fifteen minutes later.

She had taken a quick shower and was wearing a fresh white chef's apron and a new – *clean* – baking hat. She still had her shorts on, though, the ones she'd worn when she was kidnapped. Luckily, they hadn't got dirty.

"We made these! Thought we'd show you that your brothers still have the knack, the know-how, the family magic in their fingers!"

"You guys did a great job," said Rose, patting her older brother on the back. On one of the prep tables was a cup of tea and some of the contraband Kathy Keegen cookies. Her usual breakfast. Rose took a sip of tea and asked, "What *Apocrypha* recipe did Lily mess up this time?"

"This one," said Sage, handing Rose one of Lily's creamy recipe cards and the pamphlet of greyed sheets that was the *Apocrypha*.

ROLLS OF REVULSION:
To sow the seeds of hatred and discord

It was in 1809 in the Arabian village of Masuleh that the nefarious descendant of Albatross Bliss, Madame Gagoosh Taghipoor, did bake these rolls of cake filled with bitter jelly. She did feed them to all of the children in the town, whereupon they did begin to feel a strong distaste for their parents' cooking, and for their parents in general. They thenceforth ate only at the bakery of Madame Gagoosh Taghipoor, and when Madame Gagoosh Taghipoor moved away from the village, the children did wander in exile, hating their parents until eventually they starved.

"Geez Louise!" Rose exclaimed. "This one sounds totally nasty!"

"We followed the recipe part, where it says *bitter fruit*," said Sage. "Look."

Madame Taghipoor did combine two fists of **bitter fruit** *with one fist of* **sugar** *and one acorn of* **THE OBJECT OF REVULSION**.

"The only difference we could find between the original recipe and Lily's," said Ty, "was the Object of Revulsion. We thought maybe hers wasn't strong enough. Because see, she was making a much larger batch, but she didn't change the proportions. So we just added a lot more."

"But what *is* the Object of Revulsion?" Rose asked, wrinkling her nose. It certainly didn't sound very *appealing*, but then again not much in the *Apocrypha* did.

"Oh, it's this stuff," said Marge, holding up a red mason jar filled with a crumbly black substance that looked like... well, rabbit poop. "Mr Butter delivered it himself. I don't know what's in it."

Rose opened the jar and was smacked in the face

by the smell of dead flowers and old cheese and unwashed sneakers and yogurt breath and a thousand other nasty things. She snapped the jar closed, her stomach churning.

"Oh my. That is bad. So what do these King Things do?" said Rose. "I doubt they'll be edible, if you dumped this nasty stuff in."

"There's only one way to find out," said Marge, and she passed the frosted chocolate logs to the other bakers, then took a bite of one herself. "Huh," she said, wincing only slightly. "Could be worse."

Ty and Sage gave each other a rousing high five. "We did it, man!"

"But what did it do?" said Rose. "Marge, do you feel funny?"

"I feel like I have a good sense of humour, but my wit isn't as sharp as that of a professional comedian," said Marge thoughtfully. "My mother never encouraged me to develop my natural talent in the arts. I mean, I *appreciate* humour..." At the look on Rose's face, Marge trailed off. "Oh, you meant, do I feel funny as in *strange*. No, no, I don't feel strange at all."

"What about the rest of you?" Rose said to the other bakers. "Anything different?"

They shook their heads.

"Why isn't it doing anything?" Sage whined.

"I don't know," said Rose. "See, you can't just add stuff willy-nilly – there might be too much of the Object of Revulsion in there. King Things are supposed to be a lighter chocolate – these are so dark, they look like…" Rose reached into the pocket of her shorts and produced the letter she'd received days ago. There it was, in a boxed picture at the bottom of the letter. "They look like these: Kathy Keegan Koko Kakes."

As soon as Rose said "Kathy Keegan," the bakers' faces instantly contorted into looks of complete revulsion.

"That talentless witch?" Marge spat. "That *hack*?"

"Her Koko Kakes are chocolate tragedies," said Jasmine angrily.

"If I saw her on the street, I would spit her Koko Kakes right in her face," said Ning. "Right into her scaly lizard face."

Sage pointed to the cartoon drawing of Kathy Keegan on the letter. "This little cartoon lady?" he said. "With the short hair? She looks fine to me!"

With a scream of rage, Melanie and Felanie seized the letter from Sage and tore off the cartoon Kathy Keegan head. "Hey!" Sage called out, but Jasmine and

Ning had already crumpled up the portion of the letter they'd ripped and shoved it down the garbage disposal, cheering as it was ground into a pulp.

"Here, Sage, give me that." Rose held out her hand and Sage gave her the remainder of the letter. She folded it up as best she could and put it back in her pocket.

"What's their beef with Kathy Keegan?" Sage asked.

Rose shook her head. "It's the King Things." She pointed to Jasmine and Ning who were staring down the drain and clapping. "They make them hate Kathy Keegan!"

The bakers covered their hands with their ears, as if the very name of the cartoon baker sounded like nails on a chalkboard.

"Why would Mr Butter want that?" Ty asked. "I thought he wanted to take over Kathy Keegan's company?"

An image of the International Society of the Rolling Pin's meeting flashed before Rose's eyes – how everyone there despised Kathy Keegan. "It's a backup plan in case the other plan doesn't work," Rose said with a sudden realization. "If people eat King Things, and King Things make them hate Kathy Keegan, they're not gonna go out and buy a box of Kathy Keegan Koko Kakes, right?"

The bakers snarled and winced and threw metal bowls, which went clattering to the floor.

"And since only two bakeries in the country are now legally allowed to operate, that means Mostess Moony Pyes and Glo-Balls and Dinky Doodle Doughnuts are their only other choice," Sage concluded. "Tricky!"

Rose smelled the red mason jar containing the Object of Revulsion once more. "I just don't understand exactly what this stuff is."

"It actually looks like Kathy Keegan Koko Kakes," said Ty, peering through the red glass of the jar. "Like, ones that have seen better days."

"That's it!" Rose exclaimed. "The Koko Kakes themselves are the Objects of Revulsion! They've been putrefied, probably with some kind of magical rotting agent. Add the revolting stuff to the batter, and the people who eat it start to hate that thing. A lot."

Marge and the other bakers had opened fifty canisters of vanilla frosting and were assembling the white goopy stuff into something that looked like a snowman.

"What are you doing with that frosting?" said Rose.

"We're making an effigy of that useless *sack* Kathy Keegan," said Marge.

"And what are you going to do with it?" asked Ty.

Marge's eyes seemed to burst with flames. "Burn it."

Rose grabbed the *Apocrypha* and flipped through, looking for an antidote to Gagoosh Taghipoor's Rolls of Revulsion. "Oh dear. We have to fix this before they burn down the building."

PARENTAL PASTRY CREAM: To squash the seeds of hatred and discord

*The beautiful Lady Niloufar Bliss did greet the wandering band of starving children who had so violently eschewed their parents. She did create a plum tart and did imbue the pastry cream beneath the fruit with **MOTHER'S LOVE**, mined from the wailing of the estranged mothers of the village of Masuleh. When the children did eat of the tart, they wept and ran back to the arms of their weeping mothers, who kissed their faces and rejoiced.*

"Where are we going to get Mother's Love?" Rose asked.

"Duh," said Ty. "Our own mother is about a mile away. And she loves us. Like, a lot."

"Right," said Rose. "Except we don't have the key to their suite. I think I saw it on Mr Butter's key ring, but there's no way to actually lift it off his belt."

"Leave that to me!" squeaked Jacques. The mouse had been watching the proceedings from atop one of the prep tables. "You see, I used to be a thief."

"You did?"

"*Oui,*" said Jacques. "I would steal food from expensive shops in the market and give it to ze poor people."

"Like Robin Hood," said Ty.

"That was ze idea," said Jacques. "But I got very creative. In ze beginning, I would leave potatoes on their doorstep. Then eet was a whole medley of vegetables and butchered meats. Then I was constructing elaborate gift baskets from the things I stole. Eet got to be excessive. Ze poor don't need little tins of caviar and smoked oysters. And ze baskets were so heavy that I would have to enlist many mice to help me carry them. And then ze mice would start to eat ze baskets – oooooh, eet was a big mess."

"But your heart was in the right place," Rose said.

"*Absolument!* In any case, I am quite an adept thief." He drew his paws along his whiskers, cleaning them.

"When your Mr Butter comes in here later today, that key will be mine."

Mr Butter and Mr Kerr showed up a short while later. Mr Kerr had on a bright purple velour track suit. *How many of those things does he own?* Rose wondered.

Sage and Ty watched from Rose's bedroom, unseen by Mr Butter and Mr Kerr, while Rose greeted them in the test kitchen.

Marge and the bakers had completed their life-size frosting statue of Kathy Keegan. It bore a remarkable resemblance to the cartoon character on the letterhead. If the bakers hadn't been driven by blind hatred, they might have considered careers as sculptors and artists.

"What is this snowman doing here?" asked Mr Butter.

He stood behind a stainless steel prep table wearing a light-blue button-down shirt and navy slacks. The same thick ring of keys Rose had seen before hung from his belt, and as she scanned it, she saw an oddly shaped key, a brass staff with a tiny rolling pin jutting out from the end at a ninety-degree angle. She looked around for Jacques, but he was nowhere to be found. Gus, though, she could see sitting atop a refrigerator in plain sight. She'd told the cat to hide – Mr Butter clearly didn't like him – but he had his own ideas about where he belonged.

"This is an effigy of Kathy Keegan made from frosting," said Rose. "The bakers are eager to burn it."

"Are you?" Mr Butter asked the bakers, looking delighted. *"Why?"*

"Because Kathy Keegan is *evil*," Felanie said.

"Like music that plays in elevators," Melanie said.

"Or Christmas fruitcakes," Gene said.

"We were trying to expunge that ugly face from our brains," said Marge. "We only want to think of Mostess – and its heavenly, perfect food-like products."

It would have been a rousing performance, thought Rose, if indeed it had been a performance. Unlike the other times Mr Butter had come in to check on the test kitchen's progress, this time the bakers weren't faking it. Mr Butter was witnessing the true destructive power of the perfected recipes firsthand, and he was *loving* it. His eyes were bright and wide, and his cheeks were as pink as the top of his bald head. He looked like a schoolboy. A strange, old schoolboy.

"I'd like to ask you all a series of questions," he said, using his fingers to comb nonexistent hair across his shiny scalp. "Just to make sure the King Things are perfect."

"Anything for you, Master of the Mostess!" Ning declared with a bow.

Mr Butter whispered to Rose, "We'll see whether the recipe has truly been perfected. Lily Le Fay was able to achieve similar results, but her King Things weren't quite strong enough."

They're strong enough now, Rose thought. *Thanks to Ty and Sage.*

Mr Butter pointed to Marge. "What do Kathy Keegan Koko Kakes taste like?"

Marge made a face of disgust. "Rotten eggs and disappointment!"

He pointed to Melanie and Felanie. "What is your favorite thing about Kathy Keegan?"

"That she can be hit over the head with a rolling pin," Melanie volunteered.

"And smacked in the face with a baking sheet," said Felanie with a firm nod.

Mr Butter continued around the kitchen until he was standing directly in front of Gene. "Where do you think Kathy Keegan lives?"

"A sewer," he answered. "And that's where she does her baking."

Finally, he gestured at Jasmine and Ning. "And what

would you do if you ran into Kathy Keegan on the street?"

"Run!" cried Ning.

"As fast and as far in the opposite direction as I can go!" said Jasmine.

"Or build a prison out of Moony Pyes and Glo-Balls and lock her inside," said Ning.

"You've outdone yourself, Miss Rosemary Bliss," Mr Butter said just as Jacques appeared at the corner of the table.

"Why thank you, sir!" Rose said, anxious to draw away his attention. *Now please give us your keys so I can go see my mother and turn these poor bakers back the way they were.*

"In a mere four *days* you have perfected our Moony Pyes, Glo-Balls, Dinky Doodle Doughnuts, and now our King Things! By the end of today, when you've perfected the original Dinky recipe, all five of our new and improved FLCPs will be ready to go into production!"

Jacques tightroped along the edge of the table, carefully putting one tiny pink foot in front of the other, almost within reach of the dangling batch of keys on Mr Butter's belt.

"Kathy Keegan is, as you know, the devil incarnate," said Mr Butter.

The bakers hooted and applauded as Jacques, unseen by anyone but Rose, reached forward and tried to unhook the rolling-pin key. But Mr Butter was standing just an inch too far from the table for Jacques to reach.

Rose moved to the edge of the prep table opposite Mr Butter. "Could you lean forward, Mr Butter?"

"Why?"

"I... I'm thinking of shaving my hair off, and I want to see what it would look like on top." She shrugged and smiled. "It's a new fashion!"

Mr Butter cooed and leaned forward, so that his key ring clunked onto the top of the table. "This isn't a traditional girl's haircut," he said, "but kids these days!"

Rose reached forward and ran her fingers along the smooth, waxy surface of Mr Butter's head, all the while staring down at Jacques, who had disappeared beneath the folds of Mr Butter's button-down shirt.

"It's so... bumpy," Rose said.

"That's my skull under the skin," Mr Butter said.

A moment later, the mouse emerged carrying the oddly shaped key, and Rose liberated her hand from Mr Butter's greasy head. "Thank you," she said. "That was very... informative."

"You're welcome," Mr Butter said, smiling. "I aim to inform."

Jacques scampered across the table on his hind legs, carrying the rolling pin key over his head like a javelin thrower.

He was nearly at the other end of the table, ready for Rose to scoop him up into the pocket of her apron, when he was spotted by Mr Kerr.

"Mouse!" Mr Kerr screeched, and he slammed a metal mixing bowl down onto the steel table, trapping Jacques inside.

Before Mr Kerr could reach into the mixing bowl, Gus leaped from the top of the refrigerator and landed on the shoulder of his velour jumpsuit.

"Ahhh! I'm being attacked!" cried Mr Kerr, who hurled a swift upper jab toward Gus in an attempt to knock the cat off of his shoulder, but Gus had already leaped through the air onto the back of Mr Butter's blazer, latching on like a baby koala bear.

"Get it off!" Mr Butter cried, and Mr Kerr ran over to pry the cat off Mr Butter's back. Gus immediately jumped onto Mr Kerr's head and from there onto the top of the refrigerator. Meanwhile, making it look like an accident, Rose overturned a two-foot-tall stack of metal mixing bowls onto the surface of the prep table. Some landed right side up, some landed face down, and some clattered to the floor.

When Mr Kerr turned back to the prep table, he saw no fewer than seven metal mixing bowls overturned on the table. "Which one was the mouse in?" he cried.

"I don't remember!" said Rose. And it was the truth – she'd forgotten which bowl Jacques was cowering under. "I guess we'll wait to see which bowl moves!" she shouted, hoping Jacques would get the hint and nudge against the wall of his metal prison, so she would know which bowl to protect.

Mr Kerr impatiently began overturning the bowls. "I'm not waiting around for a filthy mouse."

The bowl in front of Rose moved half an inch, and Rose lifted it just enough for Jacques to scamper from beneath it into the pocket of her apron. "Nothing here!" she said, overturning the bowl to show the others.

Mr Kerr sent the last of the metal bowls careening to the ground, with no mouse in sight. He huffed over to the golf cart, sat in the driver's seat, folded his arms, and pouted. "I thought I had it," he said.

Gus released himself from Mr Butter's back and dashed away into the Bakers' Quarters.

"Were you not doing such good work, Rosemary Bliss," Mr Butter said dryly, "I would have that cat removed immediately."

"No!" Rose cried. "He's my only link to home."

"I understand wanting a link to the place you grew up," said Mr Butter, tucking into the passenger seat of the golf cart. "Just make sure I never ever see him again. Keep that beast caged up. And get started on those Dinkies now. We are so close to our dream! When you're done tonight, there will be a wonderful reward waiting for you."

As the golf cart disappeared beneath the floor, Jacques poked his head out of Rose's pocket. "*Merci,* Rose," he said gravely.

"The thanks are all owed you," Rose said. "Did you manage to hold on to it?"

The mouse held up the tiny notched-and-grooved rolling pin. "I've got ze key!"

Chapter 14

LOVE IS IN THE JARS

WITH ONE HAND on the steering wheel, Ty sped the golf cart through the maze of warehouses, darting away from the occasional oncoming delivery trucks.

"This is no big deal for me, *hermana!*" he yelled to Rose over the rush of the wind. "I'm basically a stunt driver!"

Sage sat in the back, his arms wrapped around a crate of red mason jars, empty save for a bit of heavy cream at the bottom of each. The jars clinked and rattled as the golf cart hurtled along.

Rose sat in the passenger seat, clinging to the dashboard with one hand and clutching the rolling-pin key with the other. She thought of her mother's face, tender and heart-shaped, with her wild, curly dark hair that was always tied into a messy bun, like a swallow's nest in a willow tree.

Her mother always knew the best thing to do. Was there some way out of this whole Mostess mess that Purdy might be able to see, if only she weren't locked away like Rapunzel in a tower? After finishing the antidote for the King Things, Rose only had one more recipe to perfect – the Dinky – but the real work of bringing down the Mostess Corporation was just beginning. She didn't know how she would do everything without her parents' help.

But she knew that she had to try.

If she freed her parents and escaped now, who would stop Mr Butter and the International Society of the Rolling Pin? No one. It was all up to Rose. First she had to undo the evil recipes she'd helped to perfect. Then she had to find a way to defeat Mr Butter. And *then* she could free herself and her family, and maybe together they could reverse the new bakery law....

"What are you thinking?" Sage asked, nudging her shoulder.

"That it will be good to see Mum," Rose said.

"And to break her out!" Sage replied. But Rose didn't answer him.

By then, Ty had pulled up in front of the

pastry-bag-shaped hotel, which seemed to rise up straight into the late-morning clouds. Rose, Ty, and Sage tiptoed through the empty lobby, which was so crisply air-conditioned that Rose instantly found her arms covered in goose bumps. The teenage concierge looked bewildered by the reappearance of Sage and Ty.

"Hello again, Miss Bliss," he ventured. "I see your guests from the Children with Weird Voices Association are back?"

Rose cleared her throat. "Umm, yes. It's actually a two-day tour."

"And you're giving away free mason jars?" the concierge asked, referring to the crate of twelve empty jars that Sage was clutching to his chest.

"My *souvenniiiiiiiirrrrrrrrrrrs!*" Sage roared in his weirdest voice, struggling to keep the jars from dropping. He sounded like a strange cross between an old lady and a newborn baby.

The concierge just nodded, as if glad his own voice was not so weird.

When they were all safely inside the elevator, Sage gratefully laid his red glass burden on the floor, and

Rose found the small, rolling-pin-shaped indentation in the brass plate next to the button for floor 34.

She took a deep breath and inserted the key into the small hole and heard that wonderfully satisfying click that keys always make when they fit into a lock. Rose turned the key to the right while pressing the button, and the elevator rumbled and began its ascent.

"Once we break them out, are we going to go home?" Sage asked as the glass box rose higher and higher over the Mostess compound.

Ty tapped Rose on the shoulder. "*Hermana*, if we bust Mum and Dad and Balthazar out of that hotel room, won't that Butter dude find out? And won't he think you did it and come after you?"

"We are going home, and we are going to free them," Rose answered, gazing out over the warehouses and the small house where Mr Butter grew up, all of it looking very small in the golden wash of morning. "But only after we ruin this place."

"Can't we just go home?" Sage whined. "Tomorrow night is the inaugural summer water balloon fight in Calamity Falls Square, and I'm going to miss it! I've been planning for it all year."

"Sage, our *hermana* is right. Think about it," Ty continued.

"If we escape, they're gonna zombify that Kathy Keegan cartoon lady, and then they're gonna ruin the rest of the country. We're the only ones who can stop them! But we can't stop them if we let Mum and Dad and Balthazar go."

Sage scowled. "But we *need* Mum and Dad and Balthazar to help us stop them," he protested. "This is too big for us to do on our own."

"No, it's not," Rose said as the elevator shuddered to a stop on the thirty-fourth floor. "That's why we brought the jars."

The doors parted, and Rose led Ty and Sage down the plush hallway, past the sleek wooden doors, to room 3405. To Rose's great relief, the keyhole was shaped like a rolling pin.

"You ready, Sage?" Rose asked as her younger brother opened the twelve red mason jars.

"I guess so," Sage said grumpily, opening the last jar and gathering the crate up in his arms.

Rose turned the key, and the door to the suite swung open.

Purdy, Albert, and Balthazar were lounging on a plush velvet couch in the living room, staring at a flat-screen TV whose size rivalled those of the screens at the

Calamity Falls Movie Theatre. They were cackling at a stand-up comedy special and looked very relaxed.

At the sound of the door creaking open, the three adults whipped their heads around in surprise. Albert leaped over the couch like he was jumping hurdles at the Olympics and threw his arms around Ty and Sage. "My boys! How did you get in? What are you doing here?"

"I drove!" Ty said. Balthazar, who had sauntered over from the couch with outstretched arms, patted Ty on the back.

"Good boy," he said, and Rose noticed a slight glassy wetness in her normally grizzled great-great-great-grandfather's eyes.

Purdy scooped Rose into her arms and kissed her cheeks over and over.

"You're OK!" Purdy cried. "I can't believe you're OK! We were so worried! But where is Leigh?"

"She's still with Mrs Carlson," Sage said. He broke free of Albert and began capping the twelve open mason jars.

As Purdy hugged Rose, then Ty, then Sage in turn, the bit of cream sitting at the bottom of each jar whipped and swelled into a pale-pink butter, filled with her love for her children. "What are you doing, Sage?" she asked.

"I love you, Mom," he said, and she just squeezed him harder. He twisted the lid on another jar.

"What's with the jars, son?" Albert asked curiously.

"We needed a Mother's Love," Sage answered, capping the last lid onto the last jar. "As an antidote to fix the bakers in the test kitchen. They ate the Object of Revulsion and now they want to burn Kathy Keegan."

"The Object of Revulsion, eh?" said Balthazar. "That's a nasty one."

"They want to burn someone?" Albert said, alarmed.

Rose explained everything that had happened that she'd been unable to tell her parents before – about what Mr Butter had made her do, about Lily's involvement, about how the International Society of the Rolling Pin intended to enslave the country. "I've been making antidotes left and right," she ended, "but I made all these awful recipes, too! None of this would have happened if I had just refused. But now I've helped them."

"You couldn't have refused, darling," said Purdy, clasping Rose's hands. "Mr Butter gave you no choice.

He kidnapped you, and he said he would hurt us if you didn't help him. You did what you had to do. And you did it *well*."

Even though Rose was incredibly upset, hearing that her mother wasn't mad at her – and actually seemed proud – lifted her spirits.

"So they have the nasty recipes?" Balthazar asked in a guttural voice. "The *Apocrypha*?"

"Yes," Rose said, "and no. They have some recipes on cards that Lily copied out, but they don't know the *Apocrypha* is here. And they're planning to feed some of the evil recipes to Kathy Keegan. She's their last competitor, and they're going to take her out."

"I thought Kathy Keegan was just a cartoon!" Albert said, scratching his scruffy red beard.

"Apparently, she's real," Ty replied. "And she's coming here, and then she'll be brainwashed into joining Mostess, and when she does, there'll be no stopping them."

"Oh my goodness," Purdy fretted, rubbing Rose's cheeks with her soft hands. Then, to Rose's surprise, her mother simply looked at Rose and said, "So what are you going to do about it?"

"Me?" Rose did a double take. "I don't know what to do about it! I thought you'd tell me what to do!"

Purdy and Albert and Balthazar looked at one another with furrowed brows. "Of course we'd love to tell you what to do, sweetheart," said Purdy, smoothing her daughter's black bangs. "But we're trapped here. We can't help you with the baking."

Her head down, Rose mumbled, "I know."

"Mr Butter's guards check on us a couple of times every day, and you're smart enough to know that if we disappear, Mr Butter will find out."

"I know that, too," Rose said. Her chin began to tremble. Her mother knew Rose wasn't going to rescue her, and Purdy was OK with that. "But how can we just leave you here?"

"You don't have a choice, honey," Purdy said.

"I don't know about these two," said Balthazar, "but I'm enjoying having a little time off. This is the biggest TV I've ever seen. Though I have to say, the food leaves something to be desired." Balthazar plopped back down on the couch and held up a plate filled with Dinkies, Moony Pyes, and King Things. "I don't know how much longer we can survive without eating. It's been two days, and we're pretty hungry. So hurry it up, kiddo."

Rose wailed, "But I don't know how to stop Mr Butter!"

"You will figure it out, my love," Purdy said firmly. "I know you can do it. And you won't have to do it alone. You have your brothers. They would do anything for you."

Rose pulled back and stared imploringly into her mother's heart-shaped face. Her emotions felt like cookie dough – all mixed up and swirled together. "But what if they win, Mum?"

"I have the distinct feeling that won't happen," Purdy said. She stood and gathered Rose, Ty, and Sage in front of her. "I have very special children. You are good and clever, and you look out for one another. You will be fine."

Rose wiped away tears with the sleeve of her white baking jacket. Her mother was right. They would be fine. "I'm sorry you're not coming with us."

"Oh, I'll be with you the whole time," said Purdy. "You have the best part of me in those red jars. Use it wisely."

Suddenly, a red light over the door began to blink. "Hurry!" Albert cried. "That means one of the guards is on his way up to clear our dishes! You three gotta run!"

With that, Rose and her brothers gathered back up

the jars, put them into the crate, and stumbled out into the hallway, closing the prison door behind them.

When Rose and her brothers returned to the test kitchen, they found the six bakers on the floor, tied up in a bundle with kitchen twine. Their wrists and ankles were bound, and their mouths were plugged up with cloth napkins. Gus and Jacques were splayed out beside them, panting.

"What happened?" Rose gasped.

"*C'est horrible!* They started saying we reminded them of Kathy Keegan," Jacques panted. "How I am reminiscent of a cartoon woman, *je ne sais pas*, but this is what they were saying."

"They came after us with knives!" said Gus. "We had no choice but to tie them up with kitchen twine."

"How did you even do it?" Sage asked, setting the twelve full jars of Mother's Love down on the prep table.

"I don't want to talk about it," Gus replied, swishing his tail. "Let's just say cats don't typically run, and I've done more running in the past half hour than I have in all my life until now."

The bakers snarled and made gurgling sounds through their gags.

"Luckily, we got enough Mother's Love in these jars to cure a whole army," said Rose with a sniffle.

"Where are Mistress Purdy and Master Albert?" Gus asked. "And where is Balthazar, that gnarly old coot? Were you not able to access their hotel room?"

"We were." Rose sighed. "But they couldn't come with us."

"*Comme c'est bizarre!*" Jacques exclaimed. "Why not? Did they not want to be rescued?"

"They did," said Ty, "but we all knew it would compromise the mission to take down Mostess. So they stayed. After we finally take care of Mr Butter and these crazy Rolling Pin people, we're gonna spring them loose."

"*If* we blow them out of the water," Rose said under her breath.

"Eyes on the prize, *hermana*," said Ty. "Let's pump these bakers full of Mother Love before they tear down the building."

The recipe called for a batch of the same chocolate batter they'd used for the King Things of Revulsion, but when it came time to add the Object of Revulsion, Rose instead added a heaping scoop of the creamy pink Mother's Love from one of the red mason jars. Instantly, the batter smelled like roses and clean laundry and hot muffins just out of the oven.

"I have a good feeling about this," Rose said, inhaling the comforting smells of home.

"I miss Leigh," Sage said, tears in his eyes.

"I miss my hair gel," Ty said, his voice thick, touching his drooping spikes.

"Come on, guys," Rose said. "Let's get this done."

They baked the King Things at a heat of six flames for the time of seven songs, and for the first time since arriving at the Mostess Corporation headquarters, Rose and her brothers actually sang the seven songs – Sage insisting on singing "My Way," "Fly Me to the Moon," and five other Frank Sinatra songs, all the while performing the Gangnam Style dance. "*This* is how you dance, bakers!" he cried.

When the hot chocolate logs were finished and had cooled for a few minutes, Rose and Ty and Sage untied the napkins from the faces of the bakers.

Marge screamed in a rage. "That nasty cat tied me up! That rotten Keegany cat!"

Rose shoved the warm King Thing in her mouth.

"Here, have some dessert." Ty and Sage did the same for the other bakers.

As Marge chewed on the log of chocolate cake, her brown eyes softened and her eyebrows lifted to the heavens. Her chin wrinkled and quivered. "I can't believe it!"

"What?" Rose asked.

"Angels in my stomach!" she gushed. "I feel like someone just wrapped my heart in a warm towel! I feel as if my limbs are made of love and porridge, and my brain is a nest in which only the most beautiful doves make their tender home!"

"Just a minute ago," said Rose, "you wanted to murder Kathy Keegan."

"Bite your tongue, Rosemary Bliss!" Marge snapped.

Laughing, Rose untied the twine that bound Marge's feet and ankles.

"How could I ever say anything unkind about Kathy Keegan?" Marge said in disbelief. "Why, she is one of the finest women in the world!"

"How do you know?" Rose said. "I thought she was just a cartoon."

"How dare anyone speak ill of Kathy Keegan, Kitchen

Goddess!" said Gene, undoing the last of the twine from his wrists.

"It's scandalous!" cried Melanie and Felanie, shaking their matching blonde bobs. "She *is* a paragon!"

"Keegan lets people *think* she's just a figurehead because she is too modest to appear in public," said Marge. "But I know the truth. My mother's best friend's cousin was her personal assistant. I know the whole deal."

"And what *is* the whole deal?" Rose asked, settling down on a stool next to the prep table, as her brothers untied the rest of the bakers, most of whom were now openly weeping and wishing for home, for their mothers' embrace, and a nice warm blanket by the fire.

Marge marched around behind the prep table. "The Keegan family lives in the same small town where they have operated their bakery for generations. It was the late 1930s, the height of the Great Depression, and times were difficult for most bakeries – but not for the Keegans. The demand for Keegan Koko Kakes was so large that they had no choice but to expand.

"The Keegans would never sacrifice quality by stuffing something with preservatives and shrink-wrapping it in plastic," Marge said. "So they gave their recipes to hundreds of local bakeries across the country that were struggling to stay open. The bakeries got to use the Keegan name and their perfect recipes, and thanks to the business were able to survive and flourish."

"Kathy Keegan has been alive since the 1920s?" Sage asked. "That would make her really old. She looks so much younger in the cartoon."

Marge laughed. "No, no! The *Kathy* is actually a title given to the most talented baker in every generation of the Keegan family. Sometimes it's a man, which is sort of weird, to be honest. But the current holder of the title is a woman. *The Kathy.*"

"Sort of like the Dalai Lama?" Ty asked.

"Yes," Marge replied, "only with hair and a sweet tooth."

"So Kathy Keegan is just a regular woman who loves to bake?" Rose asked. "She's not a fake cartoon owned by a corporation?"

"She doesn't just *love to bake*," said Marge, fanning herself with her hands. She was clearly getting excited. "She *is* baking. It is in her blood. I met her once. She was on the shorter side, like me, with strong hands. She accidentally touched me here, on my arm. I never washed it." Marge lifted her sleeve and pointed to a black smudge the size of a fingerprint.

"I though that was a birthmark," Rose said.

"Nope," Marge answered. "It's soot from a pan of cookies I'd burned because my oven was broken. Kathy opened it up and helped me fix it. That's just the sort of person she is. She has brown hair, too – not blonde like in all of the cartoon pictures."

There was a moment of silence while everyone thought about the sort of person who not only bakes but fixes ovens, too.

"We've got to protect her," Sage said.

"Mark my words," Marge said, raising a thick finger. "If Kathy Keegan comes here and eats the perfected Mostess cakes, bakers everywhere will lose a national treasure." She paused. *"A treasure."*

"Don't worry, Marge," said Ty, standing with his fists on his hips like a superhero. "That's not gonna happen. The Blisses are on the job."

Marge looked at Rose and raised one of her eyebrows. "That's supposed to reassure me, right?"

Chapter 15

A DINKY BIT OF
ALL-CONSUMING GREED

"Ok," said Ty, rubbing his hands together. It was early afternoon, and they had only a few hours left for the final recipe. "What have we got?"

"The final FLCP is the one that started it all: the Dinky itself," Marge said, pulling a tray of Dinky Cakes from the fridge.

The Dinkies looked just like the ones Rose had seen in the glass dome in the room above the production factory: two disks of a chocolate cookie-like substance, with a layer of white frosting in the center. "When we baked these with the former Directrice, they made us all fall to the floor. We couldn't stop kicking; it's like our legs weren't under our control. It was bad, but it didn't seem like the right kind of bad."

"Let's see the magical ingredient that witchy witch used," said Sage.

Marge dug through a pantry closet and produced a red mason jar with a knotted old piece of wood inside. "She brought it here herself," Marge said. "Made us be very careful with it. Said it was very old and delicate."

Rose peered into the jar. The knotted piece of wood looked as black as a chunk of coal. And it almost seemed like it was moving. The longer Rose stared at it, the more the wood seemed to pulse as if it had a heartbeat. As if it were *alive*.

"It looks like it's from a tree," said Sage. "An evil tree."

Ty nodded. "Let me see if there's anything in the *Apocrypha* about bark or twigs or wood."

With her brothers looking over her shoulders, Rose flipped through the *Apocrypha* until, on the final page, she spotted something. "It's not wood," she said. "It's some kind of ginger root."

IN THE BEGINNING:
THE THRUMPIN'S CURSE

It was in 1699 in the ancient Scottish town of Tyree, where the brothers Filbert and Albatross, from the long line of magical bakers called Bliss, did, while playing in the forest, meet a Thrumpin. This was the most rare and dangerous of the forest creatures, for he was a spirit of death. He did greet the boys, who both had flaming red hair, by saying, "Here is a ginger root, for ginger brothers." He did hand the boys a bit of gnarled ginger root and say to them, "Whatever you do, do **not** grate this into a batch of gingerbread."

Filbert did awake in the middle of the night one week hence to find Albatross in the kitchen, grating a bit of the gnarled root into a bowl of gingerbread batter. "The Thrumpin said not to!" cried Filbert, and he grabbed the root and hid it in a place where Albatross could never go, which was at the bottom of the pond, because Albatross was afraid of water. As of this writing, the root has ne'er been recovered from the lake, and the Thrumpin's warning still stands.

It is said that Albatross did eat of the gingerbread, but he never spoke of its effects, and they remain unknown to this day.

"Looks like pairs of redheaded brothers run in the family," Sage said, puffing out his chest like a proud red robin.

"That's not even a recipe!" Ty complained.

"Weird," Rose said, scratching her temple. "Ty is right – it's *not* actually a recipe. It's more like a warning. But clearly this Thrumpin thing is dangerous."

"What does this have to do with the Dinky, though?" Ty asked. "It's chocolate. Not ginger."

"You're right," Rose said, shrugging. "I'm not sure."

"Should we use the recipe anyway?" Sage asked tentatively.

"Maybe," Rose said. "But we don't know what it does. If Mom and Dad were here, they might know... but I – I don't have any idea." She stopped, feeling deflated.

But then a thought came to her: maybe she could just substitute the all-purpose Follow Your Bliss Bakery chocolate-gingerbread recipe for the chocolate cookies in the Dinky. As for the Thrumpin ingredient, she didn't like that she didn't know what it would do, but she didn't feel like she had another choice.

Rose turned to the bakers. "You said that when Lily used this ginger root, it made you guys roll on the floor kicking your feet?"

"Yes," Gene answered, "but she didn't use a lot. She seemed nervous. She just sprinkled a pinch in."

Rose winced. "This could be bad. Like, really bad. This

might be the thing that turned Albatross into a bad seed in the first place!"

"Nothing could penetrate the good vibes I have going right now," said Marge. "Certainly, not some gnarly dried-up old root. That Mother's Love has really got me riding high." She threw up her arms and shimmied. "Come on, Rosemary Bliss! We can do this!"

Gene led the bakers in whipping up the white frosting for the filling, while Rose opened the mason jar that held the Thrumpin's root.

As soon as she unscrewed the lid, a foul smell filled the entire room – it smelled like a mixture of gingerbread and rotten eggs. Rose immediately pinched her nostrils closed with her fingers.

"Gross, *hermana*," said Ty, doubling over.

Rose unpinched her nose and breathed through her mouth instead, sticking her hand inside the jar and pulling out the knotted wood. It jumped in her hand.

"Quick," she said to her brothers, tossing it onto one of the prep tables. "Grate a bit of it before it... well, before it does whatever it does."

Their eyes watering, Ty and Sage grated the entire Thrumpin's forbidden ginger root into a pile of fine ginger dust. The smell grew worse and worse until everyone had to pinch their nostrils shut while they were working.

Marge and Rose prepared two batches of chocolate-gingerbread batter: lobbing industrial-sized bricks of butter, ten-pound bags of sugar, five cases of eggs, enough flour and cocoa powder to fill a sandbox, and a soda-bottle-sized jar of vanilla into the two enormous stainless steel mixing vats.

It had only been four days that they'd worked together, but Rose and the Development Kitchen Bakers were a perfect team now. Gone were the frightened smiles they'd once worn for Mr Butter's benefit. Gone, too, was the maniacal neatness. They were messier now, but they were also more efficient bakers. They knew what to do and didn't get in one another's way. They were relaxed and focused on their work and… Rose felt herself grin.

"What is it?" Marge asked, pausing with a rubber spatula in her hand.

"I just – it's just – everyone looks sort of happy." Rose shrugged.

"Of course they are!" Marge said. "And it's thanks to you. All any of us ever wanted was to be able to do what we love and to do it well. You're the first person to let us be who we want to be."

To do what you love and to do it well – that was all Rose had ever wanted, too. It was why she'd fallen in love with baking in the first place – creating goodies that made people in Calamity Falls happy, made *Rose* happy.

As the vats churned and lurched like cement mixers, Rose noticed fat tears streaming down Marge's cheeks.

"Oh, Marge! What's wrong?" Rose asked.

"It's what's *right*, Rose," said Marge. "After eating those King Things with the Mother's Love, I feel light as a feather. Finally, something's clicked in my head. At first, I thought it was a filling cracking in one of my molars. But then I realized that it was a *mental* click."

"And what was the mental click?" Rose asked.

"I don't want to be here," Marge said. "Not at all. This place, this job? It is not my dream. I *like* baking and all. I have nothing against baking, and you're wonderful at it – but working here is more like being a factory worker than a baker."

Rose smiled – it was true: the Mostess factory wasn't exactly her idea of a perfect kitchen.

"But even that is beside the point," Marge continued. "The point is that my heart belongs, now and always, to the sky." She looked up at the ceiling and frowned.

"The sky, Marge?" asked Rose.

"I should have followed my girlhood dream of becoming a hot-air balloon operator. Sailing over the trees. Taking people out on their honeymoons. Sucking in the pure air of the mountain skies. That's where I belong, Rose. Up there. Not down here."

Marge sat down next to one of the vats of chocolate batter and cradled her chin in her hands. Her baker's hat fell to the ground with a soft plop.

"Well, why didn't you try to become... a hot-air balloonist?" Rose asked, crouching down next to Marge.

"Because I'm not built for it," Marge said. "I'm a round gal. Always have been. When I was young, my parents put me on a diet of string beans and boiled turkey. Didn't lose a pound. I told them I wanted to be a hot-air balloon operator. They laughed and said that the people in the balloon with me would probably never leave the ground. I was six years old, but I got the hint. Started working here as soon as I finished high school. I figured I'd fit in around cake, 'cause it looks like I eat a lot of it." Marge paused, her lips quivering. "I don't even like cake that much," she said.

"Why don't you quit and become a balloon operator now?" Rose said.

"Nah, I could never quit! I'm too old and too afraid

of Mr Butter," said Marge. "He told me I belong here." She sighed deeply. "And he's probably right."

"I think you belong wherever you want to be, Marge," Rose said, kissing the baker on the cheek.

"You know what, Rose?" Marge said, patting Rose on the back so vigorously that it nearly knocked her to her knees. "You're a friend. You're a good person. And I'm proud to know you."

"Thank you, Marge." Rose considered what these past few days would have been like without Marge – then pushed that thought out of her mind because it was too awful to imagine. "I'm proud to know you, too."

Marge cleared her throat and wiped her face with her sleeve. "All right. Good talk. Now boys, time's a-wasting, and we've barely an hour and a half to finish this recipe. Can we get that ginger root over here?"

Ty and Sage traipsed over to the chocolate vats carrying a measuring cup full of something that looked exactly like sawdust.

"I wonder how much we should put in?" Rose asked. "It should be more than a pinch, since that's what Lily used, and it didn't really work."

"I say we go all in. *Todo el jengibre*," said Ty. "That means, *all the ginger*."

Before Rose could protest, Sage had dumped the entire cup of ginger sawdust into one of the vats of chocolate. The ground root disappeared in a swirl of beige as the vat continued to churn.

"I guess we used more than a pinch," said Rose. She only hoped that this was the difference that explained why Lily's recipe didn't work.

Half a dozen songs and some cooling time later, the first batch of Dinkies was ready to be frosted. Ty and Rose spread white cream over six of the cookies and placed six more cookies on top.

"I guess it's now or never," said Rose. She pictured the six bakers erupting into flames or turning into dust or just plain keeling over and dying.

"Wait!" cried Sage. "Maybe they shouldn't *all* eat it. 'Cause we don't know what it does."

"Yeah," said Ty. "Maybe only one or two of you should eat it."

"Count me out," said Marge. "I never liked ginger." Her stomach churned audibly. "Also, I'm terrified."

"We'll do it," said Gene, stepping forward and pulling Ning with him.

"We will?" Ning gasped, throwing his hand over his mouth in fear.

"Yes," said Gene, pounding Ning on the back. "Of course we will. We're bakers, right? Let's act like it."

And before Ning could protest, Gene stuffed a piece of the nefarious Thrumpin's chocolate-gingerbread Dinkies into Ning's mouth, and then another into his own.

The two men stood still a moment, chewing the cake. Rose, Ty, Sage, and the other bakers looked on, dumbfounded. Rose couldn't hear a sound in the room except for the heavy beating of her own heart.

Then just as Gene proclaimed, "I feel fine!" he buckled to his knees and began to writhe on the ground in a frenzy. A moment later, Ning did the same. Neither one let out a word, but their eyes were open, their faces contorted in a grimace. Suddenly, their right arms flew up into the sky and began to shake. Then their *left* arms flew up in the air, like they were doing some strange sort of dance.

And then they toppled to the floor and began to shimmy around like snakes.

"What's wrong?" Rose cried, running to where the two bakers lay knotted in agony.

Gene and Ning went limp.

"Help!" Melanie cried out. "They're like wet spaghetti!"

Rose fell to her knees and shook the fallen bakers. This is why her parents should have helped her, she thought. None of this would have happened if she'd brought her parents back.

After a moment, Gene and Ning stood up, glanced at each other, then busied themselves brushing off and straightening their clothes.

"I don't think it did anything," said Gene.

"Yeah, I feel totally normal," said Ning.

But Rose could see that both of their eyes were glowing a bright shade of green – an ominous, enchanted green.

Gene and Ning noticed the tray with the four remaining cookies on the prep table.

"I think we should just... eat the rest," said Gene, and he dragged the tray toward him.

"That's a great idea," said Ning, pulling the tray back toward him.

They pulled the tray back and forth in a miniature tug-of-war until finally Ning stuffed the four remaining cookies down the front of his apron.

Gene lunged at Ning and tackled him to the ground,

reaching down his collar for the cookies. The two continued to roll and wrestle on the floor.

"Give me those cookies!" Gene screamed.

"Never!" Ning roared.

Gene scratched Ning across the face, leaving three gashes on his cheek. *"Cookies cookies cookies!"* Gene screeched. Ning looked like he'd been attacked by a panther, but he didn't seem to register the pain at all – he just responded by headbutting Gene.

"Get them away from each other!" Rose said. "They can't feel pain! They're going to murder each other!"

Ty grabbed hold of Ning and shoved him into the Bakers' Quarters, then locked the door. Gene continued to pace around the main area of the test kitchen, snorting like a bull. Finally he rammed into the door of the Bakers' Quarters with his shoulder, over and over again, trying to break it down.

"That door's not gonna hold!" Marge screamed. "We gotta cure these guys! Fast!"

Rose reread the *Apocrypha* recipe in despair. Because it wasn't actually a recipe, it seemed no one had ever figured out an antidote. She realized she would have to invent an antidote on the spot before Gene and Ning destroyed each other.

Rose tore through the red mason jars they had on hand in the test kitchen, pushing aside jars containing glowing moths and pieces of rainbows and talking mushrooms. "I don't know what to do!" she cried.

"It's like the ginger root pitted brother against brother!" Sage said.

For a quick second, Rose thought of her parents and Balthazar stuck in that hotel room. They believed she could do this. *Think, Rose, think...*

Then it hit her. *"Brothers,"* Rose repeated. She pulled out a jar that held a round, oval stone that glowed a bit in the centre. The jar was labelled BROTHER STONE.

"This!" Rose cried, running over to the second vat of chocolate batter. "What do I do with it?"

"Just plunk it in, maybe?" said Sage, and Rose dropped the stone into the well of chocolate and turned on the beaters. "And a bit of ginger for taste," Marge said, throwing in a fistful of regular old powdered ginger.

As the giant metal paddle churned the batter, the surface became like a shimmering mirror. Rose could see two boys, both with red hair, wearing old-fashioned tunics and knickers, doing a secret handshake, with a lot of laughing and stomping and turning. Then the vision went dark, and the chocolate batter returned to normal, just as Gene managed to break down the door to the Bakers' Quarters.

"Tie them up!" Marge yelled, reaching for some of the twine that Gus and Jacques had used earlier. She tossed a ball of it to Jasmine, who began to run around Gene and Ning in circles until they were tied together, back to back, unable to move – like two caterpillars in cocoons.

"Phew," Jasmine said after she had tied a double knot and a bow around their waists. Ning and Gene said nothing, just struggled to break free of their bonds, eventually falling to the floor, still and silent.

"Don't try this at home," warned Marge.

After the timer dinged, and after the cookies cooled, Rose thrust a cookie into the mouths of both of the furious men. They chewed and swallowed and seemed to calm down, the green light in their eyes fading to a glimmer and then nothing at all.

Holding her breath, she untied them.

Instead of fighting, Gene and Ning commenced the same secret handshake that the two redheaded brothers had done in the vision Rose saw on the surface of the chocolate. The bakers laughed and jumped and bumped fists, as if they had choreographed the whole thing years before, and when they were done, they gave each other a hearty hug.

"I'm so sorry, Gene!" Ning cried, looking at the scratches on Gene's face and arms.

"I'm sorry, too!" Gene said, pointing to the giant red bump on Ning's forehead. "How could we fight like this? We're family, man!"

"Family!" Ning replied, and he gathered the rest of the bakers into a group hug.

"I love hugs," Felanie said softly.

Rose carried the Dinky Cake made with Thrumpin root over to a glass display case on wheels. She lifted a bell-shaped cover and placed the Dinky Cake beneath it. On the cart beside it were four other bell jars, under which were a Moony Pye, a Glo-Ball, a Dinky Doughnut, and a King Thing – samples the team had made while she and her brothers went to see her parents.

Rose surveyed the horrible spoils of her work over the past few days. These five snack cakes, if reproduced, could single-handedly ruin the world.

Then she placed an antidote Dinky in the refrigerator where they'd been storing the antidotes, lest anyone should need one.

"What if every member of the International Society of the Rolling Pin were to eat one of these cookies?" Rose whispered to her brothers.

"It's a good idea, *hermana*," Ty replied. "But first we need to worry about fixing Mr Butter, and I don't think the Brother Stone alone is gonna do it. He is seriously whacked. He is bent on world destruction and domination like I'm bent on being adored by women of all continents. And that's saying a lot."

"The most important thing is to make sure Kathy Keegan doesn't eat any of the magical *Apocrypha* snack cakes," said Rose.

At that moment, Gus and Jacques emerged from the windowed room upstairs, Jacques clinging to the fur on Gus's head like a maharaja riding an elephant. They'd gone off for a long nap earlier, exhausted by their role in the day's events. Now the cat leaped up onto the prep table and let Marge pet him.

"The only surefire way to stop *me* from eating a snack is to have me be a different person," Marge intoned. "That's what I always say."

Rose pondered this as she looked toward the ceiling. "That's it! No one knows what Kathy Keegan looks like!"

"I do," said Marge. "I told you. On the short side, with strong hands. Brown hair."

"But *Butter* doesn't know that!" Rose said. "As far as he's concerned, she looks like the cartoon on the package: a tall lady with a blonde bob."

"Where are we going to get a tall lady with a blonde bob?" Sage said. "I mean, Ty is so pretty that he could *look* like a tall lady. But he doesn't have a blonde bob."

There was a desperate pause. Then Melanie surged forward, breaking out of the bakers' group hug and throwing her arms up in the air. "I do!"

Felanie followed after her sister, clutching the top of her head. "So do I!"

Rose looked back and forth between the twin bakers, then raised her eyebrows. "Are you both wearing... *wigs*?"

"No," said Felanie. Then, softly, "Just Melanie."

"We're not actually identical twins," said Melanie, her lower lip trembling. "We're non-identical. But we like being exactly the same, so..." She turned so they could all admire her chin-length blonde hair. Then she reached up and lifted it off her head. Beneath it was the shadow of dark buzz-cut hair. "My hair is a natural brown."

Jasmine gasped. Rose could hear Jacques whisper, *"Sacré bleu!"*

"I usually just dye my hair, but I gave myself a terrible haircut last week," said Melanie, her lower lip trembling. "I was embarrassed, so I shaved it all off and ordered this wig to wear until it grows back."

Rose looked on in awe as Melanie put the blonde wig back on. Then she glanced at her older brother, who was several inches taller than the twins.

"Ty...," Rose began, "if you pretend to be Kathy Keegan, we could protect her. We heard what they said at the Society of the Rolling Pin – she's coming *here*, to the Mostess factory!"

"Nuh-uh," said Ty, holding up his hands in protest. "And besides, how are we supposed to prevent the real Kathy Keegan from showing up?"

While the bakers huddled to try and figure this out, Gus leaped up onto one of the metal prep tables, his tail curled, and leaned forward to Rose. "I can take care of that," he whispered. "The Caterwaul. It shouldn't be too hard."

Marge took charge. "Baking team! Dirty up this kitchen so that we can trick Mr Butter. It needs to look like we have created the most powerful treat yet – the

Thrumpin's root–tainted Dinky Cake." Gene and Ning immediately began flinging the extra chocolate batter on the walls, floor, and ceiling of the kitchen.

Marge set a gentle hand on Rose's shoulder and said, "Rosemary Bliss, you need a nap. You look like you haven't slept in days."

It's true, Rose thought with a yawn, even though she'd only woken up a few hours ago. It was barely noon, but the past few days had been beyond exhausting. She reached toward the recipe cards and the jars of Mother's Love, but Marge took them from her, saying, "You leave the tidying up to us. I know exactly what needs to be done with these precious things. Maybe for the first time in my life."

That was confusing, but Rose was too tired to care. As she traipsed upstairs for a nap, she heard Marge's final command, to Ty. "And you, you handsome boy – you need to be fitted for a dress."

Chapter 16

SKIRTING THE ISSUE

TWO HOURS LATER, when the sirens and blinking red lights signalled the arrival of Mr Butter, Rose bolted out of bed, forgetting for a moment where she was.

In her swiftly fading dream, she'd been back in her room in Calamity Falls, and the lights were those of the paparazzi, and she had a moment to relive that morning over a month back when she'd wished it all would go away.

But then, as she came fully awake, she saw the kitchen through the window and remembered where she was. "I wish I were back home," she muttered, "and everything was back to normal."

From the dresser top, the cat said, "There you go wishing again. Didn't I warn you about that?" He stood and arched his back like an accordion.

"Sorry," Rose said. "I forget myself."

"It's OK," Gus said. "That was a good wish." He glanced down. "You'd best get a move on."

Rose grabbed her baker's hat and bounded down the stairs just as Mr Butter emerged alone from the entrance in the floor – no golf cart, and no Mr Kerr. He was wearing a sharp grayish-blue suit with a striped shirt and polished black loafers, and he was as jumpy as a child who knows he's about to get a whole roomful of presents.

He surveyed the wreckage of the kitchen: Gene and Ning both lay on the ground, pressing ice packs to the giant red welts on their foreheads. The door to the Bakers' Quarters lay in two pieces on the floor. And Melanie, having lent her wig to Ty, was revealed to be nearly as bald as Mr Butter himself. Ty and Sage were nowhere in sight.

"Marvellous!" Mr Butter said, dragging his finger through the gobs of chocolate dough that covered the prep table and then wiping it clean. "Looks like the new and improved Dinky Cake has done its worst, and so have all of you! What a mess! But all for a good cause!"

He clapped his hands slowly above his head. "You. Are. Heroes!" he announced. "The Mostess Corporation owes you all a huge debt of gratitude." Mr Butter walked along the line of bakers, reaching down to where they lay on the floor and shaking each of their hands. "Directrice Bliss. Wonderful. Marge, superb. Jas… mine? Yes." He approached Gene and Ning. "Ping. Steve. Excellent work."

He arrived in front of Melanie and Felanie and struggled to remember their names. "Blonde Twin One. Blonde Twin Two," he said. "Good job." He stared a minute at Melanie's buzz cut. "Blonde Twin Two, wasn't your hair blonde and long just this morning?"

"She got in my way," Felanie replied without missing a beat. "So I cut off her hair."

"Very well," said Mr Butter. "Development Kitchen Team, you've all worked very hard, but there is little time before Kathy Keegan arrives! She'll be here in an hour! So clean yourselves – you're all a mess! – and we'll begin our celebration very shortly!"

Marge led the bakers toward the now doorless Bakers' Quarters, while Mr Butter and Rose went to the rolling glass display cart that held the five sinister snack cakes.

"Behold your work!" Mr Butter said, squinting at the tiny treats.

Rose forced herself to smile, but behind her grin she was confused. The treats didn't look quite *right*. The Dinky Cake was thinner than it should be, and the Glo-Ball was frosted a peculiar shade of magenta that she didn't recall noticing before. The Moony Pye was fatter in the middle like a flying saucer, and the King Thing log was longer than Mostess regulations specified. *Someone messed with these treats*, Rose realized. She opened her mouth to say, "These aren't—"

"Aren't anything that anyone else can claim credit for," Marge called from behind her. "We bakers would like to give all the credit to our Directrice, Rosemary Bliss!"

"Hip hip hurrah!" the bakers cried again and again and again, and Rose would have been touched if she hadn't been so sickened at the thought of how perfectly evil these snack cakes were. She wiped away a tear.

"How touching," Mr Butter said with a sigh. "Now, Miss Rosemary Bliss, I have a special task for you. Your final task as Directrice is to deliver these samples to our guest of honor: Kathy Keegan. She is arriving here this *very* evening. She'll be quite impressed by your win at the Gala des Gâteaux Grands, I think – so impressed that she'll eat whatever you present to her without question."

"I don't know if I can do that," Rose said hesitantly.

"I've still got your family up there in that room," Mr Butter reminded her, making a fist in front of her face. "They could remain my guests, shall we say, for a *very* long time. As could you!"

Rose looked down at the floor.

"And don't think I won't know the difference between Kathy Keegan eating the perfected snack cakes and some other, previous version of our products," said Mr Butter. "You have done a good job so far, Miss Bliss, and you know very well how... *influential* our baked goods should be." He took a deep breath. "If Keegan doesn't start behaving like a lunatic the minute she eats the first bite, then I'll know you've tricked me, and I'll act accordingly." Mr Butter's face twitched. "Do we understand each other?"

Rose nodded.

"Now, let's prepare a special platter, shall we?" Mr Butter said. He reached into the glass domes and grabbed each treat in turn – the Moony Pye, the Glo-Ball, the Dinky Doodle Doughnut, the King Thing, and the Dinky Cake – and placed them onto a silver serving tray with ornate swirls carved into it like the billowing tails of birds of paradise.

"I'll take *this* tray," Mr Butter said. "And you'll give it to Kathy Keegan, and she will love it."

"I hope so," Rose said.

She and Marge had a plan, but she wasn't too sure of it. Marge was going to hide the antidote snacks in her purse, and at some point she would find a way to switch them with the sinister snack cakes Mr Butter had arrayed on the platter. That way, Ty, disguised as Kathy Keegan, would eat the antidotes – which would have no effect whatsoever on him. But he would *act* as though he had become a murderous, easily controlled zombie so that Mr Butter wouldn't suspect anything.

It wasn't much as plans went, but it was all they had.

Meanwhile, the *real* Kathy Keegan would be safe at home eating pizza bagels on her couch, having been warned away by Gus and the Caterwaul.

Rose heard the sound of distant trumpets.

"What is that infernal noise?" Mr Butter shouted, his ears perking up. "Who is playing the trumpet? There is a no-music rule on this compound!"

Marge and the other bakers stared at Mr Butter, bewildered. None of them was playing a trumpet.

Mr Kerr appeared through the trapdoor in the floor.

He stood there on the elevator platform, clutching his chest. "Mr Butter," he panted. "Kathy Keegan. She's here."

"Already?" Mr Butter moaned, one hand to his head. "She's not supposed to be here for another hour!"

"She's early," Mr Kerr panted.

"All right! Come on. Rose, Marge, you pile in the back of the golf cart." Mr Butter's knuckles were white as bone as he clutched the silver tray of Mostess Snack Cakes.

Marge winked cryptically at Rose and patted her purse.

"Here goes nothing," said Rose under her breath.

No one spoke as Mr Kerr drove the golf cart up to the main factory building, where Rose had been briefed when she first arrived at Mostess and where she'd seen the shrine to the Dinky Cake.

"Hurry!" Mr Butter said, pushing Rose and Marge ahead of him through a pair of stainless steel double doors. "The press has been notified! Everything is about to happen!"

Inside the factory, hundreds of the octopus-shaped robots whirred and pounded and zoomed around, manufacturing the Mostess FLCPs. They moved in perfectly synchronized waves, injecting filling into cakes, sealing cellophane packages around Moony Pyes. The factory was a wonder of mechanical coordination, and it took Rose's breath away.

And then she saw that the robots were controlled by a team of one hundred or so bakers wearing electronic white gloves. As a baker made a gesture, all the robots down the line followed suit.

"Amazing," Rose said.

"Yes, isn't it?" Mr Butter snarled. "Come along. We have to be in place before she gets there!"

A plush red carpet had been rolled out along the entire width of the factory floor. Photographers and reporters were stationed on one side behind a thick red-velvet rope, and a band of trumpeters was stationed on the other side.

The photographers snapped pictures as Rose, Marge, and Mr Butter marched down the carpet to a lavish banquet table that had been set up on a stage directly underneath the little glass room with the Dinky shrine. After a moment, the photographers raised their cameras as the double doors burst open, the trumpets blared, and the orange glow of the setting sun flooded the room.

Rose's eyes quickly adjusted, but all she could see was the silhouette of a tall woman gliding through the double doors and down the red carpet. She almost seemed to be flying. The trumpets blasted a fanfare as confetti cannons exploded behind her in a sequence of loud, colorful booms.

The doors were thrown shut, and suddenly Rose could see the whole scene more clearly: a golf cart was creeping slowly along the red carpet toward the banquet table.

The driver of the cart was a boy wearing black tuxedo shorts, a T-shirt, a chef's toque, and a pair of sunglasses so big that he looked like a praying mantis. He sat back in his seat and drove with one hand on the wheel, his elbow resting luxuriously on the golf cart door. Even with the toque and the sunglasses, Rose would know those pudgy, rosy cheeks anywhere: the driver was Sage.

And standing up in the cart, like it was her own personal chariot of fire, was a tall, lanky woman with red lipstick and blonde hair that puffed out at her ears and then tapered down to a point under her chin. She was wearing a smart navy-blue business suit, the kind you'd find on a secretary of state, and she was waving with just her wrist, like Queen Elizabeth.

"Isn't she resplendent?" Mr Butter whispered.

Isn't she my older brother? Rose thought.

The activity on the factory floor came to a halt as the gloved bakers filed in behind the trumpet players, and the robots filed in behind the bakers who controlled them.

"Ladies and gentlemen!" Mr Butter shouted into a megaphone. "Our chief competitor, Ms Kathy Keegan! She has come here today to discuss a partnership between the Keegan Corporation and the Mostess Corporation – the last two bakeries in America. Please join me in a salute to our esteemed colleague!"

When the bakers raised their white gloves to their foreheads in a salute, the robots standing behind them also saluted in unison with all of the arms on one side of their bodies. There was a subdued ripple of creaks and clanks throughout the room.

Sage stopped the golf cart just short of the banquet table.

Mr Butter helped Ty step down. "What an entrance!" he said. "Ms Keegan! My darling, you look like a queen! And so much like the cartoon on your packaging! What an... uncanny likeness!"

"You're too kind," said Ty, barely altering his normal speaking voice. He sounded nothing like a woman.

"What a… strong voice you have," said Mr Butter. "What a commanding presence."

"Thank you!" said Ty, folding his hands over a tiny sequined bag that hung over his shoulder. "I love what you've done with this factory. So shiny! All the robots and the gents and ladies with their shiny gloves…"

"Thank you!" Mr Butter said, staring at Ty the way a hungry praying mantis might stare at a housefly. "Those shiny gloves actually control the robots. Efficient little system thought up by yours truly. Team, wave to Ms Keegan!"

The long row of bakers waved back and forth, and the robot arms clattered and clanged as they waved back and forth in unison.

"What a brilliant system!" Ty said. "It's like a big… video game!"

"This allows us to use fewer workers," said Mr Butter. "This is our lead baking team, all hundred of them. Each of the factories on the compound employs hundreds of people, and those hundreds of people control thousands of robots. One worker frosts a cupcake, say, and all along the line, the robots imitate his movements."

"It gives me *chills* just thinking about it," Ty said with a shake of his padded shoulders.

"You see," Mr Butter said proudly, "the idea came to me one night, when—"

Rose coughed, fearing Mr Butter would go on all day if she didn't stop him.

"Ah, yes," Mr Butter said. "How could I forget. Ms Keegan, this is the esteemed Directrice of our Development Kitchen, Miss Rosemary Bliss."

Ty glared at Rose as though she were gum on his shoe. "Who is this little girl?" he asked in a grand voice, trying to conjure up the essence of a cooking empress.

Rose rolled her eyes.

"Rosemary Bliss," Mr Butter repeated. "She just won the Gala des Gâteaux Grands in Paris."

"The youngest winner *ever*," Rose added.

Ty stared at the ceiling as if racking his memory. "Oh! Yes, I think I remember reading something about that. The girl who was assisted by her disturbingly handsome older brother. Yes, I remember him. And I suppose this girl was there as well."

Ty shook Rose's hand, and then Mr Butter handed Rose the plate of sinister snack cakes. "Give them to her," he whispered menacingly in Rose's ear.

Rose gritted her teeth and held the tray up to Ty. "These are for you to sample. They're our new recipes."

Rose placed the platter on the banquet table, and Ty reached down and picked up the Moony Pye. "How perfectly... perfect!" he said.

Rose cast a frantic glance over her shoulder at Marge, who was standing in the shadows behind Mr Butter. Marge nodded, patted her overly large purse, and gave Rose a thumbs-up. Rose didn't see how Marge could have switched the snack cakes when Mr Butter had held the tray the whole time, but at this point she had no choice but to trust her and hope that everything would turn out all right.

"These look wonderful," Ty said, eyeing Marge. "But first, let me tell you that I, too, have brought a few hundred slices of my Kathy Keegan Koko Kake to share with *your* team. We can both sample one another's wares! It's a total photo op!"

What is Ty doing? Rose wondered. *This isn't part of the plan.*

"Oh?" Mr Butter said, surprised. "Um! Well! All right, I suppose."

Sage reached into the back of the golf cart and took out a wooden crate filled with dozens of tiny boxes, each of which held what looked like a slice of Kathy Keegan Koko Kake. Around them, all the bakers giddily removed their gloves and gathered in a line.

"Come on, Mr Butter," said Ty. "Let's help that poor golf cart driver."

Mr Butter grumbled as Ty pulled him toward the golf cart. He stood begrudgingly with Ty and Sage as they handed each of the bakers their own individual Kathy Keegan Koko Kake. The factory bakers began to eat them, many of them smiling warmly after a few bites.

"Where did those come from?" Rose whispered to Marge. The Koko Kakes didn't seem to be doing anything to the factory bakers except make them happy.

"We baked up a storm while you napped," Marge said through her smile. "You should go help distribute the Koko Kakes."

Confused, Rose joined Mr Butter, Ty, and Sage at the back of the cart.

"Hey, can I get a slice, too?" a man asked Sage. "I'm not one of the bakers, I'm just the electrician. But I do work here."

"Sure," said Sage, handing the man a box. "Those gloves you wear are awesome. Why don't the different robots get confused by all of your different gloves?"

"Oh," the man said, the slice poised in his hand. "Every baker has his own frequency for their team of robots. Except for the master control, which Mr Butter keeps for himself."

"Cool," said Sage thoughtfully. "Very, very cool."

Meanwhile, Ty was busy talking to the reporters.

"Who have been your biggest inspirations, Ms Keegan?" said the reporter.

"Oh, my… grandmother," Ty fumbled. "Also Katy Perry. As well as Tony Hawk and various other professional athletes."

Just then, out of the corner of her eye, Rose caught Marge moving toward the table. Like a stealth leopard or a CIA operative, Marge swiped up all five poisoned snack cakes and dropped them in her clown car of a bag, then laid out the five antidote snack cakes on the platter. Mr Butter was watching the reporters, completely oblivious to what had just happened. Rose laughed giddily.

"Just what is so *splendid*, Rose?" Mr Butter asked grumpily. But then he smiled in a way that Rose found unnerving.

"Nothing," she replied. "Just glad we're almost done passing out these snack cakes. My hands are getting tired."

When the last baker had been given a snack cake, Rose followed Mr Butter back to the banquet table, where he took his place beside Ty to pose for a picture. Mr Butter held a Kathy Keegan Koko Kake in his hand, and Ty picked up the antidote Moony Pye.

Cameras flashed as both baking executives – one older and bald, one younger and wearing a wig and a stylish skirt – held the snack cakes to their lips.

"You go first," said Mr Butter.

"I couldn't possibly!" said Ty. "Why don't you?"

"Ladies first is the custom, I believe," said Mr Butter. He seemed anxious and uncomfortable.

"In some parts of the world, men go first," said Ty. "Just saying."

"Oh, just eat, already!" Rose shouted.

Each watching the other, Mr Butter and Rose's older brother moved the chocolate cakes closer and closer, until the treats were almost touching their lips.

Just as Ty was about to bite into the Moony Pye, the double doors at the front of the factory flew open, and a woman staggered in, clutching her furry hat, which looked like a tea cozy.

"Who the heck is that?" asked Rose.

As the woman drew closer, Rose could see that she

was short and stocky and wearing a navy skirt suit that looked remarkably like Ty's, and that the hat she was clutching was not a hat at all, but a furry gray cat.

"Somebody! Get! This! Cat! Off! Me!" she screamed as she bounded forward, staggering down the red carpet.

The cat, whom Rose immediately recognized as Gus, leaped off the woman's head and disappeared into a dark corner behind a web of conveyor belts. What sounded like a million camera clicks exploded from all of the photographers.

"And who do you think you are, to interrupt this august ceremony?" Mr Butter demanded.

The woman shook her head, straightened her hair, brushed off her suit, and marched toward Mr Butter. "I am Katherine Keegan, of course!"

Chapter 17

LET'S GIVE THE BOY EIGHT HANDS

THE ROOM FELL silent – even the reporters were quiet.

Mr Butter glared at the short, brown-haired woman like he had discovered a dead rat on the factory floor.

"Katherine Keegan, indeed!" Mr Butter shouted. "Katherine Keegan is right here!" He patted Ty on the back. "Everyone knows that Kathy Keegan is a tall, beautiful blonde! So you, whoever you are, can walk your delusional self right off this compound!"

The woman looked calmly up at Mr Butter and placed her hands on her hips. She had a small mouth, a chiselled nose, and wise brown eyes. "You know what? Maybe I am delusional. Because as I was coming here, a grey cat with little folded lumps for ears leaped into my limousine and told me to turn around and go home. In English! So perhaps I *am* delusional! But make no mistake: I am Katherine Keegan! *The* Katherine Keegan. And *this*" – she pointed to Ty – "is an imposter."

She walked closer and looked Ty up and down, then snorted. "I think you'll find that this 'woman' is actually a teenage boy."

Ty gasped. "How *dare* you? I am clearly a forty-year-old woman! You, on the other hand – *you* are most definitely a man in a wig!"

"That is patently untrue!" the woman said.

Mr Kerr snuck up behind the woman and yanked at her hair, which stayed in place atop her head. "Ow!" she cried. "That's my hair, you velveteen beast!"

"The hair's real, boss!" Mr Kerr cried. "It's definitely a lady!"

Mr Butter stared at Ty, and Ty stared back at Mr Butter. Mr Butter reached over and clutched Ty's hair in his hand, then pulled the wig clear off Ty's head, revealing the flattened spikes of his red hair. "Ooooh," Ty said weakly.

The line of bakers gasped and stared at Ty.

"Don't eat those Koko Kakes!" Mr Butter shouted. "Lord knows what's in them! This isn't Kathy Keegan – this must be" – he glanced back and forth between Rose and Ty – "Rosemary Bliss's brother!"

Ty shrugged. "I guess I am!"

"Ty! *Run!*" Rose screamed.

Ty leaped off the stage and galloped down the red carpet toward the front doors, with Mr Kerr bounding after him. The photographers were having a field day, snapping their cameras every which way.

Mr Kerr had almost caught up to Rose's older brother when Sage screamed, "Hold it right there!" He tugged on the gloves he'd pocketed from Mr Mechanico's office, the ones labelled MASTER.

He pressed a button on a boom box that he'd pulled from the back seat of the golf cart, and the immortal strains of Michael Jackson's "Bad" pumped out from the speakers. Sage, in his black tuxedo shorts and big sunglasses, began a dance of such style, such epic charisma, that it would have made for a wonderful viral video if anyone had been recording it.

Everyone stopped and stared, even Mr Kerr. Even Mr Butter.

But it wasn't just Sage who was jumping and spinning and moonwalking and double-clapping. The thousand or so robots that filled the factory floor began to dance as well, following Sage's erratic arm-snapping and popping and locking, his grapevining and his electric sliding. The room was overtaken by the screeching metal clank of robots trampling machinery, while the bakers ducked for cover.

Sage boogied and bopped his way to a giant vat of chocolate batter, and all the robots followed suit.

Sage reached in and hurled a fistful of the goopy chocolate in Mr Butter's direction, and the robots did the same, one fistful after another. When Sage was finished, Mr Butter, Rose, Marge, and the robots were all coated in a fine layer of chocolate batter. Somehow, Kathy Keegan had managed to stay out of harm's way and was perfectly clean. And Ty was nowhere in sight, having escaped through the double doors.

Mr Butter wiped his eyes, fuming, and grabbed Rose by the collar of her chef's coat. Rose grabbed at his wrists and tried to pry them away, but skinny Mr Butter was a lot stronger than he looked.

"Enough!" Mr Butter screamed. "Do you love your sister, boy?"

Sage looked up from the vat of chocolate and froze.

"Pull off those gloves and bring them to me."

Sage gulped as he removed the master gloves. He shuffled over to Mr Butter and bowed his head as Mr Butter snatched them away.

"And you!" Mr Butter cried. "The other brother!"

Ty reappeared through the double doors. He was still wearing the navy suit jacket and skirt, though he carried the high heels in his hand. He hung his head as he made his way back through the pileup of robots that stood motionless on the red carpet.

When Mr Kerr grabbed both of the Bliss boys by their upper arms, Mr Butter finally let go of Rose, who choked and massaged her aching neck.

"Apologize to your sister for ruining what is undoubtedly the most important moment of her professional career," said Mr Butter.

"I'm sorry, Rose," Ty said through gritted teeth.

"Me too," said Sage. "Sorry we made a mess."

"You were jealous of your sister's great fame, weren't you?" Mr Butter asked.

Kathy Keegan watched the proceedings with narrowed, skeptical eyes.

"Yes," Ty said. "We were jealous. We're sorry."

"Very well," said Mr Butter, suddenly sounding jovial. He took a deep breath and approached the real Kathy Keegan.

"My goodness," he said in a fake, saccharine voice. "What a dreadful mix-up! I knew something was amiss, of course, but I didn't want to spoil our meeting. You'll forgive me, I hope. I promise that the rest of the event will go off without a hitch."

He held out his hand for her to shake, but Kathy Keegan kept her arms folded across her chest.

"You have to understand how strange this all is for me," she said. "I am invited here to celebrate a law that I did not help to bring in existence and which I do not support. On my way here I am attacked by a talking cat, who tells me to flee for my life. Which is bizarre enough in itself. But there's more.

"Upon my arrival, I find a teenage boy in a wig impersonating me, and I am accused of being a man. Then another young boy perpetuates a messy robot dance party." Kathy Keegan gave an exasperated sigh. "Can you understand how, at this point, I am less than keen to continue with the scheduled press event?"

Mr Butter took Kathy Keegan's hand and tried to kiss it, but she pulled it away.

"Of course, Kathy!" he said. "May I call you Kathy?"

"No," she said. "Ms Keegan will do."

"Ms Keegan," Mr Butter continued. "We are *so* very glad to have you here today at Mostess and would be *so* very delighted if we could continue with the event as planned."

Kathy crossed her arms. "What *is* the event as planned?"

"To begin with, as a small peace offering, we'd like to offer you a plate of our finest snack cakes," he said. "Our young protégé, Rosemary Bliss, winner of the Gala des Gâteaux Grands—"

"Yes, I know who she is," said Kathy Keegan. "I wrote her a letter asking her to come and work for me, but I never heard back."

Rose wanted to scream. *Of course I would have written back if I had known how good you were and how bad Mostess is!* But she held her tongue.

"Oh dear!" Mr Butter said, grinning gleefully. "How awkward! How awful of me to bring you two together! If I'd only known what a terror this little girl is!"

"It's quite all right," Kathy Keegan said with a kind smile. "I'm sure she's been very busy. And she clearly values her work here, so you must be doing something right."

Kathy Keegan winked at Rose, and Rose wanted to die.

"In any case," said Mr Butter, "Rose has been doing wonderful work here. She has perfected the recipes for our five top-selling items, and she would like to present them to you now."

As Rose picked up the silver tray, she found that her

hands were trembling. She nearly dropped the baked goods on the floor as she moved toward Kathy Keegan. She couldn't look the famous baker in the eye – she was too ashamed of what she'd done, how she'd perfected the recipes without trying harder to escape or staging a hunger strike or *something* that would have prevented the ugly recipes from entering the world in the first place.

"You're shaking, dear," said Kathy Keegan. "What's wrong?"

I was kidnapped and forced to participate in the evil plans of this evil organization, and I just want to go home, and I can't tell you any of this because this psychopath will hurt my parents! Rose wanted to scream. Instead she said, "Nothing, Ms Keegan."

"Why don't you put the tray down on the table," said Kathy Keegan, leaning forward and whispering in her ear. "I get nervous in front of cameras, too. It's OK. Why do you think I put a cartoon on my packaging?"

If only it had anything to do with stage fright, Rose thought, relieved to place the tray back on the table.

At least Marge had managed to switch the baked goods, Rose told herself, as Ms Keegan approached the tray and looked it over. Now Kathy Keegan was about to eat the antidote snack cakes, instead of the poisoned ones – but she didn't know that she was supposed to act crazy after eating them. What would become of Rose and her family after Mr Butter saw that Kathy Keegan wasn't turning into a nutcase?

"They look wonderful," said Ms Keegan, beaming. "Congratulations!"

"Thank you," said Mr Butter. "But those are for display only! The real treats are being kept safe in here." He plucked Marge's handbag off the shocked baker's arm.

Rose's stomach jumped into her throat. Mr Butter had seen Marge switch the treats!

"What say I eat these samples," he said, pulling the platter of antidote snack cakes toward him, "and you can have the *real* snack cakes! It'll make a better picture if we're both eating the same thing."

Rose felt she might actually jump out of her skin as Mr Butter pulled the first snack cakes, the evil ones, from Marge's purse and arranged them on an empty platter on the banquet table.

"What's different about these?" Kathy Keegan asked, eyeing the new platter of snack cakes. "And why were they being kept in a purse?"

"They're of finer quality," said Mr Butter. "I employ

Marge here to keep security in our kitchens. And a good thing, too! Otherwise that imposter would have eaten all our hard work and spoiled your little treat. Aren't you glad I noticed that little mix-up, Rosemary?"

Rose tried to nod, but she couldn't move. She felt like she'd never be able to take a deep breath again.

"Come here, Ms Keegan, stand next to me," said Mr Butter. He guided Kathy Keegan behind the banquet table, where she could look down at the tray of snack cakes – the Moony Pye, the Glo-Ball, the Dinky Doodle Doughnut, the King Thing, and the Dinky Cake, all prepared according to Lily's recipes, all perfected by Rose.

Rose sidled up beside Marge. "What are we going to do, Marge?" she whispered. "The plan failed. I failed. Kathy Keegan is going to become a Mostess puppet."

Marge put her arm around Rose and pulled her close. "You listen to me, Rosemary Bliss," she whispered. "You need to learn how to have a little faith."

"Let's begin with the Moony Pye," said Mr Butter. But when he looked down at his Moony Pye, a tiny brown mouse was standing beside it on his hind legs, playing a song on the flute. Debussy's *Claire de lune*, in fact.

Mr Butter stared down at Jacques, his eyes bulging

out of his head as he shouted, "Another mouse!" He stumbled backward into the arms of Mr Kerr, who fell into Rose, knocking her to the floor. "Ow!" she cried.

Mr Kerr rolled over, and Rose scrambled to her feet in time to see Jacques galloping away astride his trusty feline steed, Gus.

Looking dazed, Mr Butter got to his feet and stared down at his platter. "Good grief!" he panted, adjusting his glasses. "Please ignore the events of the past three minutes, Ms Keegan. Of late I have been haunted by apparitions of mice. Let us, just to be safe, begin with the Glo-Ball instead."

Rose gulped, her heart doing flips inside of her as she watched Mr Butter reach down and pick up his antidote Glo-Ball. Kathy Keegan picked up her perfected, poisonous Glo-Ball.

They clinked Glo-Balls like they were clinking glasses of champagne at a New Year's Eve party.

"Bottoms up," said Kathy Keegan.

As the two popped the Glo-Balls in their mouths, the cameras flashed, and Rose held her breath for what was about to be the worst moment of her entire life.

Chapter 18

BOYS DO CRY

A HUSH FELL over the room as Kathy Keegan and Mr Butter chewed their snack cakes.

Rose remembered the crazed reactions of the bakers when they first ate their Glo-Balls, imbued with the howling emptiness of the Hag o' the Mist. She waited for Kathy Keegan to growl and viciously demand more *more MORE* Glo-Balls.

But the sound she heard was of another variety entirely. It was a deep, guttural crying – the sound of a hard soul cracking open its shutters and letting in some light.

Rose opened her eyes. Mr Butter was draped over the banquet table, sobbing like a lost little boy.

Kathy Keegan looked over at Mr Butter, confused. "What's the matter with him?" she asked. "I mean, they're delicious, don't get me wrong, but I don't know if I'd *cry* over them."

Rose felt like her head was about to explode. Why was Kathy Keegan unaffected by the perfected recipes? And why was Mr Butter crying over the antidotes?

Rose tugged at Marge's sleeve. "What the heck is going on? Why isn't Kathy Keegan going crazy?"

Marge wore a small but devilish grin. "I whipped up a different batch of treats back in the Development Kitchen," she said. "While you were taking your nap, and while the rest of the team was preparing the Koko Kakes."

"So Kathy Keegan is eating the antidote cakes?" Rose asked.

Marge shook her head, her eyes gleeful. "No, she's eating the same thing Mr Butter is eating."

"But why is Mr Butter reacting that way? Why is he crying instead of running around begging for more Glo-Balls?" Rose asked.

Marge stared ahead, grinning as Mr Butter reached out, sobbing, for a hug from Mr Kerr.

"Hug me!" Mr Butter sniffled. "Would someone please hug me?"

"Marge," Rose said. "Explain yourself."

Marge cleared her throat. "I couldn't let anyone eat those evil Mostess cakes. And the only way to make sure of that was to destroy them and their recipes for good.

"So, while you were taking your little nap, I got busy baking some extras of the five antidote snack cakes, and I put a heaping pat of that Mother's Love cream into each one. Those were the cakes in the display case, and those were the cakes in my bag. I threw out all the cakes and things made from those evil recipes. But as you can see, the antidotes don't affect everyone the same way." She gave Rose a tiny, tight-lipped smile. "I learned that in that *Apocrypha* booklet you left lying around."

Rose threw her arms around the Head Baker and wept. "You're the greatest, Marge! The greatest!"

"It said that the Mother's Love buttercream fills in the holes where a person is missing his or her mother's love," Marge said, giving Rose a gentle squeeze back. "Katherine Keegan was clearly loved all her life. But Mr Butter, now, he's something else entirely."

"You're a genius," Rose said. "You've saved us all."

"It was *you*, Rosemary Bliss," said Marge. "Well, you, and the Mother's Love you fed us back there."

Mr Butter was rolling back and forth on the floor with his arms outstretched. "I'm so sorry!" he sobbed. "I must apologize! I must send a personal letter of apology to everyone in America for even *thinking* of hurting them!"

Mr Kerr knelt next to his boss and shook Mr Butter hard by the shoulders. "Jameson Butter! Snap out of it! What the heck is wrong with you? Are you dying?"

"I am dying of joy! Of... love!" Mr Butter shouted. "Have a King Thing!"

Mr Butter handed Mr Kerr one of the chocolate logs.

"I'm not hungry," said Mr Kerr.

"You must have it!" Mr Butter cried, and he stuffed the whole thing into Mr Kerr's mouth.

"Watch," Marge whispered to Rose. "This should be a sight like none we've ever seen."

As Mr Kerr chewed the King Thing, his furrowed brows melted into a look of tender love, and he groped around for the nearest thing that looked remotely like a mother, which happened to be Kathy Keegan. He slid under the banquet table and curled up at her feet. "Mama!"

While the photographers frantically snapped pictures and the reporters held out their microphones, Kathy

Keegan said, "Would someone mind telling me what's going on?" She stepped out of Mr Kerr's clutching embrace. "Why are these men crying? Why is there a talking cat and a flute-playing mouse? Why was this young man pretending to be me?" When Ty flinched, she smiled. "It's OK, honest – you look good in a skirt!"

"Thank you!" Ty exclaimed.

"It's a long story," Rose said.

Kathy Keegan sat down on the edge of the stage and pulled the platter of treats toward her. "There's nothing I like better than a story while I'm snacking."

Much later, after the reporters had taken all the pictures they wanted and gone home, after the workers had been dismissed and the baking team had gone back to the kitchens for a well-needed rest, Ms Keegan sat with Marge, Rose, and her brothers at the banquet table on the factory floor.

"So it didn't matter which cakes we ate," Ms Keegan summed up.

On the floor in front of them, Mr Butter and Mr Kerr had fallen into a troubled sleep in each other's arms.

"It was the only way to be safe," Marge told Rose. "I

couldn't bear the thought of something going wrong with the plan."

"It maybe wasn't the best of plans," Rose said.

"That was very crafty of you, Marge, to switch *all* the cakes," said Kathy Keegan.

Marge blushed. "Oh my! I can't believe Kathy Keegan just called me *crafty*. I need a minute." She took a deep breath and fanned herself with the empty platter.

"She's a big fan of yours," Rose told the woman.

"It appears she saved my life," said Ms Keegan, "so I think I'm a fan of hers, as well!"

"It wasn't just me!" Marge said, hyperventilating into her bag. "It was Rose! She gave me the courage to fight for what I know is right!"

Beside her, Sage sat with the master gloves on, his arms extended and crossed at the wrists, his hands rocking back and forth like he was riding an invisible horse. From somewhere behind him came the sound of many segmented mechanical limbs repeating the moves in time with him.

"And the cat... Can it really talk?" asked Kathy Keegan. "Or had I already been poisoned by these Rolling Pin people?"

Gus leaped up to the banquet table and brushed up

against Kathy Keegan's side. "I ate a magical biscuit when I was young. As one does. Sorry for giving you a fright."

"That's… all right," said Kathy Keegan, staring warily at the grey cat. "It's just not something you encounter every day."

"I should hope not," Gus said. "I pride myself on being unique."

Jacques scrambled up and sat atop Gus's head.

"And you," said Kathy Keegan, eyeing Jacques suspiciously. "You actually play the flute?"

"Did you enjoy?" the mouse asked anxiously. "I have been practicing *Claire de lune* for years!"

"It was beautiful," Kathy Keegan said, laying her hand over her heart. "Now this Rolling Pin group, they're the ones behind the Big Bakery Discrimination Act?"

"Yes," answered Rose. "They all worked together to get the law passed in Congress. We thought you were part of it, too, since it benefitted your bakery."

"I did no such thing!" said Kathy Keegan, aghast. "There isn't any discrimination against big bakeries! It's the silliest thing I ever heard. I came here today to try to talk Mr Butter into coming with me to ask Congress to overturn the law. It's ridiculous."

"Even if you had convinced Mr Butter," said Sage,

"you'd have the other members of the International Society of the Rolling Pin to contend with."

Kathy Keegan rose and took a stroll around the banquet table, then down the red carpet, winding her way between pairs of robots doing Gangnam Style dance moves.

"Sage," Rose hissed, "stop it!"

"If these people – the International Society of the Rolling Pin – use magic," Kathy Keegan said at last, "then we need to fight them *with magic*. I have the resources to launch a national campaign. I've done it before, and I can do it again. What I don't have is magical know-how. I don't use magic in my baking – just recipes that are very, very, very good."

It sounded much like the appeal Mr Butter had made to Rose when he first brought her to the Mostess compound and asked her to work on the recipes – only this time, Rose had a feeling of lightness and calm in her stomach. She could tell that Kathy Keegan meant well.

"If we team up, we can overturn the Big Bakery Discrimination Act and get your family's bakery up and running again," said Kathy Keegan. "And then we can create a line of products that targets these Rolling Pin people, whoever they are, and cures them of their misery and greed."

Rose smiled. She thought this sounded like a great idea.

"Did you ever get my letter?" said Kathy.

"Yes," said Rose. "Actually, I have it right here!" She pulled the crumpled and torn-up letter from the back pocket of her shorts. The top was missing, and it was wrinkled and stained, but it was still legible. "I have to warn you, I'm not really great on camera."

"Oh, never mind that!" said Kathy Keegan. "I'm terrible on camera as well. Did you read the other side?"

"Other side?" Rose shook her head and turned the letter over, which, just like the *Apocrypha*, had its own sweet little antidote to what had been typed on the front. There was a handwritten paragraph from Kathy Keegan herself:

Dear Rose,
You are a remarkable young woman and your passion for baking is obvious. I know you're an integral part of your family's bakery in Calamity Falls, but I would love for you

to come and create some new recipes for us. Just for a week,
if you can. I'd love to work with you.

Cheers,
Kathy Keegan

"Wow." Rose laughed. "That would have been a lot more fun than the week I spent here."

"The offer still stands," said Kathy Keegan.

"I think I should ask my parents and Balthazar first," said Rose. "Would you like to meet them?"

"They're here?" said Kathy Keegan.

"Yes," said Rose. "We just have to go and rescue them."

"If we do it really fast," said Sage, "I can still be home in time for that water balloon fight!"

Epilogue

LADY ROSEMARY BLISS

THE GORGEOUS MORNING light of Calamity Falls poured in through the bedroom window as Rose yawned herself awake. She didn't feel any different, but she knew that she was.

Rose looked over and saw Leigh snoring in her bed, sucking her thumb and holding a plaid blanket in her other hand, something Mrs Carlson had given her during the regrettable time when Leigh had lived apart from her family at the Carlson house.

"Wake up, little one," Rose said to her younger sister.

"Hehnmh," Leigh said from her bed, her eyes still shut. "I'm sleepy."

Rose pulled on a red tank top and a fresh pair of shorts, then swept Leigh into her arms – still in her pyjamas – and carried her downstairs. Today was a special day, and she was excited to celebrate it with her family.

The Bliss kitchen was empty. A pile of mail was sitting on the breakfast table next to a copy of the *Calamity Falls Gazette*.

Rose slid Leigh onto a kitchen chair. "Morning, Rosie," Leigh said, her voice still heavy with sleep.

"Morning, Leigh," Rose said, glad to be back with her sister – and back at home.

Rose glanced down at the paper. A headline was emblazoned across the front page in fat letters: BAKERY ACT REPEALED! Rose smiled, knowing it was only a matter of days before the Bliss Family Bakery had its grand reopening. Rose had just got back from a week with Kathy Keegan, where they had discussed important plans for the future, and she knew she had only a few days of summer freedom left before school started up again. She intended to enjoy them.

Rose left the newspaper on the table but grabbed a couple of postcards and her little sister as she stepped out into the backyard, where Gus and Jacques were sunning themselves in miniature lawn chairs.

"Have you ever even *tried* fish?" said Gus. "How can you so despise something you've never even tried?"

"Non mais je rêve!" Jacques retorted. "I don't believe it! I could say the same for you and cheese!"

"How can you love something that smells like feet?" Gus asked.

Jacques twitched. "How can you love something that smells like fish?"

Rose laughed as she stepped over the furry duo.

"Rose!" said Gus. "Look, I've got a tan!" He parted some of the fur on his gray belly, revealing more gray fur underneath. "You can't really see it, but I've got a tan."

"That's great, you guys." She smiled. "You're real beach bums."

Rose stepped out toward the shed and the tree with the tire swing, to where Ty and Sage were fighting – virtually, of course.

Ty wore one pair of robot-controlling white gloves and Sage wore another. They both stood on opposite sides of the giant trampoline and punched the air, while two robots from the Mostess compound bounced up and down on the black vinyl, swinging at each other with padded arms.

As far as Rose knew, the entire Mostess compound had been dismantled, the red mason jars taken away and destroyed under her great-great-great-grandfather's supervision. Mr Butter and Mr Kerr, transformed by the Mother's Love Marge fed them, were now working for Kathy Keegan, detailing everything they knew about the International Society of the Rolling Pin. The Mostess Corporation was no more, its factories closed and its workers at last gone home.

The robots, however, had come to Calamity Falls with Rose's brothers.

Ty's robot took a jab at Sage's robot. Sage dodged out of the way, and his robot fell clear off the side of the trampoline, landing in a heap on the grass. It buzzed and thrashed and was still.

"Oh well," said Sage, bounding off toward the shed. "Time for a new robot." He slid open the shed door, revealing a collection of fifty or so identical metal robots. He dragged out another and heaved it onto the trampoline.

"You know, you need to be more careful," said Ty. "One day, we're gonna run out of these things."

Rose turned her gaze away and shuffled through the postcards. One in particular grabbed her attention: it was a photograph of a woman waving from a hot-air balloon. The balloon was so far away that Rose could barely see her face, but Rose knew exactly who it was.

"Guys! We got a postcard from Marge!"

Ty and Sage kept swinging punches at each other as Rose read the postcard aloud.

Dear Rose, Ty, and Sage,
Guess what my new job is? Hot-air balloon operator! No one's ever gonna hold me down, ever again. I will just fly away if they try. Love, Marge

Rose pressed the postcard to her heart. "I'm framing this," she said to her brothers.

"No one could hold Marge down in the first place," said Ty, swinging a series of quick jabs that landed Sage's robot in another smoking hunk of metal on the grass. "She just didn't know it."

"Oh, man!" said Sage. "I gotta take boxing lessons."

Rose continued to flip through the postcards. Her eye settled on one that was just a blank, cream-colored card embossed in the center with a radiating silver rolling pin.

Her blood ran cold as she flipped over the postcard and read Aunt Lily's unmistakable calligraphy.

Just because you turned Mr Butter into the King of
Sunshine and Daisies and destroyed the Mostess
Corporation doesn't mean you've defeated the Rolling Pin.
See you soon. Love, L.

"Ty! Sage!" Rose cried. "Look at this!"

Ty and Sage dropped their gloves and sauntered over. They passed the postcard back and forth.

"It smells like flowers," Sage said, holding the card to his nose. "It's really from her."

"But better show Mum and Dad and Balthazar, just to be safe," Ty said.

At that moment, Albert and Balthazar drove up in the Bliss family van. The back door of the van slid open, and Purdy and Kathy Keegan stepped out onto the driveway.

"And why can't we manufacture Mind Your Own Beeswax Buttons?" Kathy Keegan asked. "They'd be a wonderful addition to the Kathy Keegan dessert line. They'd stop tabloids and gossip columnists in their tracks."

"Because the Dread Swarm of the Tubertine needs time to regenerate," Purdy explained patiently. "These magical ingredients can't be had en masse. You need to use them responsibly."

"I see," Kathy answered, scratching her chin thoughtfully. "You'll have to forgive me. This whole magic thing is new to me."

Rose handed her mother the postcard. "It's from Lily," she said.

Purdy glanced at it and tucked it into her pocket. "Never mind about that. We have a surprise for you, Rose."

Purdy and Kathy pulled Rose into the kitchen, where Albert had pulled the shutters closed, just like the first time he had showed her the secret hiding place of the *Bliss Cookery Booke*. Ty, Sage, and Leigh followed behind.

"What's going on?" said Ty.

"Shhh!" whispered Purdy.

The kitchen was dark, except for a few ribbons of light flowing in through the shutters. Balthazar entered from the front room carrying a pink cake, with thirteen tiny candles sticking out from the top. When Balthazar got close enough to set the cake in front of Rose, she could see that they were actually thirteen Blinding Beetles hovering above the frosting, sparkling in different colours.

"Happy thirteenth birthday, Rosie!" he cried.

She'd forgotten what day it was. *How could that have*

happened? she wondered, but she knew the answer already. Sometimes life was just so full that you lost track of things. "I – I forgot!" she said.

"Time to blow out the Blinding Beetles! And don't forget to make a wish!"

Rose smiled and blew as the Blinding Beetles scattered into a cloud of coloured sparks that lit up the room, while everyone clapped and cheered. "Yay!" Leigh cried.

"Did you make a wish?" Gus asked from down at her feet.

"I made two," said Rose looking down at the cat. "But I can't tell you what they are. But you can bet I was careful."

Gus said nothing in reply, just purred and butted his head against her shin.

In one of her hands, Albert placed the whisk-shaped key that opened the secret storeroom behind the walk-in refrigerator; in the other, he set the grey pamphlet of questionable recipes and their antidotes: *Albatross's Apocrypha.* "Go put this back where it belongs, please, Rosie."

Rose took a deep breath and opened the walk-in refrigerator. The Blinding Beetles followed her to light her way, like little fairies, past the wall of eggs and milk and sugar and chocolate. She pulled back the green tapestry on the far wall and inserted the whisk-shaped key into the hole in the wooden door. She pulled open the door, and the Blinding Beetles followed her inside to illuminate the centuries of Bliss family portraits that lined the walls of the secret room.

Rose found the hollowed-out place in the thick back cover of the *Bliss Cookery Booke* where the *Apocrypha* was stored. She noticed that a new recipe had been added on the final page, in careful printing:

CHOCOLATE-GINGERBREAD OF BROTHERHOOD:
For the Cessation of the Thrumpin's Curse

It was in 2014 in the American state of Pennsylvania that Lady Rosemary Bliss did, under greatest duress, create an antidote to the gingerbread created from the ground ginger root first offered to Albatross Bliss by the evil Thrumpin. She did create a chocolate-gingerbread batter and add THE BROTHER STONE, whereupon the bakers so afflicted did feel a sense of brotherhood once more.

Rose nearly wept as she stared at her name, printed in the *Bliss Cookery Booke*: *Lady Rosemary Bliss.*

She had been welcomed into a tradition as old as time. She had invented her own antidote, and she was a real Bliss family baker. The look of her name, printed in that ancient calligraphy, was the most beautiful sight she'd ever seen.

Rose closed the book and reentered the darkened kitchen, where her family and Kathy waited. "You're a real Bliss Baker now!" Purdy exclaimed. "You're part of the history books, honey!"

Rose fell into her mother's arms. "That was one of my wishes," she whispered, overwhelmed.

"You were born to it, darling," said Purdy. "And the other wish?"

Just then, the kitchen door creaked open. Rose peeked out from her mother's arms and saw Devin Stetson peer into the kitchen.

"Oh, sorry. I didn't know you guys were having a ceremony," he said. "I just wanted to know if Rose wanted to come for a birthday bike ride."

Rose turned back to her mother. *That was the other wish,* she wanted to say. But she thought that she would keep it private, just for herself.

"Well, Rose has a lot of baking to do," Balthazar began. "Seeing as how she's an official Bliss family baker."

"Actually," said Rose, "I think the world can wait for a little while."

Her mother kissed her head and released her. "Have fun, honey. You deserve it."

And so Lady Rosemary Bliss did ride off into the blistering light of afternoon, on the morning of her thirteenth birthday, with the Blinding Beetles showering streaks of orange and green and purple light behind her, and she did no longer feel exactly like a girl.

Instead, she did feel almost like a Lady.

ACKNOWLEDGMENTS

Thank you to my mother, for providing a safe haven in which to write this book, for the late-night movie marathons, and for the all the kale you bought me. You have rescued me from the Mostess Compound many times.

Thank you to Katherine Tegen, Katie Bignell, Amy Ryan, and all the book chefs at Katherine Tegen Books and HarperCollins Children's Books for believing in the Bliss family and for putting them into the hands of readers.

This book, and indeed this whole series, would not have existed without the patient guidance and wild creativity of Ted Malawer and Michael Stearns at The Inkhouse. Thank you for allowing me to tell the story of the Bliss family. There aren't enough baked goods in the world to repay you.

ROSE BLISS IS ALWAYS COOKING UP
MAGIC... TURN THE PAGE FOR
MORE BLISS BAKERY BOOKS.

"It was the summer Rosemary Bliss turned ten that she saw her mother fold a lightning bolt into a bowl of batter and learned – beyond a shadow of a doubt – that her parents made magic in the Bliss Bakery."

"They had only just arrived and Rose
was already in trouble..."